The Last Flight of Poxl West

ALSO BY
DANIEL TORDAY

The Sensualist (a novella)

The
Last Flight
of
Poxl West

Daniel Torday

ST. MARTIN'S PRESS

NEW YORK

THE LAST FLIGHT OF POXL WEST. Copyright © 2015 by Daniel Torday. All rights reserved. Printed in the United States of America. For information, address St. Martin's Press, 175 Fifth Avenue, New York, N.Y. 10010.

www.stmartins.com

Designed by Jonathan Bennett

Library of Congress Cataloging-in-Publication Data

Torday, Daniel.
  The last flight of Poxl West : a novel / Daniel Torday.
    pages cm
  ISBN 978-1-250-05168-4 (hardcover)
  ISBN 978-1-4668-7181-6 (e-book)
  1. World War, 1939–1945—Veterans—Fiction. 2. Families—Fiction. 3. Loss (Psychology)—Fiction. I. Title.

  PS3620.O58747L37 2015
  813'.6—dc23   2014036360

St. Martin's Press books may be purchased for educational, business, or promotional use. For information on bulk purchases, please contact the Macmillan Corporate and Premium Sales Department at 1-800-221-7945, extension 5442, or write to specialmartkets@macmillan.com.

First Edition: March 2015

10 9 8 7 6 5 4 3 2 1

For Erin, Abigail, and Delia

The bomber will always get through.

—BRITISH CONSERVATIVE LEADER STANLEY BALDWIN
DURING A PARLIAMENTARY DEBATE, 1932

The Last Flight of Poxl West

Acknowledgment: Prologue

Before halftime on Super Bowl Sunday, January 1986, my uncle Poxl came over. He was just months from reaching the height of his fame, and unaware the game was being played. He wasn't technically my uncle, either. He was an old friend of the family. For years he had taught at a prep school in Cambridge, where my grandfather had served as a dean. After a massive heart attack a year after I was born left my grandfather as much a memory to me as thin morning fog, Uncle Poxl came to fill the void. That Sunday he sat down in the living room and, speaking over the game's play-by-play, started a story he could barely clap his gloves free of snow fast enough to tell.

A miracle had occurred that afternoon. His neighbor had died a few months back, and though my Uncle Poxl was consumed with the details of the upcoming publication of his first book, he'd advised the neighbor's sons on the handling of the estate. The neighbor was an obscure literary novelist who'd enjoyed acclaim early and then none. Their father had left nothing more than his immense library—and thousands of dollars of debt from a mortgage on a house too far in arrears to sell. Uncle Poxl had become immoderately involved in figuring a way to help them, though it wasn't clear what expertise they felt he could lend—decades ago he'd quit a job at British Airways to take a Ph.D. in English literature, then later dropped his dissertation on Elizabethan drama to finish what would in time become the successful memoir of his time flying Lancaster bombers for the RAF. Maybe they assumed that because he had owned a number of houses and apartments, he had a certain familiarity with ownership. Maybe people just assumed from listening to his confident tone that my uncle Poxl knew what he was talking about.

He was falling behind in grading for his classes, and in the early spring he would hit the road for his book tour, but something hadn't let him give up this neighbor's case.

"Then today," Uncle Poxl said as Steve Grogan missed a receiver with a pass, "the deus ex machina!"

I had no idea what he meant at the time—I was barely fifteen, and what mattered back then were the Patriots and the Red Sox, a girl named Rachel Rothstein I was after in my Hebrew class who couldn't have cared less for some wizened British war hero. But that Sunday I was too drawn in by his unerring voice, its dry gravity and utter self-belief, not to find out what happened to his neighbor's sons. Somehow his voice had found the only register that could drown out the game's clamorous announcers.

"Willie, the younger son, asked me if I'd help pack," Uncle Poxl said. "He figured he'd give the books away."

Poxl had noted my eyes on him now, not just my parents'. The volume of his wry voice rose perceptibly.

"We were a dozen books in when I dropped Saul Bellow's *Herzog*. I picked it up, and a crisp hundred fluttered to the ground. Willie and I looked at it like it was—well, like it was a rabbi on a football field."

He looked at me. The Bears scored. I missed the play and the replay.

"Julian had used hundred-dollar bills as bookmarks in every one of his books. He'd get paid two hundred dollars a review, and put half back into the books. They hadn't counted it all yet, but there must have been near to a hundred thousand dollars in those books—he didn't write a review every week, but he wrote for that paper regularly, and others. Maybe he thought his sons would find it all. Willie doubted it, and I did, too—we were a pile of cardboard boxes away from handing his estate to the Harvard Coop!"

Uncle Poxl kept talking, hauled along by the wonder of the thing. I'd rarely seen him so animated. This was the first time we'd spent alone with him since he'd finalized copyedits on his memoir, and his appearance at our house was a surprise, given the frigid air and snow outside. We'd assumed we wouldn't see him again until his first reading, here in Boston, scheduled for the week after the book's publication date. I'd been longing to see him, my eccentric European uncle who'd lived so much life. But now the Patriots were in the Super Bowl for the first time, and my tongue buzzed like it did after I woke from a nap. My mother changed the subject, and by then I'd stopped caring about the game. Would the contents of a book ever carry the same meaning again?

This image of hundred-dollar bills spilling out of the pages of books would plague me for years. I tried to watch the end of the football game, but Grogan was awful, and a three-hundred-pound Bears lineman known as "the Refrigerator" scored a touchdown, and I couldn't set my mind to anything but my uncle Poxl and when I'd finally get to read his stories between bound pages.

As I say, my uncle Poxl would reach the apex of his own literary success in the months ahead, after his book finally made its way into the world. Every season for as long as I could remember, Poxl had taken me to the opera, the symphony, to the Wang Center to see plays and musicals. If there was a performance of Shakespeare anywhere in our city, Poxl would find a way to take me. This wasn't the kind of thing that should have interested me—a trip to Fenway was my idea of a cultural outing—but my uncle Poxl was built like a power forward and moved as fluidly as a Bruin, and he was everything the other Jewish authority figures in my life weren't. On Monday and Wednesday afternoons I suffered two hours of Hebrew school, where

our aging teachers would ply us with tales of woe, melancholy stories of the survivors of death camps and ghettoization. I remember
seeing for the first time, when I was only ten, the black numbers
tattooed on a classmate's grandmother's wrist. I can see even now
my young brain being tattooed with anxiety and pensive fear. My
grandfather had survived that period and reached the States—only
to die before I'd gotten to know him. It compounded my sense then
that history was some untrammeled force acting upon us, leveling
any hope of heroism like some insuperable glacier flattening moun-
tains to plains.

Even the new young rabbi at our synagogue, Rabbi Ben Schine,
who had come straight from Berkeley with a nappy beard and hair
past his shoulders, calling us *dude* and trying to get us to talk Jewish
mysticism, sat nodding solemnly as these stories were recited, fingertips tracing his copy of *Night*. I recognize now, of course, why we
were being inundated with these truths. But I was fifteen, and what
I needed was a hero—and hope. We might be able to see God's body
in the Kabbalah's ten Sefirot, but it was 1986, barely forty years since
our grandparents' generation sat desperate and fated in their East European neighborhoods. *Never again*, our teachers incanted to us Monday after Monday, Wednesday after Wednesday. But when I picture
myself in those rooms in the basement of our shul, even now I can
only hear the incantation's reciprocal: *It will happen again*. Beware.
Be always aware. But I was growing to see myself as an exception
then, too, for I was learning on those outings with Poxl West that I
had an antidote in my family: There was more thunder in my uncle
Poxl's senescent face than in one strand of Rabbi Ben's unkempt
mane. Trailing him like the sweet whiff of cherry tobacco from a
pipe smoker's coat was the fact that he'd been a pilot for the Royal
Air Force, a Jewish war hero, the only one I'd ever heard of.

I would've followed his broad shoulders into the ballet without
embarrassment.

Though his teaching job held a certain prestige, Uncle Poxl was an aspiring writer when we started on our trips. It was all he'd wanted in his later years, to get down stories based on recollections of his youth, and all he did with his free time. But in more than a decade, three novels had been rejected by New York editors. No matter how proud he was, his shoulders slumped a bit farther forward with each turning away. Regardless, my parents felt it an inherent good that Uncle Poxl serve as my monthly Virgil through the vague cultural life of downtown Boston—no accrual of rejections in New York could undo cultural currency in our small city, and any time spent with Poxl would do me good, they said.

What I learned from my uncle Poxl on those outings didn't come as we listened to Daniel Barenboim play the *Moonlight* Sonata. After each event Uncle Poxl would drive us out to Newtonville, where over sundaes at Cabot's he would read passages to me from his latest project, this one not a novel but a memoir. After his return from a trip to London for the funeral of a captain he'd served alongside in the RAF, he'd finally decided he would write a memoir of his life during that time. He'd felt more comfortable writing fiction, but if it was a memoir the world needed, he'd write it. It wasn't much different from the novels he'd read to me from in the past. They were full of strange, awkward depictions of sex, scenes that, looking back, I now realize I was too young to be hearing. This new book felt overwrought at times, a feeling I wasn't too young to pick up on. But with this new project, suddenly the scenes he'd written were vibrant, absent the hesitations and wanderings of his earlier works. The sex scenes, while still graphic, were somehow easier to hear. Even today I feel a pride that borders on embarrassment intuiting that those scenes were crafted to make my younger self accept them.

"This next section," Poxl said one night after four long hours of *Don Giovanni,* "is the most gripping scene of all, when the reader sees what we were really up against. The story of when the 'S-Sugar' bomber went down in a lightning storm."

His hands flew up near his curly auburn hair. Uncle Poxl had one of those pointy red Ashkenazi faces whose very shape carries confidence and import. The bridge of his nose was so thin it simply faded into his high red brow. Atop his head he wore a trademark porkpie hat, the brown felt of which was always brushed. The hat's name wasn't lost on him: "It's the closest to anything *trayf* I ever come," he said. Out from the hat's sides stuck shocks of his remaining translucent hair, which took light like a polished garnet. Lambent crimson ran to his cheeks through gossamer veins. But there was nothing varicose about my uncle Poxl's face: He was hale and lissome, a man of indeterminate age but whose virility was discernible in the very color of his cheeks. He wore a black tweed Brooks Brothers suit with narrow lapels and a collar he'd popped against the Boston winter. He saw no need to smooth it down now that we were inside spooning pralines and cream.

"My squadron flew into a thundercloud over Lübeck," he said. "That's when the S-Sugar began to fly into the thundercloud, too. Crack, boom, blue lightning! You've never seen anything like it." I asked him to read it to me instead of telling me about it—he'd written it down, after all, and I wanted to hear—and so he put his face to the loose pages before him and read. The world around us dropped away as I listened to my uncle Poxl read from his book. His hands spun dense nimbus clouds in the air between us as he narrated the bomber's bravery. This was an entirely different kind of war story than the ones we read at Hebrew school—a story not of survival, but of action. It was as if he was crafting his great account before my very eyes, and I don't know that I've been so close to history since. My uncle Poxl was born in a small city north of Prague but he had a diplomat's accent—his cars had *r*'s, his parks, too, and unlike the living survivors we met or whose books we read in Hebrew school, his tongue wasn't thick and muddy with Slavic consonants. As he described in the middle chapters of his book—I'd heard each of them as we talked over fudge and whipped cream—he had been sent to London by way of a year in Rotterdam. By the time the Luftwaffe began bombing the East End, he was enlisted as a squaddie. Poxl was a Jew who had flown for the Royal Air Force during the war and lived to write about it. Though he carried in his broad shoulders the complicated burden of his own actions in those days, he had wrested his fate from the inevitable bearing down of history upon his fellow Ashkenazi Jews. And not only that but he'd lived to write about it, too.

And write about it he did. Each time he finished a new chapter he would take me somewhere new and recount to me his finest similes, the clearest arisen memory, the complicated feeling that arose as he remembered things he'd obviously spent most of his adulthood trying to forget—all for the sake of literature. For the sake of those who came after him. We talked about the fact that this is why men wrote: to leave behind their stories for those who would come years later.

"The pages are flowing from me faster than ever before," Poxl said one afternoon. We'd just gone to stare at the Renoirs at the Museum of Fine Arts. He had an innate knack for spotting celebrity, and that afternoon, like two little kids spying on the neighbor's wife, we watched Katharine Hepburn as she studied the great painter's brushstrokes. But now we were again at Cabot's, and he had promised to read to me from the middle of the book, pages he'd only recently completed. I asked him what the new scenes were about.

"Well, until I started writing, I'd entirely forgotten about the day I enlisted. The officer called me into his office," Poxl said. "'Weisberg,' the officer said, 'we need to talk. If you're shot down over Jerry soil, a man with a Jew name like yours will be torn to pieces.' So that's how they came to call me Poxl West—the kind of name men remember." He looked at me, and I looked back. I implored him just to read to me, and as he always did, he shuffled the pages in front of him and settled back into his tale.

I sat and stared at my uncle as if he were the only hero we'd seen that day. Who needed some prune-faced old actress I'd never even seen in a movie when my uncle Poxl was there to recite his stories? Even when he stopped midsentence and stared at the shimmering window behind me, an odd blankness coming over his face, as if he might stop, I felt I could read the story he was telling in the ageless lines of his sharp red face.

By the time I was a sophomore in high school he had finished the book. As I've said, this one quickly found a publisher. A small but prestigious press bought it, offering a respectable advance. A book tour was arranged, he completed his copyedits, the first edition was printed, and before he even had a chance to give that first reading in Boston—not three short months since that moment when he'd come to my parents' house and interrupted the Super Bowl—the book began to get real notice. Before we saw him again we read the review on page twenty-three of *The New York Times Book Review*. The reviewer was laudatory and honest: "*Skylock* is not a perfect book. There are some odd formalities in its language at times, and its second half is stronger than its first. But the story Poxl West has to tell is truly unique, a history we need, and there's something undeniable about the quality of its details, the precision of its observation. Having finished it, I don't think I've been so moved by a book in recent memory." Without even talking with him I could imagine my uncle Poxl's response: "There are some criticisms in there, Eli, sure. Even *The Great Gatsby* isn't a perfect book. But my book! Reviewed in *The New York Times Book Review*. *The New York Times*!"

I imagined the glint in his eye over a sundae we would share later that year. I knew even if I chided him, nothing would sway Uncle Poxl's new, implacable optimism in the wake of its publication. He'd received an advance against future royalties, and notice in the paper of record.

Now my uncle Poxl was a writer.

Before the ink had dried on the newsprint in the *Times,* Poxl had moved out of his tiny apartment in Somerville and rented an apartment in Manhattan—the place was in Spanish Harlem, but it was a place in New York. Though he held no Ph.D., having been ABD for longer than I'd been conscious, he was offered an adjunct class at Columbia in the fall. He planned to take a leave from his job teaching ninth-grade English. He had syllabi to write and readings to conduct. He'd called my father one afternoon when I was at a basketball game, and I can still feel how my skin prickled with jealousy that I hadn't been the one to answer. I could only hope and imagine he'd honed those very passages of his book on those Cabot's trips of ours. Somehow I'd been a part of the writing of this book—I'd touched history, fame, and heroism all in one small passive reach, and though it later nudged me down my path, it gave me no solace at the time. Uncle Poxl was to be a known writer, but as a result our Brahmin cultural outings were to take a hiatus.

I wrote him a letter congratulating him and briefly bemoaning not seeing him or the Rodins at the museum for a while. He wrote back with the promise of complimentary copies of his book—which we wouldn't receive until we saw him for his reading in Boston. Those books hadn't arrived. I allowed myself to assume he was simply too busy to send them along, or his publisher had forgotten to fulfill his request, but my parents could see the disappointment on my face each time mail arrived without copies of his book. I tried to remember what Poxl had written, but there were so many gaps to be filled, and what is the memory of words compared with reading the pages of a book? I longed to hold the object. I wanted to see Poxl West's name on the cover.

But what I did get was that letter. I hadn't flown his mind entirely. It was written on stationery, at the top of which was embossed *The Algonquin Hotel* in red letters, the color of which matched his face.

"As soon as my tour is over," Uncle Poxl said at the end of his handwritten note, which I still keep in a desk drawer today, "I'll take you down to the island of Manhattn. We'll go to the Galerie St. Etienne and I'll show you the Schieles there—oh, the Schieles there! What a treat you're in for, Elijah. You'll come down to New York. Then you'll really see something for once."

Skylock

The Memoir of a Jewish
RAF Bomber

ACT ONE

I.

I grew up in Leitmeritz, a small Czechoslovak city forty miles north of Prague. My father owned a large leather factory called Brüder Weisberg. It was a business he ran for his family, out of filial duty and love, and if this story is to be about something, it is love, not war. And if we are to understand romantic love, we must first understand the languid, sedentary love of family.

My father was among the most well-to-do Jews in Czechoslovakia. We lived in a large house on a hill above the streets of Leitmeritz. Its long stone façades overlooked the city all the way down to the Elbe, over the tufted green hills where I played as a child and endured the bullying of instructors at a strict gymnasium. When I was young I worked at my father's factory. I learned the trade, and on holiday accompanied him to the aerodromes, where the fortune he'd accrued allowed him the luxury of flying private aeroplanes. One day, I was to take over the factory.

Every Sunday, while my father flew his planes, my mother took me into Prague to see her mother, my grandmother. We arrived at the main train station and she walked me through Wenceslas Var, across the Charles Bridge and up to the castle

mount to buy some *smazeny syr* before crossing the city to my
grandmother's town house. Black bulbs at the top of the cathedral stood out, imposing against the marbled sky. Walking up
the cobblestone streets we passed cafés and bars where men
stared at my mother's beauty as we passed. From the top of the
mount we witnessed the drone of the Vltava pushing in its
absolute grayness, bisecting Prague like some great creature
finding it easier to keep watch over a city divided.

On one particular visit when I was thirteen, the city was overwhelmed by a gray, damp chill. It was late October and cold
enough to erase most odor from the air. Only the pungent smells
of meat held the power to waft by on our walk to my grandmother's immense town house in the Zizkov district. Cobblestones made a trail from the river, and beneath my feet I saw
$2 \ldots 4 \ldots 16 \ldots 132 \ldots 17,424$ and on into infinity millions of
cobblestones smudged to a variegated mix. The sky throbbed
with fast-passing clouds. I walked with my arm in my mother's
until she stopped. I looked up and saw pasted to a stone wall
posters drawn by the Art Nouveau painter Alphonse Mucha.

My mother stood staring.

She was an amateur painter, a habit my father supported with
a complicated reluctance I could not understand. On our trips
to Prague she would always divert us when my father was absent, eager to see what art she could. While she stopped, two
men paused alongside us to look at these posters, as well. Green
vines enwrapped the bodies and breasts of stark naked women,
in their hands bunches of grapes. One of the men next to us said
to the other in a shallow, informal Czech:

"Wouldn't you like to have one just like her?"

"Flat up against a wall like that," the other replied.

They both laughed and looked at my mother, expecting to have offended her.

She smiled at them.

She was not embarrassed by the nude women before us. The men's lecherous leers and ugly comments did not faze her.

They looked at me, and my skin prickled.

They walked away.

I watched a change pass over my mother's face: The skin about her eyes drew back and I saw there a kind of giddiness my father at all times looked upon with impertinent disdain.

We walked to my grandmother's. She lived at 30 Borivojova, in a town house painted canary yellow. The components of its face were those chisel-cut rectangular stones one might find all across the city. On the front steps leading to the door sat a pair of angry lions. Inside the entranceway the air was close. Grandmother Gertrude, whom we called "Traute," held my head to her bosom. She kissed me on my cheek and rubbed the invisible stubble over her upper lip against my nose. I longed to get away and departed for the lav, and when I reached it, I tended to myself. In the cobblestones that rose out of my memory came Mucha's women—only overlaid by that scrim of stones, they grew even more angular. This new image seared itself across the backs of my eyelids. I felt the warmth of their painted bodies come to life under my skin.

While I was cleaning up, I heard footsteps.

I froze.

They veered off into a room nearby. As I moved toward the sitting room where I'd left my mother and grandmother, I noticed the door to a little-used room off the main dining room was open. Inside, I found my mother standing before half a dozen paintings propped along the far wall. A burlap tarpaulin that must have been used to cover them was strewn across the floor. The angular girl in the painting before my mother sat with her legs spread, her hands below her small breasts and a mossy tuft just covering her exposed pink sex.

The two paintings next to it contained more of the same.

My mother took note of my presence. She blanched. Her shoulders drew back. A look crossed her face.

"I suppose I'm glad to see you like them," my mother said. "They're the work of a great painter, an Austrian called Schiele."

I looked away from the first painting and to one of an emaciated, naked older woman who appeared to be writhing in pain. My mother pushed it off to the side to reveal a portrait of a similarly angular woman with her legs spread as if to form a wishbone, between them heavy brushstrokes of dark gnarly brown. My mother explained that she had posed for Schiele when she was young, during summers she spent in Neulenbach, outside Vienna. There she would go to his atelier to see him with his woman, Wallie. She took my mother to buy beautiful hats until Schiele was sent to prison.

But I could not listen to her words—for on the face of the second Schiele girl, I saw something fantastic, something I hadn't noticed in the midst of my preoccupation with the fact that certain deep brushstrokes had been used to create the deep pink roundness of the areolae on that girl.

The face in that second painting was very young. But it was clearly my mother's.

If that realization wasn't enough, these paintings were the

exact images overlaid by cobblestones that I'd seen when I'd closed my eyes in the bathroom minutes earlier.

I blinked hard.

It was as if I had crafted Schiele's style in my mind just minutes before. While I marveled at this coincidence, my mother said that before her marriage to my father was arranged she had sat for "her Egon" when Wallie was away. She had been the subject of a number of his paintings. Grandmother Traute had tracked down the others some time later, wishing them to be kept private.

"So what do you think, Poxl?" she said.

Again that look crossed her face.

"Let the boy to his tea," Grandmother Traute said. She had arrived in the doorway—when I couldn't say. "He hasn't had a thing to eat."

My grandmother sent me off to my tea. Voices rose from the other room and then cut out altogether. Something passed between my mother and grandmother. They returned to the drawing room. We ate. Mother sent me off for our coats and I heard corrugated words pass between them yet again. Soon we left without my learning what had transpired.

Then we were going home to Leitmeritz. My father planned to stay on another night in Prague to steal skyward one more day in his new plane. It struck me only later just how often one or the other of my parents was in Prague alone, each taking trips south almost weekly. Though in the years to follow I would learn from my father how to handle those small propeller planes that prepared me for the Tiger Moths I would later train on, my mother and I now rode the train home alone.

"Now that I know what you thought of the Schieles," she said, "tell me. Would you want to try your hand at painting one day?"

I'd only ever shown interest in books, and in my father's leather. The latter was the only viable option for me. The former could survive in mind only as a potential avocation.

"I'll take over Brüder Weisberg one day," I said.

"Well, yes, but you could paint on the side."

"If I was going to do anything," I said, "I'd write, or at the least study books, I suppose."

Her eyes grew gray. I did not know a thing about painting, but I knew my mother well enough to see I'd disappointed her.

I tried to say I could show her some of my writing if she wanted. But her eyes only darkened. She was staring out at the fallow fields alongside our window. Stands of sunflowers grew diffuse in the thickening evening light.

"Your grandmother felt very strongly against my having posed for Schiele when I was a girl," my mother said. She continued to stare out the window as she spoke. "I was just the age when a woman is supposed to have her marriage arranged. My parents decided your father was the man for me. His family still lived in Prague then. They were a good family. This was before the riots, just before you were born, before we moved to Leitmeritz for good. But that summer I lived in Neulenbach and Egon—" She stopped for a second. Not looking at me, she started up again. "The painter Schiele, whose work I've introduced you to, showed me how to paint. He suffered for his art. He was jailed after everyone in town complained he was corrupting their—that he should not be painting the portraits as he was painting them. It was only after his death that *Vater* would even let us keep his paintings in our house. Then Grandmother Traute became obsessed with tracking them all down, owning them."

Again she stopped and looked out the window.

We both stopped talking. My mother went to sleep. She was a small woman with the curly rust-red hair a minority of Ashkenazi Jews are blessed with. A pair of earrings dangled from her lobes, each with a piece of amber the size of a child's shooting marble. I put my head against her clavicle as I always had when I was a child. In her half-sleep, she pulled me to her, then took the amber from her ears. She clacked them against each other in her left hand. Only when the knocking of amber quieted did I know she'd passed fully into sleep.

I put my finger to her ear as I had when I was a child, as I would never stop longing to do. She lay against the door, stilled, sedentary, a woman frozen, having been captured in paint and only half-released back to the world moving past her. Her earlobe grown soft, ceding to the amber's pull, drooping, awaiting the next trip to Prague.

2.

My name has appeared as pilot at the top of more flight manifests than I could possibly count. But you will not find a written record of the most memorable time I rose skyward. It was little more than a year after that trip to Prague with my mother.

After many years left standing in a field at the aero club my father belonged to, watching him fly off and waiting for minutes, hours, until his plane appeared again in the sky—he a distant cloud obscuring the sun as I waited below—when I turned fifteen we drove down together to fly in his new Beneš-Mráz Be-50 monoplane. Business must have been going well, a real fortune accruing, for this was the first plane he owned outright. For weeks prior, my father had quizzed me on flight safety, and I had complied. And now here we were.

There was an overcast sky that early-spring morning. We'd left Leitmeritz before the sun rose above Radobyl and spoken little in the morning haze coming down, and we were alone at the aero club when we arrived. My father liked very much to teach me about the leather business, but there was a newfound energy in him that morning—one I'd observed many times before and now could finally share for the first time. In the small hangar I was overcome by the smell of petrol filling the air. As my father went about his work, prepping the parts of the wooden wings of his new plane, we talked with a freedom I rarely experienced with him. His hands were busy, and when your hands are busy, it liberates your voice.

"Do you like the books you're studying at the gymnasium, Leopold?" he said. Only my father called me by my full name. Everyone else just called me Poxl. "Your mother tells me you long to study books. Perhaps you'll be a writer."

"I didn't tell her that," I said. "I want to take over the business. But I told her that if I were not to take over the business, I'd be more interested in books than I would in painting."

His hands stopped moving along the wood of the ailerons

he'd been working on. I watched him make twin fists, knuckles pink against white skin, and then release them. Then he began again at his work.

"Yes, your mother and painting," he said. "Very hard to get her off that topic once she's begun."

I agreed with him and though I thought of mentioning the Schiele paintings, asking him about my mother's life before I was born, before they met, I quickly thought better. I recognize now that of course my father knew more about my mother and her business than I possibly could have gleaned, but I was her son and a teenager, so what really could he have told me? Here we were together. It was precious time, this time alone with my father, and I had none of the petulance of a teenager that morning. I had a goal and that goal was to get into my father's new monoplane and see our world from above.

And so we flew.

My father sat in the cockpit and I sat in the passenger berth behind him, both of which were open, and he called out to ask me if I was ready, and when I said I was, we began taxiing. As the nose of the plane began to lift, I could feel the middle of my stomach dip toward the balls of my feet, and then the ground was lifting away from us. The field drew in at its edges below us and the Be-50 made a mighty racket, a whirring I could feel shaking deep inside my ears—but here it was! The gray of overcast skies pushed cloud masses against my eyes, and with the wind stiff and bracing against our faces in those open seats, the smell of petrol blew away. Instead, there was now the smell of droplets of water in my nose, the fresh morning smell of clouds. My father veered west, and soon we were passing in the sky above the old city of Prague. From thousands of feet above we could see every block—down below was my grandmother's house in Zizkov among the many terra-cotta roofs, I knew, and to the west the castle mount, and what I remember most then was how I longed to talk to my father about it. I wanted to tell him what it looked like to see that city from above, how close it all seemed and how absurd that a walk from the Charles Bridge up to Grandmother Traute's should feel significant, now seeing that one was but a thumb's length from the other.

But even a shout was lost in the racket of the air in those open areas, and my joy at that flight came in my simply sitting back and taking it in, knowing that my father was taking me skyward. While he had a certain genius at business, in all other venues in life I could remember him only as passive—it was as if he was saving up all his energy and mastery for the two things he cared for most: selling his leather and flying his planes. I do not blame him for it; I know he didn't see that it could make my mother feel he did not give her the attention she deserved, or that it might make me want and need more than he could give.

As we flew southward all the way down to Český Krumlov, where we could see the great oxbow in the river, my father's right hand shot out to the leeside, pointing at the massive medieval castle at the village's center. The cloud cover began to burn off, and while wisps of cloud might appear far ahead, that's not what I could see, and it's not what I remember. What I saw for that whole long flight each time my neck grew too stiff to continue craning, to look out at the land below, was the same thing I would see every time I flew with him in the years ahead, the same thing I would see when my father bought a Tiger Moth biplane the following year, that same invisible guide that would be emblazoned on my eyes whenever I flew: I saw before my eyes the back of my father's helmeted head.

3.

March 21, 1938.

Hitler marched on Austria.

The Anschluss was under way. I was eighteen. Much to my surprise, my father came to me that afternoon not to keep me close, but to present me with an unexpected wish: I was to leave for Rotterdam as soon as arrangements could be made. There was business to be done there with his Dutch counterpart in leather sales. But that was not the immediate reason for my flight. My father felt it wasn't safe for me to stay in Czechoslovakia. I was a young Jew with a future to protect. He himself refused to leave. He would take care of Brüder Weisberg, and see to his planes down at the aero club, but I was to leave. He and my mother had had an arranged marriage. I was to have an arranged emigration.

Until that moment my life had had a single trajectory: I was to take over the tannery. I'd had an education that might allow me to cultivate interests like my father's in his aeroplanes or my mother's in her painting, or the life of books that held my interest more, but my central concern was the factory. And so in my mind it was equally settled: I would stay, no matter what my father's arrangements.

On a Tuesday two weeks later I had lunch at my uncle

Rudolf's. His daughters, my cousins Niny and Johana, had departed for a new life in London the year before. My father's demands ran through me like current through a wire. I excused myself as soon as I could. I would plead with my mother to convince my father I should stay. And I would have succeeded, had it not been that that afternoon I discovered more about my mother than I'd ever hoped to know.

The first thing I saw on my return from my uncle's was a large, hard suitcase our maid Josefina had packed for me days earlier in advance of my planned departure. I walked into the hallway, where it had sat since it was first packed. A pair of wool pants was folded on top of a sweater on the luggage. Then I saw a pair of canvas pants hastily left crumpled on the floor, covered in variously colored splotches of oil paint. My father did not own such a pair of pants, and his only hobby was flying. If a pair of his pants were to be soiled it would surely not be by oil paint.

I saw my mother next.

She was on her knees. This is not a position to which I was accustomed to seeing my mother, who knelt for no one. The only time she'd ever acted against her will was in accepting her arranged marriage to my father. My view of my mother was obstructed by the most unpleasant sight. When her eyes opened and she saw me, she stopped the business at which she was engaged. She stood bolt upright. This action only doubled the discomfort I was already feeling.

I'd never before seen my mother naked—I'd seen that young version of her in the Schiele portrait years earlier, I suppose, but surely I had not seen her so in person, and not at such lascivious business. None of the involved parties had the wherewithal to alleviate the awkwardness of the moment. My mother did not cover up, but simply said, "Oh—Poxl. Oh."

The hairy thing in front of me was not my father. What he revealed to me presented a proper exclamation point to their act, evidence that was now rapidly becoming detumescent without achieving its ends. My mother stood and turned her back to me, which, again, did very little to alleviate the awkwardness of the situation.

My failure to speak or depart from the doorway in which I stood also did little to help. I know I'm not without blame for not simply fleeing right then, but what would you ask of an eighteen-year-old upon finding his mother in such a state? My luggage sat in the hallway opposite from where I now stood. Until that very moment I'd not allowed myself a real thought of leaving Leitmeritz.

Now it was the only option.

I would not be able to keep this event from my father. What this, coupled with what was now clarifying itself about that Schiele afternoon with my mother years earlier, was coming to show me was that a different kind of trauma was accruing in my parents' home. I looked up and before my eyes was a flash of memory of an afternoon along the Elbe, but as quickly as it arose, it disappeared. The eggy smell of river water entered my nose and evaporated.

My bag was already packed.

A visa to Holland had already been arranged.

A rucksack with my books was sitting on our porch.

I walked across the room and lifted the trunk, but its lid was not latched. I'd not thought to latch it—the main intent of my actions was overwhelmed by my trying not to look at this unclothed man—and its contents tumbled to the floor. Now here they were, all the clothes I was about to take to Rotterdam with me, crumpled on the hallway floor. While I assumed the beast before me could do no worse than receive oral pleasure from my mother in my father's house, effectively exiling me from my childhood home, the hairy golem proved me wrong.

Not only did he charge over to pick up the contents of my trunk but he *still* had done nothing to cover himself. His paint-splattered canvas pants still sat in the corner opposite. In charging over in so disrobed a state, and rapidly going flaccid, he also pronounced quite explicitly that he was not a Jew himself—as evinced by a rather ugly piece of pachyderm skin, which proved that, unlike Abram five thousand years earlier, he'd not made the essential covenant with the Lord that my people had made with every male birth since.

I had to put up a hand to stop him from taking another step.

He stopped.

All this time my mother continued to stand in a corner. I latched the trunk and collected my rucksack and was out of the house and down the hill to the Leitmeritz station without having said a proper good-bye to my mother or my father. The smell of the river lodged in my nose and piggybacked along with it was the image of that cuckolding suitor of my mother's, and a heat rose up into my cheeks I couldn't cool.

I got on the next train south.

As I left the house that day I expected anger—but marrow-deep anger follows action after a lag of days, not hours. The sulfurous river smell returned to my nose as I descended the hill toward its source from our house, and before me was the memory that longed to gain purchase:

I was too young even to know how young I was, before my father ever took me up in his plane. My cousins and I had just returned from an afternoon sunning along the Elbe, one town over, in Schalholstice. This is where our fathers' leather was tanned, where the current was strongest and could lend the most power to the mill wheel. My father would select the hides of cows in Prague, in Brno, in Budapest, or travel to the port in Rotterdam, and the raw hides would then be dipped into these huge oak barrels dug into the ground and covered over with straw. From there they would be taken to the factory for finishing, packaging, and shipping.

We reached those huge circular vats dug deep into the muddy soil alongside the river, where the mill wheel of Brüder Weisberg turned day and night. And there between sunken vats my mother was holding my father's hand. They were only bodies against the backdrop of leather tanning vats, looming above holes in the brown ground. My father stood stiff. His shoulders were held perfectly parallel to the ground. None of the ease I'd witnessed in watching my father full of life before flying his plane was evident. He looked stiff—and uncomfortable. My mother tugged his sleeve toward her, French cuffs I knew so well pinned together with links adorned with Czech amber, the liquid solidified millions of years long since passed. My father did not move. My mother pulled herself by his sleeve, pushing her chest against his arm. She was flirting, but he was not flirting back. Even as young as we were then we could see it. They were standing only a few feet in front of the nearest vat to one side, closer even on the other.

Still my father did not move.

Only now, as my mother went around him, she lost her footing. Her foot dunked straight through the straw into one of the vats. She and my father both looked down at it. My cousins and I were too far to smell it, but we saw the way my father's shoulders dipped perpendicular to the horizon as he lifted my mother from the ground, expertly held her in his arms, and ran her to the river to soak her in its waters. I recognize now the opportunity that had passed—that my father never had a chance to loosen up, to give my mother the love she wanted. But I suppose it's too hopeful to imagine he would have changed. Who could say how many more times this scene had played out, or one like it, my mother needing something my father couldn't, or wouldn't, give. But I didn't see all that then. What I saw was my father acting when action was needed, carrying my mother riverward. The last thing any of us saw—was I the only one to see it? Did Niny and Johana see it as well? Or was it so dark none of us could see it, and I've only invented it in my memory over the years?— was the look on my mother's face: the relaxed eyes, the taut, smiling lips of a woman who has achieved happiness so momentary it is a flash more fleeting than the look captured in a painting.

My cousins and I did not say a word to one another. We walked back down to another part of the river to swim.

4.

In Prague I was forced to wait for the evening train. When night came, we rode out of Hlavni Nadrazi. Lights scattered across the Zizkov hills like trails of a thousand small fires burning. Holland lay before me, five hundred miles west. I closed my eyes, and when I opened them again the Vltava flowed dark alongside my window. In the distance, the peaks of St. Vitus Cathedral pronounced themselves against the night sky. The church was lit from below as if to say good-bye to her departing Semitic son. A flock of waterbirds lifted off the dark water in unison. The moon lit the river not yet signifying a bombing, but only Czechoslovakian night.

I arrived in Rotterdam two days later and was let off at the station not far from the harbor. My mouth was full of a long night's cigarette smoke, my head not a fit for my brain. Already I'd fared poorly—the bag our housekeeper had packed was lost on the train. I only had money enough for a couple nights' sleep in a hotel until I could find work. Once I was settled I would seek out whatever business connections my father had set up for me there. First thing, I found a room above a small restaurant called Café le Monde on Schiedamsedijk, and at the café a job busing tables.

The first night there was a Saturday, and as the dinner crowd thinned, a group of musicians filed in with their large black cardboard instrument cases. They set up outside, and inside the café I could feel only the thud of the double bass. Toward the end of their set I went out front. They were a quartet, a pair called the Tennessee Sisters, backed by two men, and they played a kind of music I'd never heard before.

That bass and a banjo backed up two young women, who sang high harmonies.

The lead singer was called Maybelle Tennessee. Her face was the color of untreated pine, dusted with ground cardamom. Her dark hair wasn't quite black and was kinky as if even the ends of her hair longed to stay as close as they could to her head. There was a gap between her two front teeth wide enough to slip in a chapbook of love songs, and in this slight imperfection she was only more alluring. Next to her ear, a brown-pink scar drew bright against her earthen skin before she sang. I stood there and watched. Here I was, alone in the world, listening to two Dutch girls sing American folk songs.

After their set, I cleaned the tables out front, where people had sat to listen to them.

"Do you have a deep, enduring love for the American folk-singer Bill Monroe?" Maybelle said to me. She said it in English, of which I knew only a little.

"Am not a waiter," I said, using the tiny bit of English I had learned from my grandmother's American cousin. "I find one."

"I do not want a waiter," she said. She spoke to me in German now, having picked up on my accent. "I saw you listening to us. From looking at you I thought you were an American and perhaps a fan of brother-duo singing music. But you are not."

"I am not," I said.

"You should know!" she said. "He is the greatest American folksinger of all American folksingers. Bill Monroe, one of the brothers in the Monroe Brothers, along with his brother Charlie Monroe. They are the finest of all brother-duet singers in America, the Monroe Brothers."

"I don't know their music," I said. And with a boldness I would never have had back in Leitmeritz, a young man on his own in a new life, prepared not to repeat the mistakes he'd witnessed in his father's reticence, I said, "But I'd like to hear more of it."

"We're here every Saturday night," she said.

Although I'd begun working at the café I did go to see Johann Schmidt, my father's business associate, who might have provided me some lucrative work but who told me he would be leaving for the United States in only a matter of weeks. He was sorry he could not be of more help, and he handed me a wad of guilders to absolve himself of whatever guilt he felt. It was enough money to give me some freedom for a month or two, and I did my best to convince him I was simply grateful for his generosity.

The following Saturday, the Tennessee Sisters were to play again, and again I listened. With every song she sang it seemed that the lead singer was looking right in my eyes. I'm sure, looking back on it, that every man there felt that way, but I only knew then that I did. I was leaving for a walk along the Nieuwe Maas when I saw some boy about my age attempting to talk to her. Accosting her, more like. He was speaking loudly when I approached, and when he saw me, his voice dropped to a guttural growl.

"Finally, he has arrived," Maybelle said. She and this dark boy both turned to look at me. "Are we to go listen to some of the music of Bill Monroe and his brother Charlie now, as you promised? The new LP from Decca Records just arrived from America."

The boy thrust his hands low in his pockets. His shoulders moved forward and there was a bulge down where he held his hand. We had not talked again since that first meeting. I did not want trouble with this boy.

"You were going to meet me at the front of the café," I said, picking up her meaning. The pink scar beside her cheek drew brighter as she smiled, took me by the arm, and took a couple steps away from the guttural boy.

"Next time we will decide to speak in either Dutch or German," she said.

We walked quickly away before the boy could speak again. We walked all the way to the Nieuwe Maas, gas lamps lighting the path to the harbor.

"Will you tell me your name, then?" she said. "I am Françoise."

"I thought it was Maybelle Tennessee."

"That's my stage name. I'm Maybelle, and my partner Greta is Lilly. These names work better with Tennessee than our own."

"I'm Poxl," I said. She looked at me. "Leopold Weisberg. Leopold, Leopoldy, Leopox, Leopoxl, Poxl."

We walked together up the Nieuwe Maas. I told her about Leitmeritz and about my passage on the train from Prague just the week before. We walked near each other as we passed under the lights along the harbor's edge. Uneven cobblestones lined the embankment.

"What was that boy after?" I said.

"Something he could not afford," she said. She was looking at her hands when she said it. Now she looked up at me. "But," she said. "Thank you."

Now she grew quiet, as if in showing her gratitude she'd ceded some ground to me she wished she hadn't. In our silence she walked upright and reserved for the first time. In the quiet of the haze lifting off the river, the air lightened between us. I noted something I'd not seen on that evening of our first meeting: In Françoise's ears were earrings similar to those my mother wore— pellucid amber, shaped like playing marbles, casting tawny shadows on her cheek. Mist grew thick around the yellow glowing gaslights, comingled with Françoise's earrings. I found myself telling her that my mother had earrings just like the ones she wore.

"It's not a good idea," she said, "to tell a girl you've just met that she reminds you of your mother."

I spent some of the wad Johann Schmidt had gifted me on dinner and she talked to me about music I'd never heard of.

"Bill Monroe is not only the greatest American folksinger," she said. "When he was a young boy, he was cross-eyed. He could not see. This is why he learned to play the mandolin the way he did." She paused and took a breath. "When I was a child, I was cross-eyed, too. My mother saved all her earnings for many years. We had my eyes fixed. I believe it is why I can hear the music of Bill Monroe so clearly. But you can't tell they were ever crossed, can you."

"No," I said. Over the smell of meat I could detect the heavy scent of patchouli oil on her skin. "No, I would not ever have known."

5.

One night two Saturdays later, after her set ended, Françoise asked me if I would like to accompany her to a party. She led me ten blocks into the thick of the city and over to Rochussen. Two girls Françoise's age awaited us. They were her bandmate

Greta and their friend Rosemary. The party would be just the four of us, Françoise explained on our walk over. When for the first time I asked her what her friends did, how she knew them, she simply looked at me.

"We work in the brothel," she said. "We play with our band there at times. And."

I put my hands into my coat pockets and pushed my fingers against my palms. In Greta's flat, Bill Monroe was on the phonograph. We drank wine thin as vinegar. Greta arose to dance and pulled me up alongside her. I protested with the little Dutch I had—I told her I was not a dancer, that I would prefer to watch. While my facility with Dutch wasn't enough to let me argue with them, I could comprehend their conversation.

"So he is that kind, is he?" Greta said.

"I haven't yet discovered what kind he is," Françoise said.

"You'll have to find out yourselves," I said.

I stood up and took Greta's hand. Did I imagine I was my tepid father in those moments of action, slipping along the Elbe away from my mother's flirtations? I didn't. I pictured myself a painter unafraid to stand in another man's home without a stitch of clothing, my paint-splattered trousers on his floor, attempting to speak reason to his son. Greta was a substantial girl, her brown hair twisted up like a bundle of kindling. She changed the record to some big-band music and danced up close to me while Rosemary moved against Françoise on the velvet-upholstered sofa on the opposite side of the room.

Rosemary stood and began to dance behind Greta. Then her hands were up under Greta's shirt. Greta began to kiss Rosemary. I had never seen women kiss each other. They grew more sensual. Rosemary lay Greta down and undressed her, then put her face down into Greta's lap and pleasured her until she let out a little shriek. This was the first time I had ever seen female genitalia, let alone tended to so. Françoise was watching along with me, and without giving me time to anticipate it, she kissed me. She'd had a lot of wine. I'd had a lot of wine.

"Take me back into Greta's bedroom," she said. She pointed behind me to a thin silk curtain.

"Do you think we could find somewhere less out in the open?"

"These are my friends," Françoise said. Her freckled skin grew bright with embarrassment. "They won't mind."

"I can see," I said. "It's just that," I said. I could feel the heat slipping from between us. "It's just that I haven't ever seen that before. Or, you know."

Her face brightened until it was almost brown. I could only imagine the shade of red mine now turned. She took me by my hand. Her palms felt as soft as uncooked rice.

Back at her flat, it was as if Françoise was returning to adolescence. She was nervous, as if this was her first time as well. She turned on a softly glowing lamp. She walked over to the stovetop in the corner of her room, turned the governor on low, and lit a burner with a match. She placed a black teapot on the burner and pulled some chamomile tea from a cabinet above her stove. While I stood silent in a corner, she waited for the tea to steep, poured two cups on the countertop, and then walked over to me.

"I love the smell of this tea, don't you?" Françoise said.

Before I could answer her, she kissed me. Her hand was clutching me. On the coarse pallet on her floor, I took Françoise's clothes off. I was a miner seeking some long-sought vein—only after its ore was heated could the precious metal be extracted. Something different happened to Françoise than was happening to me. After I'd finished she grew as cold as the tea on her counter.

"I won't ask it again," Françoise said. "It's been a very long time since I asked it of someone, but with you I feel I can."

The room filled with the smell of tea. Until she stood and walked over to the lamp by her bed to turn it out I didn't understand what she was asking, but then I saw: she wanted the quiet privacy of darkness. In the slick, dim room she moved beneath my fingers until she was done.

When I woke the next morning Françoise had already left. There was no note, no sign of her. I gathered my things and returned to my flat. That night I worked my shift, and the next two, and did not see her again until the next time her band played. When they finished, she told me to meet her at her flat in an hour.

She was in just a robe when I arrived. She had her mandolin out. She began to pick some American folk song she'd learned from her records. While she played, I had a chance to take in her flat with the lamp lit. Clothes lay upon its floor in squalor. But I soon came to learn that if we needed to leave, she always knew just where to find a blouse, a sweater. She kept a fresh tulip on her windowsill each afternoon. Years later, when the war was over, an old Dutch woman would tell me of friends who ate the tulips from their gardens when they were the only thing left to eat. But there in the serenity before the war broke out in earnest, the splash of violet or carmine or vermilion on Françoise's windowsill lent order to her room. She may have been born cross-eyed, but Françoise as I knew her could see and see and see.

6.

One night Françoise invited me to the home of a couple she knew well, and whose complicated role in her life would grow clearer to me in the weeks after I met them. The Brauns lived in Delfs-haven, a quiet neighborhood fifteen blocks from Françoise's flat—236 Heemraadssingel. Their block followed a canal up from the Nieuwe Maas. Over the glassy, still surface of their canal, languid willows dipped their arms down to the water as if searching for something just below its surface.

Inside we encountered Herr Braun, a dentist, and Frau Braun, his wife, who had been Françoise's teacher. By the time she was sixteen, Françoise had already been at work in the brothel for a number of years. Frau Braun had been attractive then—now she was obese, but the clear blue of her eyes allowed me to imagine her in her youth. One afternoon as Frau Braun sat alongside her before an old piano, Françoise had put her hand on her teacher's arm. Frau Braun had pulled it away. Three years later, when Françoise was no longer attending school, Frau Braun had seen her performing with Greta at Café le Monde. They returned together that night to her house, and Françoise visited the Brauns' home regularly in the years to follow.

That night the four of us ate sauerkraut and bratwurst.

We looked out on their garden. The Brauns were attentive to Françoise's needs, which they seemed to anticipate even before she asked for things. There was a familiarity between them that felt almost paternal. They were cold to me, and at first I didn't know if it was because they were protective like parents—or if they felt some other kind of propriety with Françoise.

"What of your work?" Herr Braun said.

"I've just found something permanent," I said. "Working in the cranes. In Veerhaven." I'd been walking down Schiedamsedijk when I heard the familiar sound of a man speaking Czech. Along the canal were dozens of cranes, which served to take the cargo from ships entering the harbor. This Dutch shipping company had bought cranes from Czechoslovakia, but all the men who ran them except him had been called to the army because of the fear of German invasion. In the weeks and months to come, I used these cranes to unload shipments. The money Johann Schmidt had given me was beginning to run out, and it was providential for me to find this work.

"Poxl has done quite well since he arrived," Françoise said. The Brauns nodded and dragged their knives across their bratwurst. "I've even taught him to play some guitar."

We'd settled into some after-dinner port when the Brauns' daughter joined us. Heidi was eleven. She had wiry black hair and skin tawny as if she'd been too long in the sun. She seemed a bit shy with me, but she immediately walked over to Françoise. It was clear they knew each other well.

"Heidi," Herr Braun said, "would you like to sing a song for our guests? Why not one of those American folk songs your mother has taught you?"

Françoise and Frau Braun were suddenly quiet. Now even

Herr Braun grew red at the collar. Heidi walked over closer to Françoise. She blanched white as if a cloud had passed between her and the rest of us.

"You want to sing and you won't, so off with you, then!" Herr Braun said.

"Poxl can play guitar for us," Françoise said. "Heidi, we could do that new Rice Brothers Gang song."

Heidi's soft skin regained its color. She looked Françoise in the eyes. At the back of the Brauns' house I picked up a guitar and began to hack at the only three chords I'd learned since arriving in Rotterdam—G, C, D. It took me a second to change between each chord, setting each finger slowly on its fret, but I could essentially manage it now when given the time. Françoise had been playing that Rice Brothers Gang record incessantly, and in particular a song that was new at the time but has grown quite familiar to listeners in the years since, "You Are My Sunshine." It was the only song I knew. Françoise sang the end of the verse: "If you leave me to love another, you'll regret it all one day."

When she came to the chorus, Heidi sang a perfect tenor, three notes above. Her voice was naturally a few steps higher than Françoise's, but it was as if the same voice was singing the two parts together.

One night the following week, when we'd just arrived home from one of her performances and had had a lot to drink, Françoise said we needed to talk. I was full of wine and ready for bed, but clearly something was eating at her. Hazy as I was, I sat and listened.

"For a long time I've wanted to tell you the story of my

childhood," she said. "Now that you've met the Brauns, and
will surely see them again before long, I'll tell you. But before
I tell you, before I do, first I must know something from you,
something I've been needing to know: What do you think of
my work? Of what I do for money?"

She turned on a lamp, stood and lit the burner on the stove,
brewed some tea. This wasn't going to be a quick conversation,
and I steeled myself for it. Unlike our first time together, now
when Françoise made tea for me, we would go through the ritual of allowing it to steep, and then actually drink it. I'd learned
to wait patiently while she finished this ritual before we could
talk again. It gave me time to consider an answer. I was not dis-
pleased with her. I did not long to leave her. I'd never known a
different version of her—this was simply Françoise, the same
Françoise I'd first met. I'd tried in the past, against my better
judgment, to think of her with her clients, but all I could think
of was my mother and her cuckolding painter. I grew angry, but
not at Françoise. I did not know where to put the anger. In our
time together I'd learned not to ask. I did not know then what
I even thought love was—I only knew that in the moments when
I was with Françoise I did not want to be anywhere else in the
world.

But I could not say any of that now. When Françoise returned
with our tea I said, "You do what you do. It's the only way I've
ever known you. What can I say? When I'm with you, I'm happy."

Françoise handed me my tea. She did not look me in the eyes,
but sipped at her tea while I sipped at mine.

"I think I knew that," she said. She sighed, and we were both
quiet.

And then she started in on her story.

Françoise explained that her father was a colonialist who had gone to the Congo, a Dutch protectorate at the time, to oversee an investment, and had returned with her mother, who was herself the daughter of a colonialist. Her mother, Françoise's grandmother, was Congolese, though from my time growing up in Leitmeritz, I'd never encountered anyone with such a background, and I did not know until she told me that Françoise was one-quarter African. She was taupe. Freckled. There was a touch of albinism in her tan skin, which to the eye of one who knows such things might have been a distinguishing feature of her background. To a young Czechoslovak who for the first time was seeing a Dutch woman in Rotterdam, she was simply bronzed.

As Françoise told me this I sat up on a sofa in her apartment, giving her full attention, attempting not to slouch. Françoise was sitting across from me, her legs tucked under her on a straight-backed chair. When I think of her now I think of the way she was that night: The lightness of her freckles was very light then, the brownness of her cocoa nipples very deep. Her eyes were wide, trained on me as she spoke. She was so young and so unblemished in those days, days when she seemed the most worldly woman I'd ever met.

When Françoise's parents returned to Rotterdam they found the house her father had grown up in destroyed by fire. Her father's investments in the Congo had come to nothing. He sank into a deep depression. Her mother was unable to find a respectable job. The fire and penury led Françoise's mother to work in a brothel near their home. She sometimes brought home more money in a night than Françoise's father earned in a week, if he was seeking work at all.

"By fourteen, I began to work the ships in the harbor myself," Françoise said, "where sailors had comfortable accommodations belowdecks.

"I was good at my work. Being good meant many things. Different things. Some men liked to have me simply for how young I was. Some liked to give me things—mandolins, records, bottles of French and Spanish wine. But I had one immediate need myself in my endeavor, and that was that I not get pregnant. And somehow I was lucky even in that realm: I never had even a scare. It appeared I was barren."

Françoise put her head down again on her pillow. She turned to me and expressed a truth I was coming to learn: Sometimes even the most steadfast facts of our lives can be undone by time and chance.

"Then when I was sixteen," she said, "I noticed one day my menstruation had stopped. Years of work each day the same, each day a different challenge but the same results. Here I was now. Suddenly pregnant." Her mother told her she must not keep the baby. Her father had recovered himself during that period, and had made plans to return to the Congo, where he would be embroiled in a business transaction that could keep them from returning to Rotterdam even to visit for years. Her father was lucky to have found work again. Françoise would not be able to join them if she was with child.

At that moment in her telling me all of this, a new tear appeared in the outside corner of Françoise's eye like the tear that comes upon first waking. It rolled down her cheek and into her ear. Now her face was all hot and wet. It was the first show of defeated sadness I'd ever observed in her. Being full of wine herself, her energy started to flag. She came over to the sofa where

I sat and buried her nose in my neck. We lay down together on the long sofa.

"Isn't it silly?" she said. I had my arms wrapped around her now. "The choices we make."

And then, before finishing her story, she closed her eyes. "It's hard even to think of it now," Françoise said. She stopped speaking. Her breathing grew slow and heavy. Minutes passed with us lying that way. I did not have the heart to wake her. While I waited, too lit by the story to sleep myself, I was plunged into the memory of my last moments with my own parents: The week before my father told me I was to leave for Rotterdam, the three of us had traveled to Prague together. My father had just made a major upgrade to his Tiger Moth biplane, and he wanted to take us each up in it. But when we arrived, my mother refused to join us, no matter how my father implored her. She was afraid of flying, she said, though she'd been up before, and she didn't want to go.

"Take Poxl," she said, her hand distractedly playing with the amber of her earring. "He likes to fly with you. I'll take the car to town for the afternoon."

There was some loose skin around my father's eyes that twitched when he was most agitated. It twitched then without abandon. It wasn't until this moment, lying alongside Françoise, that it struck me this might have been a sign my father knew of my mother's indiscretions.

We took to the sky that afternoon while my mother was in town. A second throttle sat in my rear seat. After flying me faster and more recklessly than my fastidious father ever had before, he shouted back to me, "Take over, Poxl."

For the first time after all those flights watching the back of

my father's helmeted head, first in his Be-50 and then in this
Tiger Moth, I took that plane upward. The slightest nudge
of the throttle sent us down at an angle that seemed to me to
cause mortal danger. I straightened us and then my stomach
made quickly for my feet. But soon I had us horizontal. A
kind of ease overcame me in my seat. Thin fog passed through
us like the skin of vacated bodies, and when I looked far
enough across our leeward side, I saw that these were the wisps
of clouds we were inside of. Wind forced us up and I pushed
in, sent us down. I'd been flying I don't know how long before,
for the very last time, my father's invisible hand retook control of the throttle from me, and he again maintained control
of us in the sky.

"Ace flying, my boy," my father said. By the time we returned
to the hangar, my mother was again with us. A new pair of larger
amber earrings were in her ears.

"Do you like them?" she said. She did not look at my father.
I told her I did, sure. "I met up with Grandma Traute," she said.
"We shopped down in Wenceslas Var."

She and my father didn't speak again until we arrived in Leitmeritz. I nodded off on the ride and in my head I was back up
in the clouds—my body had maintained that altitude, and the
clouds that passed through us or we through them were all
around us again, and I was untethered. When I came back from
my reverie, Radobyl was to our northeast up in the distance, and
we were driving past the fortress walls of Terezin, which then
held none of the meaning it later would, just the remnants of
another, more belligerent time in the town to our south, walls
I'd seen a thousand times before.

Presently Françoise woke again and broke me from my

memory. She sat up, so that we were next to each other on the sofa.

"There is one more part of this story I've been telling you," Françoise said. "Where was I? Right. Of course I did not go with my parents on their new junket in the Congo. I was going to keep the baby. My mother was furious at my decision, and she and my father left me.

"I might have been in real trouble had it not been that around that time I had just begun seeing the Brauns. At first I worked for only Frau Braun, but she began to take me home to her husband as well. They were paying for it, but they were gentle and generous with me, nonetheless, and I came to trust them both. I don't think I sought them out for the sake of the baby at first— honestly, I didn't know what I'd do. But Frau Braun had wanted me, and here was this wealthy couple who had no children of their own. I began to see that it was providence, their having come back into my life.

"When the dentist noticed my swollen belly, he erupted at first, thinking I was claiming it was his, that I wanted money from him. Strange as it might sound, when he came to understand that the baby *wasn't* his and that was not what I was asking, he calmed. And at that same time, a preternatural peace seemed to come over Frau Braun.

"I have learned from my work how to read people. I saw something in Frau Braun's face—something I'd come there looking for. So I stopped pleading. I made my proposal overtly." And so I came to understand that this was what had taken her back to the Brauns that night. There was some safety in her knowing her baby would have a comfortable home with them, and that she could go to see her if she wished.

She stopped talking and looked at me.

"So, you see," she said. "Heidi Braun, the Brauns' little girl—she's mine."

And with her story complete, Françoise said she was tired. There was nothing more to say. It occurred to me, among other things, that Françoise was a good bit older than I'd assumed her to be. But surely I wouldn't remark on such a fact—now, or ever. We crawled off to her bed and went to sleep.

7.

Inside my door one afternoon weeks later I found a travel-worn envelope. My father's rendering of my address there on Scheepstimmermanslaan was barely legible. The first part was dated August 8. It had long been delayed in its arrival.

"Dear Leopold," the letter began.

> Thank you for your letter no matter how brief or belated. Your mother is fine and I am fine and little Pitzky the dog is fine. We have all been wondering about you. We are each fine. In spring Hitler slept the night in Hradcany to spit in our faces. The German soldiers took over Prague with tanks and guns, but not Leitmeritz. I have written the national bank in Prague and I have heard nothing back but we can no longer maintain our funds and we can no longer make purchases and we can no longer liquidate our assets.
>
> I have not heard from Johann Schmidt and I learned

only the other day he has left for New York and could
not have provided you with leather work so you cannot
have work from him. What are you doing to keep aloft,
my son? Please write to tell us. It pains me that we did
not say good-bye to each other before your departure,
but your mother explained you'd had a fight over
money and so you left. I'm sorry that I was not there
to see you off and know that I worry about you. Please
understand I will do for you what I can from afar. And
that I already have. Poxl you should go to the Leather-
sellers College in London. It will be possible for you to
obtain a student visa to attend the school there. Johana
and Niny can provide you a place to live and an
introduction to the city. I have made arrangements with
an associate in the consulate for you to have an exit visa
from the Netherlands and a visa into England. You
should leave immediately.

You ask after our lives here—the Bauers' sugar
factory outside of Prague has been taken. I have gone
to the Central Jewish Office and registered. I have
papers and no one else has the expertise to run Brüder
Weisberg. At the office in Prague they say they will
send up a *Devisenschutz Sönderkommando* to look over our
records. A troop of German soldiers has come through
our neighborhoods in Leitmeritz, asking, and we are
sure to see them again. One came up the Muehlengasse
a few weeks ago and asked after our business and I
asked was he the *Devisenschutz Sönderkommando* and he
asked after my papers, but I told him I didn't have them

and he said he would be back. He was the man who
came through to find out. I would see others soon
enough, he said.

Here there was a break in my father's letter. After the cae-
sura my father had written the new date, September 22, in a hand
substantially less neat than the one that proceeded it.

I write again without amendment or revision. The
Devisenschutz Sönderkommando has come to the house.
We will not control Brüder Weisberg and I would not
tell you Leo that I put up a fight. But what could I do?
There was nothing to do. What will become of it
anyway? No one could tell you, least of all me.

Leo I am looking to London, from where we might be
able to reach Palestine now and you must do the same
and come from Holland this minute if you have not
already. You must go to the British consulate in
Rotterdam where I have arranged for a visa in London.

Your father

I did not note at the time the absence of any mention of my
mother at all in the second part of my father's letter: the cease
of majesty dies not alone, but like a gulf doth draw what's near
to it. Wise as my father's advice might have sounded, and wise
as it clearly was in retrospect, leaving Rotterdam meant leaving Françoise.

I reread the letter.

I thought of Heidi, and it made me think of Françoise with

the Brauns, but that was not enough to rend me from her. I sat down at my desk and wrote a long reply. I told my father I wished him and my mother well in their travels to London and hoped they would arrive safely. He should write me at the address I gave to tell me he'd arrived. I'd met a woman now, and while I didn't tell him it was love that was keeping me—who can say in the moment what makes him do anything?—I told them that I was happy to be there with her. My home now was in Holland, with Françoise.

8.

War broke out across Europe. My father did not write again. The Tennessee Sisters played their gigs at the Café le Monde. Greta lent a high close harmony a third above Françoise's leads as they sang "What Would You Give in Exchange for Your Soul?" Their English was still a little rough, a little full of umlauts I now understand one does not generally find in a bluegrass song. Their clients had provided them with rawhide boots embroidered with colored leather, and shirts with studs and peaked shoulders. They looked the part. If he wears the uniform long enough, even the most peaceable man may grow to be a soldier.

I tried not to think about where Françoise had gotten those clothes each time I saw her play, but on the Saturday-night gig after my father's letter, for the first time it began to eat at me. My father's letter had begun to place some new thought in my mind: I imagined him at work the day I found my mother with her painter, going about his business while my mother went about hers. Was I so different now here in Rotterdam? Well, I

knew about Françoise's profession in a way my father didn't
know of my mother's surreptitious actions. But was that only
rationalization? There was a visa to London. I was staying here
with a woman who received all these things in exchange for—
what?

Françoise's and Greta's voices blended beautifully. There was
something to the act of harmonizing itself that smacked of precision: two voices doing two different things, diverging so they
might come together as one, greater than either alone.

Françoise looked as happy as she ever had that night. Fifty
Dutchmen were in the crowd. Who had come to listen, to see
them, knowing them in the many ways a man can know a
woman? Who'd simply stopped on the street upon hearing two
Dutchwomen singing American gospel songs? I will never
know. Françoise's fingers traveled deftly up her instrument,
pulling out double stops and picking loose melodies over
Greta's guitar playing. When they finished, Françoise showed
me her mandolin case, which was piled full with guilders she'd
received as tips, and she was too happy then for me even to
think of starting a serious conversation about the future.

I suppose there are men who when they are in love know to
call it love, who know its shape, its demands. Who are able to
tell when its wings have begun to rust. You will not find my
name anywhere on that manifest. My understanding of my
concerns was somehow more immediate in those days. Since
the afternoon I'd fled my mother's house I had only one direction and that direction was forward. To stop and survey,
to stop and understand how I was feeling, would have been
fatal. Perhaps it was this myopia that caused the most cata-

strophic decisions during that period of my life. Perhaps that's too easy.

When I think of it now, I can say that I do know what happiness looked like then. On Saturdays when we did not need to work, afternoons before she was to play gigs with Greta, Françoise and I would borrow bicycles from my boss and ride east out of Rotterdam, the direction opposite from the harbor. Not ten miles out of the city was an area where upon the horizon the green and brown of flat grasses gave way to brilliant swatches of color: tulip fields. Françoise would strap her mandolin in its case to her back, and I would strap a guitar to mine, and after ditching our bikes we would secret ourselves back amid acre upon acre of those definitively Dutch flowers. No farmer would disturb us on those weekend mornings, and after we made love, Françoise would teach me to make new chords on the guitar. She was a mandolin player primarily, but now I saw she knew how to play guitar as well as Greta. She would hold the instrument in her intelligent hands and show me three new voicings of G chords that sounded more open and fuller than the basic version I'd first learned. One morning in early spring, the first of a spate of warm days after winter's chill, I asked her to show me another new voicing of a G7, with the diminished seventh in the bass of the chord. But for some reason, she began to fumble with it.

"It's odd," Françoise said, giving up on it for a moment and cradling the guitar between her crossed legs. "I can make that chord easily if I don't think about it. But thinking about it now, trying to *think* where to fret it, I can't make my fingers do it. It's just muscle memory, making these chords. You wouldn't be able to think about it fast enough when playing in time if you tried.

So you make your hand make the chord over and over until you don't have to think it, exactly. You just go to make the chord, and there it is."

She looked up at me, and in her face I could see she felt she'd expressed herself perfectly. But I didn't have that muscle memory, and I didn't fully comprehend. I told her I didn't know quite what she was talking about. Now the skin on her lips bunched together, and I watched the skin around her eyes tighten.

"Perhaps you need to listen better," Françoise said. She was no longer looking me in the eyes.

"I mean, you know the chords, right?" I said. "Of course you're thinking about it."

"Well, I know them, yes," she said. Her eyes were still narrowed and diverted from mine. "But I don't think, C, and then a C chord arrives. I just know I'm about to play a C chord and my hand is gripping the neck. I don't *think* it. I just do it. Maybe if you learned how to give yourself over to it, you'd learn how to play quicker yourself."

I looked down at my hands. I wished so much then that I understood what she meant—how to give myself over to it, to develop the muscle memory. But I could make chords well enough, I thought.

"You really don't see what I mean, do you?" Françoise said.

"Not really."

To my surprise, after I admitted again that I didn't understand, something eased in the tension that had gripped Françoise's face. It pleased her I'd confessed, at least, what it was that confused me.

"To act," Françoise said. "I just act with you now, Poxl, too."

"What do you mean?"

"For so many years I've learned how to perform for men. I read what they need from me, and I give it to them. That's the transaction: for me to fulfill their needs. And that's the right word: *performance*. But with you, Poxl . . ."

She stopped speaking. I do not know if a conversation like this is what it is to be in love—to disagree but to stay around and find out why, so it is no longer a disagreement. To do something so simple as to talk honestly, and then to listen. But I do know it's what it means to begin to know someone: confession, revelation, reconciliation.

"What is it?" I said. "I want you to tell me. Honestly."

"It's like undoing the notes of a chord and then making a whole new chord. Then practicing long enough to make a new muscle memory. For years being with men was like the same basic chord. But since we've been together it's like I've begun to unlearn how I've voiced things in the past. And it grows more complicated. I tried something like this once before—"

"Before?"

"It's where I got these instruments. There was an American, I've mentioned him before. He gave me all these records, gave me my first mandolin, my first guitar. He seemed not only to want things from me but to want to give. He told me he would take me back with him to the American city of Nashville. I believed him. Then I never saw him again."

We were both silent. If love shows itself at times by giving us a sense of propriety, I suppose I came close to understanding it in that moment: I didn't want to hear about her American. I'd kept tucked away any jealousy that might accompany our relationship, her work, but for the first time now I felt it. Blood came to my cheeks. Off in the distance the wind swayed the flowers, a huge patch of yellow tulips dipping away from us and then back in our direction. A cloud passed over the sun, dimming the world around us and honing sharp teeth in the cold air. I almost spoke, almost said that I didn't want to hear about her American. Perhaps if I had then, if I'd admitted that feeling, things might have gone differently in the days ahead. But the smallest thing can change us if we let it, and I did not speak. The cloud blew past, left the sun, and our world again warmed.

"I've never told you why I left Leitmeritz when I did," I said. Françoise looked up from her guitar, where her left hand had begun to form chords again while she listened, though she did not strike the strings with her pick. The skin around her eyes drew slack, bearing relief at having told me about her American, and gratitude for my not pursuing it when she'd finished. "That afternoon," I said, "I came upon my mother in the drawing room of our house with, well, with a painter. Some man. Some man who wasn't my father."

"And you didn't know of your mother's infidelities."

"No, I didn't know! Of course I didn't."

"How did you know he was a painter, then?"

I told her that I'd seen his paint-splattered pants in the corner.

"I'm sorry, Poxl," she said. "I'm sorry, but I do hope you'll think about what must have pushed your mother there. I hope you'll consider how complicated a marriage must be, years down the road."

Now I stopped talking as well. No cloud came to darken those fields, but I drew inward. What did I want in those moments? To argue with Françoise, to defend my father or defend my mother? To parse that old memory of seeing them in the leather yard when I was a kid, to understand what had passed between them? What I found was not what I expected: I simply felt as if my burden had eased, having spoken it aloud. The bright sun lit the tulip field beside us like a sail filling with wind.

Françoise's left hand gripped the guitar again. She struck the chord.

"That's the G7," she said, and she handed me the guitar.

I suppose there are men who know to call it love when they've fallen. Though it's pained and even ruined me over the years, I know only that if I'm happy in a moment I don't want it to end— only to move on the next day, to the next desire, then the next. I have much reason to long for forgiveness, but for that I'll never apologize. I took the guitar back and played the new chord myself. I moved slowly, putting down my ring finger on the high E string, my index finger on the first fret of the low E string, fumbling only to grasp it later. My hand didn't yet have the muscle memory to get it at once. Only time and practice could make that happen.

9.

One evening a month later, as spring was just fully upon us, my gaze fell to the harbor, whose waters were choppy in the wind blowing out to the great open water along the longest port in Europe. Thirty feet below my perch, Françoise, Greta, and Rosemary were standing next to a small dinghy that bobbed along the choppy surface. I saw Greta stick out one of her legs toward the boat and nearly fall forward until Françoise grabbed her arm. Rosemary followed. Then Françoise got in.

I called out to her, this woman I'd stayed in Rotterdam to be with at great personal risk. "Françoise! Up here!" But with the sound of the wind she did not hear me. I tried to return to my work. Ten minutes later three men passed in their sailors' woolens. These men were around my age, perhaps more properly boys than men, as I now understand I was at that moment. They, too, entered a dinghy to return to their boat out in the harbor—the same boat Françoise had just paddled out to. I could swear to this day that one of those boys was the same boy I'd seen talking so gruffly to Françoise just after she and I met. These boys must have been en route between some far shore and the great expansive continent. Perhaps they were Americans, even. Perhaps one of them was the very American who'd given Françoise her mandolin and her records. It was unlikely, I know that now and I'm certain I must have known it then. But it could have been the case. It wasn't, but I might have believed it. This boy I recognized wasn't the painter of my mother's cuckolding, either. But he might as well have been.

I tried to return to my work. A seabird landed on its perch, returning from wherever it is seabirds are always going to and returning from. It looked at me with its black beady eye. Was I my father in his evasive way eluding my mother's grasp alongside the Labe, a river he veritably owned? Or was I my own man, newly aloft in a new city I'd now lived in long enough to call home?

I crawled down from my perch. I found an idle dinghy. The oar left knocking against it was rotted. As I traveled into the harbor gloaming, the boat tossed in the waters of the Nieuwe Maas. Mists rose. Drops sprinkled my face, sending my memory back to the days of my youth by the Elbe, when the mist of the river was lifted to our faces in Schalholstice by the big turning wheel of my father's factory.

I pushed on.

Though for some time I saw nothing but waves, I finally spied the destination Françoise and her friends had reached. For more than a year I'd been unaffected by my knowledge of her profession. Here, faced with the tangibility of this ship, I found a crack I'd known was there splitting into a deep fissure. I found Françoise's dinghy tied to the ship's prow. I managed to square mine alongside it. The deck was slick with harbor mist. I stood by the bow. The only sound was the harsh break of waves lapping at the ship's starboard side. Twenty-five feet ahead of me a portal glowed against the evening's half-light. Looking down through the window, I saw three women pleasuring three young sailors. Strewn over the arms of a pea green ship bed and two desk chairs were wool sweaters with roll necks bunched up like chastised house pets. On the floor, a white cotton undershirt like spilled milk.

Françoise was the most active of the three women. She was sitting up atop the insubstantial, hairless body of that same young deckhand I'd observed paddling out to the ship, moving all about with an energy I'd never seen her take on with me. She had on no shirt. She was utterly undressed, naked in a way different from that she'd ever been with me. I saw a guitar leaning up against the wall in the corner of the berth. I allowed myself to be sure now I'd seen this boy speaking to Françoise that first night I met up with her. As I knelt on the deck of that ship watching Françoise on top of this boy, the guitar in the corner, I tried to convince myself it was nothing. Was it nothing? Then Bohemia and all that's in it is nothing. Seasickness gripped my stomach. Though it went against the most difficult decision I'd made in those months, I resolved at that moment no longer to leave myself subject to the feeling I had then, the same embarrassment my father had so clearly left himself subject to. The facts began to matter less and less. It was what I was feeling that mattered, and I had only one instinct—to flee.

I turned from the window. Just as had been the case that last day I was in Leitmeritz, there was no decision left to be made. It had been made for me, before my eyes. My body *did* have muscle memory after all, and it wasn't the memory of making chords. It was the memory of leaving Leitmeritz that afternoon I saw my mother with her painter. One foot before the other, all the way to the train station. My body knew just how to leave.

That night I packed. Next morning I left my flat for the British consulate to get the visa my father had arranged. With U-boat attacks on ships in the Atlantic and the North Sea all winter long, travel was dangerous, but my body was determined to reach London. In a room at the back of the consulate I was provided a secondhand longshoreman's sweater and a ticket for passage to Britain. I would enter the country at the port of Grimsby, from which I could travel by land to London.

On my way to the harbor I stopped to see if Françoise was at her position at the café. I was about to risk death to put the North Sea between us, but my mind was like melody and harmony in counterpoint—there was a second kind of memory in my muscles and it longed to see Françoise once more.

But she was not there.

When I think of it now, do I recognize what I was doing, the mistake I was making by leaving Françoise without saying good-bye? If you have had such wisdom in the moments when you were driven by emotion, by jealousy and confusion—well, *nostrovia*, as the Russians say. Had I taken a day more to think about it, had I taken Françoise back on a bicycle to the tulip fields, where we could have talked about it, could she have alleviated the anger I was feeling? Would it have changed what I was feeling? I'll never know. What's done can't be undone.

My decision was made. My body was in motion. I would not vacillate further. So I traveled along the same path as during the previous day's trek, and only an hour later a large ship run by William Muller and Company had a space for me, and I boarded.

We embarked.

10.

The open sea was cold. I spent the long passage out the Nieuwe Maas up on deck, looking north and gazing at the waters trying to imagine I could see the U-boats circling us, seeking our demise. While up there I experienced a feeling of the loss of love I'd only experienced something close to one time before. When I was twelve, most of my summer was spent by the oxbow in the river below my father's factory. Evening would arrive as we relaxed upstream from those waters, which served as the waste bin for whatever refuse was sloughed off by the workmen at Brüder Weisberg. Each afternoon before dark the children of Leitmeritz would walk down to the Elbe to the same bend in the river where my cousins and I had spied my mother and father in their broken flirtation when we were too young to know what we'd seen. There we swam. Fifty feet out into the middle of this stretch of water our father's fathers had built a birch-wood dock. Across from this dock dangled a rickety ladder.

One day I walked amid the din of afternoon cicadas crying in treetops. We children of the little city of Leitmeritz worshiped at the brown river's ankles. My cousins lived between my family's house and the river, and I picked them up for the walk. I could think that day only of a little girl named Suse. My pursuit of her had become an idée fixe. She was in Niny's class at the gymnasium, the daughter of one of my father's workmen. I'd known her father, Vladek, since I was a child. He was a dedicated worker who did not speak much. His disdain for his station and for my father was never obvious, but I'd always surmised it must be present.

Suse was a mediocre student. She wasn't dim, but she never seemed to hold an opinion of her own. Even at that young age she was a person who is not living her own life, but waiting for someone to live it for her. There was something not wholly unpleasant in this manner—a certainty to her acceptance of life and its hardships that smacked of a kind of counterintuitive confidence—and it was, for a boy coming from a home like mine, immediately attractive. I told Niny, my sole conspirator, about my design.

"You'll help me speak to Suse today," I said.

"Do what you will," Niny said. "I won't help, but I won't get in your way." Even then Niny knew how to handle me.

She returned to conversation with her sister. I spotted Suse. She was the only girl in our class who'd grown breasts. In the hamstrung light of the evening my eyes settled upon her shape. Niny and Johana and I swam our bodies content while all along I tracked my whereabouts on the banks of the Elbe, always knowing where in the water Suse was. I found myself at day's end resting on that birch-wood dock, next to Suse and Niny.

Niny had always been my favorite. We'd taken long train rides to visit the other Weisberg cousins outside of Debrecen, Hungary, when we were little. We would play games, seeing who could count all the yellow sunflowers outside the train window. By the oxbow behind Brüder Weisberg it was always Niny who would walk upstream from the mill wheel to explore the dark woods that sat a couple hundred feet above our land. Niny's presence provided me confidence in speaking with Suse each time she returned to shore. I said, "You're cold—let's put a towel around you." She only greeted me and then returned to conversation with Niny. I listened. They were talking about their Czech history class.

"Bratislava *was* once the capital of Hungary," I said.

Suse just looked at Niny, not knowing how to respond, not knowing really what I was talking about. Niny laughed at me. She knew if she was too much in my corner, it might tip Suse to my desires. Suse followed her lead and laughed, too. She was not snobbish or curt about it, which gave her a new power over me.

Soon we were all dressed. An early-evening moon stood sentinel over us, lucid in the receding sky. The banks of the Elbe were suddenly new to me, the fields of some distant planet we'd been transported to. Flies lifted out of the low grass in ululating swarms as if shaken off the earth's floor by the vibrating strength of my desire. A low waft of fragrant pollen rose in the night air. Johana joined Niny at a game of cards. I stared up at the purpling sky. The sun was too far behind the western bank of the river and the trees for us to see it set.

Across the way Suse was out of sight. She had trekked off to the stand of trees away from the river. I walked to the cusp of the wood, on the other edge of the purple tamarisk blossoms, where she'd gone to pack her swimsuit. She heard me coming. I said, "I believe I'm in love with you." Something in my honesty held her there long enough for me to speak again. "But I can see you're not interested in me."

A sudden wave of shyness overtook me. I turned away. Behind us the setting sun threw its light onto our little mountain Radobyl. The breeze was slow at my back. It was so close to dark now, I thought there might not be time to await Suse's answer. Then, a couple of steps away, I heard the crunching of footsteps on early-spring wood fall.

Suse's hand was at my back.

I closed my eyes and pushed my lips hard against hers. Suse kept her mouth open while stroking my neck with just the tips of her fingers. Her tongue felt huge against mine, covered in bumps at its side, which presented in my mind the image of a large squid. She pulled me toward her as if she were the man, something I could imagine her father, Vladek, doing to her mother, something I knew in my bones already would have been wholly out of character for my father.

When the sound of crackling branches came again I was so caught in our dark vertigo that I didn't react. Suse was not so intoxicated. She broke away and we turned to see that twenty feet from us a boy from one of the older classes at the gymnasium, whom I'd seen many times but whose name I did not know, was looking at us. My hand had been snaking up under Suse's shirt and had almost found its way to its goal.

He pointed at us and in his loudest voice said, "Little Suse is kissing the Yid from the leather factory! Suse and the Yid, kissing in the trees!"

She pushed me away. My hand sprang toward her again, snarled in her shirt. The boy ran off, yelling to his friends to come see, come see. But before anyone could arrive, Suse ran away home.

When I saw Suse in the future, she did not speak to me. Ours was not a Jewish town, but we Jews lived in relative peace at that period with our Czech neighbors. My insecurities kept me from seeking her again. It was not clear if I had jilted her or had been jilted, only that I no longer had what I wanted. Soon other boys were with her. By the time Suse and I were sixteen, the particular blankness of her character had begun to develop into a hollowness in her eyes. She was tiring from the variety of relationships she had with so many of the boys from Leitmeritz. She became everything to the men who needed her, even men who would point at me and call me malign names.

In turn she became invisible to everyone but the men who had lost her. She lingered in my mind like the wisps of cloud I moved through—or which moved through me—when I was aloft in my father's plane. Some men would embarrass her. Their hungry hands would be all over her in public, hands that seemed guided by lascivious spirits uncontrolled even by their owners. Others were gentlemen. None elicited an observable response, but they weren't thrown off until their own insecurities or boredom drove them away.

Many years later, Niny would tell me that she had learned Suse took up with an SA officer who came to love her during the occupation. When the Russians liberated Leitmeritz in May 1945 on their push through to the German border, she was dragged into the street. Townspeople, all of them men, tore her clothes. They pushed her to the ground. Many were the same men who had made love to her before the war, groped at her, and then left or were left by her.

It was their vicarious shame, Suse's consorting with the Nazis.

She became the living declaration of their own helplessness in the days after the occupation. We lived in a time where such things were possible—when the abstractions of our day could be encapsulated in the body of a living woman. What idea I was leaving behind me then, in the body of Françoise, I could not yet comprehend. It hadn't even fully hit me yet what I'd done in leaving her to begin with—only that I'd lost something, and it was too late to return.

Acknowledgment: First Interlude

The next time I saw my uncle Poxl, it was two weeks after his book was reviewed in *The New York Times Book Review*, at his Boston reading. There was a monsoon outside. Rain sheeted down the windows of a large bookstore just off the corner of Harvard Yard. The carpeted room was packed to the walls with academics and book-club readers, Poxl's former prep school students and his colleagues. We found a seat near the middle of the space, behind a graduate student in a Guns N' Roses T-shirt. The kid wore horn-rimmed glasses, his shoulders covered in a downy layer of flaked scalp skin. I recognize only now that he was everything I tried not to be when I began grad school myself more than a decade later.

On the walls around us were musty used books. Out front were piles of new ones. Chief among them, on a wood-laminate table with folding metal legs, were a couple dozen copies of Poxl's memoir. Since our copies had never arrived, it was the first I'd seen the book in person. On the front was a brown painting of a Lancaster cutting through high cirrus, chased by an Me-109, bullets pinging its side. It was almost cartoonish, the edges of the planes somehow too bulbous, the colors too bright. Had the book landed with a bigger publisher, perhaps it would have had a better cover. Still—it was my uncle Poxl's book, in the flesh. Finally. I looked closely, but no matter how hard I looked, I could not make out the face of a pilot inside the cockpit of the Lancaster bomber. It was as if it wasn't being piloted at all.

But on the back was a full-page grainy black-and-white photograph of my uncle with his arms crossed, feet spread to the width of his shoulders. He stood in front of a tall oak. It was the kind of photograph you'd find on the back of a Stephen King or a John Irving novel at that time—in the days when a writer could become as famous as an actor or an athlete and ascend to the most visible ranks of American public life, could hope to meet Norman Mailer at a party, be reviewed in the *Village Voice Literary Supplement.* A kind of literary fame that's hard even to fathom, let alone remember, now.

Uncle Poxl was everything a sententious musical at the Wang Center could never be.

"Can we get one?" I said.

"Poxl said he'd send us each a copy," my father said. "He said he signed one for you already. Have some faith. It'll come." I didn't argue. But whatever Poxl West did for me, in all the years after the publication of his book, he never did send me that copy. Some part of me will always be awaiting it.

I sat between my parents, who were still in their work clothes. My father was a tax lawyer at a corporate firm downtown, and my mother worked as an administrator at Mass General. They were more markedly not my uncle Poxl than almost anyone in my life—he was a writer and an artist and a war hero. He was about to stand up in front of an audience while they sat watching. My father's father had come from Latvia after the war and worked all the way from janitor to dean at the prestigious school where Poxl taught, before his untimely death. My mother's parents had left Romania after World War I and opened a bakery on Myrtle Avenue in Brooklyn. We saw my mother's parents in New York only a couple times a year. My parents did their duty, making the best of their parents' hard work, their modest but tangible successes. I did not want modest successes. I did not want to be a professional. At that point, I don't know what I wanted, other than a hero. I wanted to listen to my uncle Poxl.

When Poxl caught my father's eye on his way to the podium, we felt we'd been some part of that life he'd led, a life so Odyssean and outsized we couldn't help but listen. Some young hip professor from the Brandeis English Department in a pair of paint-splattered Guess jeans and a salmon sports coat rolled to his elbows talked for five overstated minutes about Poxl West's nearly instantaneous place in the canon of Jewish chroniclers of World War II. His speech was full of humorless references to Eastern European writers I'd never heard of, writers who'd not even been translated into English yet.

Then Uncle Poxl stood.

Without shaking the professor's hand, he put his mouth very close to the mike.

"Before the night is through I would like to read to you from the climax of my memoir, a memoir that is ultimately about love and love's limits, but which contains certain inevitable passages describing as yet unspoken vengeance against the German horror," he said.

Speakers popped. He moved back from the microphone a few inches, found his place behind the podium.

"To begin, I'd like to show you a little of how the Lancaster bomber S-Sugar came to drop bombs on Nazi soil."

Rain ticked against the windows as if to dispel the validity of the pathetic fallacy. Uncle Poxl read from a chapter describing how he and his cousins felt when they first learned of their parents' fate during the war. Heads bowed toward chests all through the audience of maybe a hundred listeners packed into that small space when Poxl described what he knew of his mother's deportation to Terezin. Poxl himself never looked up from his text, which was enormous and imposing as the Pentateuch in his narrow red fingers. Thin red spindles rippled out across his face as he turned to a passage describing his trip from Rotterdam to London by freighter, the fear of U-boat attacks present at every moment. And when he finally gave us what we wanted—and that audience wanted so much from Poxl West, the first Jew so many of us had heard of who had not only survived the Nazi threat but had combated it, literally—and narrated what happened the night he crawled into the cockpit of a Lancaster bomber, when he piloted a plane so that his bomb aimer could drop blockbuster bombs that created a firestorm that destroyed almost every building in Hamburg, it was as if every villain in God's unholy world had been burned in the cauldron of fire my uncle Poxl had lit.

After he finished reading, after the thunder of applause that matched the tempest outside had subsided, the impertinent dandruffed graduate student we'd seen on our way in raised his hand. His was the only head that I hadn't seen dropped in solemn sympathy during the reading. He'd watched, but there was something defiant in his demeanor.

"Mr. West, with all due respect, isn't it possible we've reached a point of saturation with all the first-person accounts of this particular war?"

A hush fell. When I became a professor, or even just when I was a university student myself, I would have recognized this as the overzealous application of a graduate student's desire to question everything he receives. Frankly, it wasn't wholly unlike my attitude toward the stories of survivors I'd heard in Hebrew school. But I didn't see the connection then. I wasn't a professor yet, or an undergraduate. I was a kid at a reading, there to bask in my uncle Poxl's glory, and here was some kid stepping all over it. I expected to see the nostrils on Poxl's sharp nose draw in as they had the few times I'd seen him challenged. But we were close enough to see that no cloud passed his face.

"I haven't ever considered such a question," Poxl said. "This is my life as I lived it. I simply sat down and reported the heroism in which those around me on those harrowing days partook. I don't think of things like 'saturation,' or other stories previously told about it."

The audience had drawn just inches forward in their seats like grass pushed by wind when the question came; now that my uncle had handled it with aplomb, backs touched seats again. Clearly everyone expected that would be the end of it. But the graduate student continued.

"You haven't," the kid said. "Huh."

An older man next to the kid stared at the side of his head like he might do something. Someone said, "The nerve," with a bluster and propriety that sounded as if he had been the one in that Lancaster bomber and not my uncle.

Uncle Poxl's demeanor still hadn't changed. He stood in his chocolate brown Armani suit, with his shoulders drawn back, his hands along the wooden sides of the podium.

"I'd just say there's a certain saturation point with a certain kind of story," the graduate student said. "You know, in the way that Propp posited that there are a finite number of stories to be told at all, there are surely a small number of these. I just wonder what you can say that Primo Levi or Jerzy Kosinski or Elie Wiesel hasn't already." We'd been assigned *Survival in Auschwitz, The Painted Bird,* and *Night* at Hebrew school. I'd read Kosinski closest, and my uncle was no painted bird. He was a Jew who had killed Germans, who had sought the fight when others fled. He was the master of his own narrative. No one had handed me any Borowski, and Kertész hadn't yet been translated into English, I don't think. Not that it would have made much difference to me. I understand now of course that they had all fought their own battles, but I was a teenager, and wholly without patience.

Poxl West was the only hero I needed.

Now my uncle Poxl's face spidered with red lines. He began to respond, but he stopped. A gray old man made a move toward the kid. My uncle's face grew ever redder. The hipster Brandeis professor who had introduced him bumped the microphone with his rolled-sleeved arm on his way up to the podium. Speakers popped as they had when Uncle Poxl's lips first hit it.

"That will be all," the professor said. "Mr. West will be in the back to sign books. Please, just one to a customer."

My uncle Poxl shuffled to the back. The professor whispered something in his ear as they walked to the signing table. The graduate student strolled leisurely out toward the back. He came close enough

I might have reached out and ripped the earring from his smug punk ear, but as soon as violence rose in me—I was too young really to have done anything, and I don't know even now what I could have done—he was already past. My parents and I didn't need books signed; Uncle Poxl had promised copies. We stood to the side of the room as he signed. The line was so long ten minutes passed, then a half hour, and still readers and students stood with books. I was standing before the *B*'s in the Used Fiction section. Right at eye-level was a green old dust jacket that read "Bellow—*Herzog.*" A smell like dead cumin arose from the thing as its pages flapped freely in my hand. My father looked at me. I hadn't even realized until after I'd done it that I was half-expecting a hundred-dollar bill to fall from it.

Every story my uncle Poxl told moved through me like radiation.

My mother said, "We could be here forever. I'm sure we'll catch up with Poxl before he leaves town." My father agreed, but he wanted to catch my uncle's eye before we left.

Uncle Poxl was talking to a thin young man with blond hair cropped tight to his head, and a tweed jacket. When I looked down, I saw something in Uncle Poxl I'd never before seen: He sat with his shoulders hunched forward, his feet one on top of the other like they were trying to hide under his chair. He seemed not to be answering any of the questions he was being asked by this young man, but only wanted to move him along. Maybe he wanted to be done so he could come see us; maybe he was simply tired after a reading that had gone on longer than he'd intended, ended with a question he'd not expected amid the personal triumph of bringing his book to publication.

But where he'd shimmered like a flag in a strong wind when he'd walked into the room, now he looked older, shaken, vaguely defeated. It was hard to reconcile it with the fame he'd just attained, the triumph of his narrative voice. We left without getting to talk to him. We never even got to congratulate him in person on his success.

* * *

Uncle Poxl didn't come to call on us after his reading like he'd promised—my father said Poxl had left a message pleading for our leniency amid the chaos of his trip. He was off to New York and then the West Coast only four days later, and he hoped to visit Harvard, MIT, and Radcliffe before he left Boston. It sounded more like an invention than an actual excuse, but who could blame him with this new light shining upon him?

But this didn't mean we would wait any longer before reading, finally, his book. On the kitchen table in front of my father, as he told us this story, was a thick plastic Waldenbooks bag. Inside were three hardcover copies of *Skylock*, one for each of us Goldsteins.

"We'll have him sign them when he's through with his tour, Elijah," my father said. "But at least now we can read it."

Uncle Poxl's memoir was well over two hundred pages long. I read and read and read that first night after I got it, but my energy began to flag halfway through. I'd read more than enough to see that the stories as he had put them down were somehow fuller, more real and true than when he'd read them aloud from his manuscript pages. It's no longer a surprise to me to find that first-person accounts are more evocative than the historiographies I teach, but at the time it was a revelation. My uncle Poxl's stories now, between two covers, were so full of wandering detail, flashback, and of course, of the action that he'd recounted to us that night in Boston.

But more than that, they were typeset, printed, and bound. Somehow the permanence that binding his stories had received made them more believable, more important as I read them than they'd even been as he read them to me. As Poxl's Tiger Moth pitched and rattled, as the ailerons on his Lancaster iced over and lightning struck his bomber mid-flight, the image doubled: In the front of my mind, sun glinted off the Perspex of Uncle Poxl's cockpit, drawn near-blindingly bright by adjectives and precise images. But in the back of my mind flashed only images of a youthful old man, lit from behind by some terrestrial sun, his hands gesticulating wildly around his head as he read to me from these same stories over a bowl of rapidly wilting whipped cream.

Though I had finished only half the book late the night after my father handed it to me, before I closed it I instinctively turned past the final pages, to the material that came after the narrative of the book had ended. There I found a list of those people my uncle Poxl had wanted to acknowledge for their help in the production of his book, in bringing this life goal to fruition for him—the culmination of so many years of work. There were plenty of names there, but I didn't let my eyes linger. Because I saw only one thing, standing out as if bolded and italicized—a lone tree in a forest—in a list toward the bottom half of the page:

"And thanks to Elijah Goldstein, my first reader and constant listener. I've told these stories to you, and for you."

Poxl had noted me. There was my name, my full name, in print for the first time. When I published my first paper in an academic journal decades later, and every time since, it has felt simply a reiteration of that first moment I saw my name in Poxl's book.

Would I be lying if I said seeing it was better than it would have been to be standing on stage at the Wang? To have a painting hung on the walls of the MFA? All those painters were long dead. My head felt lifted toward the ceiling by a sense of importance you might call ego—a sense that, if I'm honest, I've sought ever since without being sated, no matter how many journals accept my work. Spidery fingers ran up the back of my neck.

My reverie was broken when my mother called my name. The book clapped shut on my egotism. I yelled to my mother that I knew, I knew, and I turned out the light only to turn to dreams of my own grandeur mixed with my uncle's.

I bragged of my uncle Poxl's success for weeks after that night I got his book. The first weekend after, I read the second half, all in one sitting, a whole Saturday afternoon lost in Poxl's European world. Now as I read, my energy didn't flag. In the weeks that followed I read it over and over. Some days I came home and ran upstairs just to stare at the acknowledgments page again. I had been at work for months on a sententious poem, modeled on the Keats we'd just begun reading in English class, entitled "Upon Being Acknowledged." It wasn't quite an ode and it wasn't quite a love poem, but it encapsulated all the self-seriousness and ardor of both.

Though I'd only read Poxl's book, not lived his life, now I peppered conversation with both the language of the memoir—"Have you ever seen a nacelle?" I might ask a friend. "Do you even know what one is?"—and the broader life experience it implied. I'd only just kissed a girl for the first time at summer camp the year before, but now I felt I knew what it was like to have been with prostitutes in brothels in Rotterdam, to have fought in a war whose aims we now understood to have been wholly noble. I'd read and knew that there were mitigating factors, of course, the complicated relationships Poxl had been through, but somehow those passed between my fingers like water. I was reading for airplanes and heroism, and that's what I found.

I told anyone I could all about Uncle Poxl's accomplishments. The book received another glowing review in the daily *Times* the week after his *Book Review* triumph, and in the very same *Boston Globe* Poxl's neighbor had written so many reviews for over the years. A week later it landed on the bestseller list. Not at the top of the list, but it was official: Poxl West was a bestselling author.

I'd stayed on at my synagogue, Beth-El, to be confirmed in the years after my Bar Mitzvah. On Monday nights, I'd head out Route 9 to a Hebrew class Rabbi Ben offered for the handful of us who'd stuck with it. His class was relaxed, more catching up on our social lives and our spiritual lives than arduous Hebrew study. When I arrived one night soon after Poxl's reading, Rabbi Ben interrogated me about him.

"So your uncle's book got published," Rabbi Ben said.

I'd just pulled up one of those desks that was attached to a plastic chair. Our classroom was in the basement of the shul. The heat of the building's massive boiler pushed in on us. The room smelled of must, and of Ben's patchouli oil.

"Way more than just published," I said. "It got a glowing review in the *Times* this week. It made the bestseller list. It's a great book. The *Globe* said it's destined to be a classic."

"Maybe you could get him to come talk to our class," he said. "Like, in between our Hebrew lessons we could talk to him about writing, about making images and stuff. Oh, or man, we could get him to come along with a songwriter and a poet or something, and have them talk about craft." Rabbi Ben was always trying to catch our ears by talking to us about what he thought we wanted to hear—it was all poets, and song lyrics, and if we'd let him, talk about Kabbalah, the study of Jewish mysticism. We wanted to learn Hebrew and flirt. What made him think we'd care about some esoteric sixteenth-century mystics was beyond me.

"I bet it's really expensive to get him to give a talk now," I said. I had no idea if that was true, but it sounded right.

"He's your uncle, right?" Rachel Rothstein said. I'd had a crush on her since the third grade, and even though we were in school and went to shul together, I don't think she'd ever acknowledged me before. Even the confidence I'd gained from that summer camp kiss hadn't helped. My uncle's memoir was paying off in ways I couldn't have imagined. "You couldn't get him to come?"

"I guess I could," I said. "I mean, he's not my real uncle." Rachel Rothstein looked disappointed. I needed her not to be disappointed. "I mean, he's more like a grandfather to me."

Rabbi Ben looked at me. The other six kids in the class were looking at me now, too. I only looked back at Rachel Rothstein.

"I guess I could try," I said. "If he's in town for some other event or something."

Everyone seemed happy with that. Even Rachel. We returned to our Hebrew text. The attention withdrew from me, and for the first time since I'd read his book, I was glad we weren't talking about my uncle Poxl.

Time and again during the weeks that followed the publication of *Skylock,* my father would come back with a magazine or a newspaper that had reviewed Uncle Poxl's book. This was more than a decade before the advent of the Internet. The only way to find out what was being said was to seek out those periodicals themselves. There was a cigar shop and newsstand in Jamaica Plain, near my father's office, that carried every magazine you could think of. On a Saturday afternoon in late April my father told me there was a piece on the book in *The Economist.* We should go seek it out, he said.

I'd never even heard of *The Economist* before. Why, I asked, would a magazine about the economy run a story about my artist of an uncle?

"It's the biggest magazine in England," my father said. "It's about everything happening in the world. And it will be a real feather in your uncle's cap to have been mentioned there. Not just because so many people will read it but also, since he lived in London for so long, because it will be another kind of triumph."

So that afternoon, one of the few Saturdays in that period my father didn't have to head into his office to work, we left our house in Needham for the city. As we passed through the back roads of Welles-ley, across the road that passed before the reservoir, I looked out my window to see a family of deer shocked by the whir of our Volvo engine, heads up, from their stolid meal. We made the long drive along Route 9 and into Boston. Puddles had begun to collect in the woods alongside that small highway, the last remnants of the snow that had covered the ground winter long. Bare trees popped buds like tiny green lightbulbs all up and down their branches.

This was the first time I'd made that trip on a weekend since my

uncle Poxl's book had come out—after months and years of riding
into the city with him for our cultural outings, now I was returning
to downtown Boston. Only this time my trip was to see Poxl through
the scrim of space and time, through the window the magazine
provided into his life. The only time I'd been with Poxl in the past
weeks, it felt, was at night, when I was reading his memoir. It was as
if the Uncle Poxl I knew now was a teenager, set adrift across the
Continent with the onset of war.

We parked. Even though spring was upon us, the damp air brought
a biting chill, somehow colder even than the frigid nor'easters we'd
just endured. My father popped his coat collar against the cold. We
arrived at the newsstand, and there, in the back of the magazine, was
a review of Poxl's memoir, complete with a photograph of his ruddy
Ashkenazi face. Under the photographer's flattering lights the garnet red of my uncle's face seemed almost to glow, giving off a sense
of import and beauty. He wore a Harris tweed jacket and a burgundy
tie and looked every bit as hale as he had in the days before his Boston reading—it was as if that dandruffy grad student had never questioned him, as if no one had ever questioned Poxl West once in his
whole Nazi-killing, war-enduring life.

The piece was not quite as glowing as the *Times* review, but it felt
as if a consensus was building that Uncle Poxl's memoir was an important one, no matter its flaws. At times the book wandered, the
unnamed reviewer said (I didn't understand then that all the articles
in *The Economist* were unbylined, and the fact seemed all the more
curious in the light of Poxl's success and in the glow of having seen
my own name in print). At many (many!) times it was a bit more sexu-
ally graphic than the reviewer might have liked. And while the details were revealing of a certain kind of war experience most readers
hadn't seen before, the reviewer felt its depiction of England was "too
broad." In the final paragraphs he went on to praise Poxl's writing
and to suggest that the book would likely be read in the years to come,

but each henpecking at the book's details ate at me. I could see only the criticisms.

I felt like reaching across the page and punching that unbylined reviewer in his mealy, unbylined mouth. My uncle Poxl's memoir had hit the bestseller list just weeks after publication, and here was some anonymous reviewer trying to pick at it. I didn't understand then that the book's early success was part of what drew it attention, scrutiny.

Now the damp cold cut through my jacket when we exited the cigar shop. My father and I walked back to the car, traversed the city, and as we drove the roads of Jamaica Plain and into downtown Boston we crossed the same streets where my uncle Poxl had once taken me for our weekend outings.

"Wanna head over to Cabot's for a sundae?" my father said. "I know you and Poxl used to go there after your days together."

"It's a little cold out for a sundae, don't you think?" I blew into my hands.

"Well, then, a grilled cheese," my dad said. "We could get a grilled cheese. Or something."

But I demurred. My father stood there in his lawyer's jacket and with his lawyer's stolid face. Every event that kept me too far from my uncle's book in those days felt like a burden, a jilting—and after reading that review I just wanted to look at the book again, to remember its heft, its import. The ride back on Route 9 seemed to take twice as long as the ride out. This time no deer appeared beside the road. The trees looked like they'd never again wear leaves. My father and I barely talked.

"It's a very particular book," he said as we neared home. "It's not for everyone. You know Poxl suffered so many losses—including losing his wife—and some of it can be hard to read. His confessions about Françoise can be hard."

"It's a perfect book," I said. "That reviewer has no idea what he's talking about. I mean, he couldn't even put his name to it? Cowardly."

My father tried to say something more, to explain the magazine's policy, but I was too distraught from the effect of the review to listen.

When I got back to my room Uncle Poxl's book was facedown on my bedside table. That book didn't need to press itself up against the paucity of content of *X-Men* compendia, *Bill James Baseball Abstract,* or even the classics of American literature we read in class. I sat down on my bed and touched the back cover, my fingers lingering over Poxl's face. The back of the book lifted a little on its own, Poxl's author photo moving from the table toward me almost like one of Shakespeare's ghosts, with the natural levitation cracking the spine at the acknowledgments page.

ACT TWO

I.

I arrived in London after my long trip on the Batavier Line and was admitted to the UK at a port in the small northeastern city of Grimsby. After my first sight of that precious gem set in the silver sea, I arrived in London by train four days since last seeing Françoise. I found my way to the little two-bedroom flat in Bermondsey where Niny lived with her sister.

"Poxl, you're here! And just after I've had the most terrible night," Niny said.

She approached me at the threshold to her flat as if it was the most natural thing in the world that I was now suddenly in London. She held me tight. Niny was a slight brown variety of cousin. She had a smattering of dark moles across her face that longed to be read like Braille, the most pronounced just above her upper lip. She wore dark-rimmed glasses and a printed linen dress. Her shoulders hunched forward as if she was forever trying to inch closer to you, the hollows of her mole-speckled clavicles grown obscure with shadow.

"You feel very skinny," Niny said. "Let's get you a meal."

Niny favored her left leg as she walked toward the small kitchen in her flat. Her toe was wrapped in tissue soaked through with blood. She saw me eyeing the injury and said, "Oh, I've stubbed it trying to get off the train. It's so dark between the blackout and there being no moon or streetlight."

Given the effects of my arrival, fatigue, and the comfort of seeing Niny's face, I'd not noticed the blackout curtains drawn against the evening. The room glowed with soft yellow light sent infinitely back upon itself. Even my cousin Johana's little ceramic spitz, which I remembered from their home in Leitmeritz, seemed to emit a halo of refracted light.

"Your eyes adjust as much as they can," Niny said. "In the end you can't see a thing. Just a dim blue bulb when you reach your station."

She unwrapped the tissue from her foot to reveal a half inch of flesh lifted off her big toe. The bleeding had stopped, but it was still a mess. I took her into the kitchen and washed it.

"I'm happy to have you here," she said.

The hand on my shoulder gripped tight. Then, with her toe freshly wrapped, Niny was off to the kitchen, where she prepared Wiener schnitzel as we ate it back home, enough for Johana, too, as well as some cucumber sandwiches with cream cheese on soft white bread. Amid rationing for the war, these were luxuries. I was telling her of my trip from Rotterdam when the jingling of keys signaled Johana's arrival.

"Well, out with it, then," she said as soon as she'd settled into her seat at the table. "Let's hear all about the fun you had in your protected Netherlands while we were here, awaiting the next trauma."

Johana was a small, ruddy-cheeked woman in her mid-twenties whose husband, Vaclav, had sent her to London with her sister while he stayed in Prague to see to his work at Brüder

Weisberg, all with the empty promise that he'd travel to London when he could. Johana and I never got on when we were children. Now here she was in London, an adult. She wiped her hands on her napkin.

"I said out with it, Poxl," she repeated.

"There are many stories to tell of Holland," I said. But I didn't tell any. My cheeks burned with a longing to be alone with Niny. Ugly embroidered pillows covered the threadbare sofas in the flat. In the corner, Johana's ceramic spitz was looking on at us.

"You are in London now, and you must speak English," Johana said. "Speak German here and they'll think you're a Fifth Columner. Send you off to be interned."

I hadn't even noticed I was speaking German. Niny seemed to agree there was some sense in this. So in what English I had I told them of my passage across the North Sea. Then silence ensued. I broke it to inquire after what they knew of my parents and theirs. Niny told me they knew nothing of them.

They hadn't heard a word in weeks.

2.

The early spring of 1940 found me using every method I could at the Leathersellers College to tan hundreds of pieces of leather. Away from my father I was at once home again—and the farthest I'd ever been from it. In the glowing eggshell light of the model tannery, I stood alone with hide that bore the old Brüder Weisberg death smell. My nose had learned to know death long before my eyes ever did. Bristles poked at my hands as they had back at the factory. Shivers at once pleasant and dour rippled over my skin.

One afternoon in those first days I came upon a newsstand where the front page of the *Evening Standard* read LOWLANDS TAKEN; ROTTERDAM BOMBED; NETHERLANDS HITLER'S. German troops, the story below it told, had descended on Belgium, Luxembourg, and Holland. Dutch warplanes engaged in dogfights with Luftwaffe planes, which were dropping bombs all over Rotterdam.

I'd missed the invasion by only a matter of weeks.

Now that city lay in ruins, an untold number of its citizens killed.

German troops were parachuting into the streets.

I rushed home, but what was I rushing for? The flat was empty. Nothing I could do at that moment would allow me to undo the decisions I'd made. My first thought was of course that Françoise might be dead—she and all her friends. My second was a flash of Françoise alone in those tulip fields we'd gone to together, playing her mandolin. Where did she think I'd gone? Then my anger at watching her at her work returned. Probably I thought then it was best I'd left. That I'd not been there during the bombings. But if Françoise was dead—some part of me felt that even in leaving Holland, even leaving in such a huff, one day I might be with her again. What had I done? I'd never lost someone so close. Janos Heider committed suicide when we were in sixth form, but my parents hadn't taken me to the funeral. I'd been to my grandfather's funeral, but I was too small to remember it.

Neither of them was to me what Françoise was. What had become of the Café le Monde? The Brauns down on Heemraads-singel? The only thing I could do was write a letter. I sat down to draft one—not to Françoise, but to Herr Braun. I asked if they were okay, let them know they were in my thoughts. If Françoise was okay and she wanted to contact me, she would surely learn of this letter and get in touch.

While I was drafting this morbid letter Niny arrived home. She instantly recognized my distress. She put her hand on my shoulder and let me write my letter. Later that evening she came to my room, and I told her of my history with Françoise.

"So easy to fall in love," Niny said. "You always were. I'm sorry, Poxl." She seemed to understand the pain I was in. She looked off out the window. It wasn't yet dark. The blackout curtains were still open. Light slanted in and lifted my mood. "But when you left, you must really have been hurting."

"I was," I said.

"You weren't even thinking of what she must have thought when she found you gone."

"I wasn't."

We both sat back in our chairs and looked at each other. Niny took up the newspaper I'd brought home. I could see that she wanted to continue, to bring home to me what I'd done, but that she could tell how distraught I was already.

"Half the city's buildings destroyed in one day," she said. "That's not half the people, Poxl. It's buildings. Two wholly different things." As she spoke I watched the motes in the slanting light. "You'll wait to see if you get a letter back. Meantime, you'll have no choice but to continue on."

There was a sound at the door. Johana had returned. She looked in on us but didn't say anything. Niny left me alone, too, after kissing me on the forehead. I heard Johana in the kitchen opening cabinets and closing them. Not long after she'd started banging around in there I caught a whiff of a smell so familiar that it carried with it memories: my mother's face; amber earrings clacking against each other; the thin fog of cloud as it surrounded my head in my father's small propeller plane; the dark purple outline of Radobyl in the near distance. Johana came into the room with a plate of fried cheese. She put it down in front of me.

Smazeny syr.

During the weeks that followed I heard on the radio that Holland had capitulated before the Luftwaffe had begun bombing—the queen had, like me, fled to London. The last few Dutch pilots turned west and kept right on flying across the North Sea until they, too, landed on British soil. It was as if everyone in Rotterdam was absconding for the UK. Still no word came from the Brauns, and no word from Françoise, either. Perhaps now she didn't even want to hear from me. It had felt powerful, the regaining of some propriety, leaving for London when I had. Now I was entirely powerless even to know what Françoise was thinking—if she was even alive.

My mind was given over to thoughts of flying. Each BBC report of the overwhelming power of the Luftwaffe made me think of the planes I'd flown with my father outside of Prague.

A new idea set in for me.

I could fly.

It was a matter of figuring out how to enlist.

There in London, Churchill took over. The next week,

300,000 British soldiers evacuated Dunkirk. Londoners settled into routines. Those with means sent their children out of
the city for fear of bombings. I rode my bicycle up to Downing
Street and watched as buildings on Whitehall were plied with
sandbags. Soldiers put up Browning machine guns. We were
lucky to have the freedom to observe it: Many of the Jews who
had arrived from points east were now being detained in refugee camps on the Isle of Wight. But since Johana and Niny had
established themselves, we were lucky to be spared that burden.

3.

One morning in early June a pamphlet came to our door. It was
entitled *What Can You Do If the Invasion Comes?* I arrived at a section entitled "How to Protect Oneself While Walking About,"
then this pair of sentences:

"In Holland, Dutch soldiers were gunned down in the streets
by German soldiers. Be certain to have your wits about you, and
if you see your own soldiers engaged in battle, do steer clear of
them."

And so I took to the streets of central London to seek out
an enlistment office. If it wasn't hard enough for me to get
around this new city already, street signs had been removed
now, so if a German attack accompanied an invasion, the soldiers would have a hard time navigating London. Pillboxes
went up all around the city disguised as huts or petrol stations. They disoriented me, obfuscating the few landmarks I'd
come to recognize. I rode my bicycle across London Bridge

and applied for work with the Civil Defense Department.
There was a limited amount I could do in the active war effort
as a refugee.

By mid-August, when I stopped, as I did every day, to check
in with the Civil Defense Department, I was offered a job driving a mobile canteen. This was not yet joining the RAF. Driving
a truckful of potables was not countering Luftwaffe planes.
But it was a first step.

My Czechoslovak passport declared me Class C, "friendly
alien," and though back at the end of May, Churchill had had
all the Austrian and German refugees interned, I was hired. My
canteen was a Chevrolet truck donated to Bermondsey by the
people of the American city of Chicago. In the bed of this truck
was a small superstructure we would load up with food and
drive out to the Home Guardsmen and the ack-ack operators,
who had yet to fire their flak at Luftwaffe planes.

My first week at the job, I was partnered with Clive Pillsbury, a lank Brit in his mid-twenties. His face was blanched save
for scattered freckles across his nose and the upper parts of his
cheeks. He had the face of a teenager, the manner of a much older
man, and he was possessed of a gravity and wit that made him
a welcome companion.

That first day we went out together on the streets of London
I was forced to depend upon him for directions. I studied the
city maps, marking the main avenues, but I was hopeless. "This
right here on Oxford Street—no, right, make a right," Clive
would yell. "A left here. Poxl, a left, my boy. Oh, we've missed
it again, then. Mightn't we consider trying to find another
driver?"

I looked at him.

"I know, I know, my license and all. But it will be something if we're able to get there. And now—there—no, you've missed it again."

"Why don't you have the wheel yourself?" I asked.

He didn't respond, only turned a bright red at the skin above his collar.

"Drive on, then," he said.

I had been told by our dispatcher that Clive had lost his license after driving the better part of the previous year, all throughout the Phoney War, until an unfortunate drunken incident left him unable to drive. I hadn't learned what kept Clive from driving, but I assumed I was better off not pushing it. The subject of driving was a sore one for irascible Clive.

While I became inured to our paths across London, we found ourselves circling neighborhoods. British planes were fighting the Luftwaffe on the coast, and our charge gained urgency. Where wounded soldiers had been spotted returning through Waterloo Station after Dunkirk end of May, now homeless suburbanites trickled into the city for respite.

"We shall get used to it in time," people would say. "Business as usual."

At night a pink glow rose from the southeast. Bombs hadn't yet fallen on London proper. In the evenings, Clive and I would drink. Clive's self-control in the public houses made the story I'd heard about him losing his license even more suspect. He was completely self-possessed. His secret to holding his liquor: Every three pints of bitter, he would drink a cup of coffee—ersatz coffee, amid rationing, but it was a drink he preferred to the tea his fellow Brits commonly drank. I took to having a cup myself amid all the drinking, coming to like the rectitude implied by such routine.

4.

When we heard the sound of the air raid siren at home—the sound of a couple hundred banshees all letting their voices cry upward and downward to signal that bombers were soon to be overhead—we dropped what we were doing and huddled in the Anderson shelter out back. It brought me and my cousins a new closeness, an ease like we'd had back in Leitmeritz. And something new. We would sit together, imagining this could be our last moment on earth. And something changed in us. Johana would let her fingers grip mine while her other hand gripped Niny's. We weren't children, cramped together in a tiny metal shelter, awaiting Luftwaffe bombs. We weren't adults, either. We were three cousins pressed together, not knowing what would come next, unable to predict what the next second held for us.

Those self-same banshee cries came to define much of that autumn for us—for all of us in London at the time. One night the first week of September, Clive and I sat in a pub near Bermondsey. Another air raid siren went off. I tipped my beer back before turning for the exit. But this was not the proper comportment. As they did each time the sirens went off, as I'd soon realized the previous spring, the bar's patrons remained seated. This might seem the kind of apocryphal story those who've been through war tell once it's long over, misremembering or embellishing somehow. I can attest to the fact it was this very attitude that allowed the war to continue until Luftwaffe attacks could be subdued.

Here at Smithwick's Pub with Clive Pillsbury, I found myself sitting in a bar whose windows might implode with lethal shards, whose stone walls might fall and crush us. But we weren't going anywhere. Conversation in the bar continued as if we were a group of thanes all pretending not to notice the king in heated argument with an invisible ghost. Whole notes of the air raid siren rose and dipped. No one changed his demeanor. The barkeep pulled me a Whitbread. I returned to our table. Clive sat with his coffee. He went about trying to create the admixture of milk and coffee, while all the time the sound of the siren rose and fell. Three times Clive filled his mug to the point of overflowing, then sent it back. Though he made a mess of his place at the table, Clive was repelled by disorder. Coffee drew ever more toward the top, the liquid topped off at the lip of the mug, and his hands would work—first milk, then spoon in after. His eyes never left the mug. He was at this business, the two of us ignoring the sirens, when suddenly he stood.

"I'm off to the lav," he said. The sirens continued. I know now that bar was never hit by a bomb. But I still sat waiting for the roof to crush me. What would happen when glass shattered? When the world ended for me with no one even by my side to witness it? Clive returned. The siren stopped and we sat through minutes of silence. Later in the war we would hear dogfights overhead. But this had not occurred yet. We heard nothing but Glenn Miller playing on the radio. Then a higher-pitched cry, all one high C note: the all clear.

We were quiet again for a moment before Clive's confession came. It came all at once. He said, "No one ever thinks that he's anything but the best behind the wheel. They all think they're the best driver in London.

"Bollocks."

Around us people returned to speaking at normal volume.

"Everyone gets a tad crazy behind the wheel," Clive continued. He still had not lifted his eyes from the lip of the mug. "Me, I get angry while driving, sure, but I never see red. I see black. I get blind. I come to lose myself."

This was the talk of a man who speaks more the more nervous he becomes. I noted this strange progression: He'd been in perfect command of himself during the threat of a raid, but now that that was past, something changed. Rills of coffee the color of river silt were spilling all over the sides of his mug. I looked around for a waiter but he was with the barkeep sipping a Watney's.

"It wasn't seeing black kept me from driving," Clive said. He continued to look down into his coffee. "Do they tell the story around the station, then?"

"What story?"

"'What story?'" Clive mocked. "What do you think? I can see it all over your face. The story of how Clive Pillsbury isn't driving the canteen truck because he cracked."

"People say you were drunk."

"Too much drink has kept me from driving?" he said. "If only. A few too many whiskies, a man recovers in a day." At a corner table a squat man with a gleaming head told a joke that kept his two companions laughing. A crescendo had been building in the minutes since the all clear. Clive was sopping away at his mug, into which now he continued to pour milk from the small pitcher at its side.

"Might be good to take a sip if you don't want to spill over any more," I said.

Clive's cheeks flushed.

"'Might be good to,'" he said.

For the second time in five minutes he'd mocked me—and the second time he'd ever done so.

"It might do to take a sip, Poxl. But I can't. Same reason I can't drive the truck." He fell silent again. "You see, I get in this way so I can't do a thing."

"Can't do a thing?" I said.

"Like with this cup of coffee here." Clive looked down at his mug and then put a finger to its rim. "For a long time I knew how I liked my coffee. I knew it more and more, until I could drink it only if it was the right combination." I told him that everyone has a way he likes his coffee. "Not like this," Clive said. "I can see the color without tasting it: caramel, only not. September clouds, only not gray. And this"—Clive was pointing down at his coffee—"is not right."

"One time I'd gotten into my car at the end of a long day," Clive said after a pause. "As I was driving I thought I'd hit something. Could have been a dog. I drove back. There was nothing. The next week it happened again. This time I was sure I'd hit something. Still, I got half a mile from it before turning back.

"Nothing.

"A couple of days later I thought I'd hit something again. This time I decided I must not have. I got ten miles away before I turned back and found nothing there.

"It began to happen more and more. The bump would stick in mind until, when I got back to the location of the first incident, my mind had made it into a human-size bump. Even when it was a man I'd thought I'd hit, I'd convinced myself I'd hit nothing. I would almost get home. Then, a hundred yards from my door, I'd go back.

"Only now, on the ride back to the scene, I'd hear a new bump. In my mind it was a man again. Do you know the guilt, believing you've killed a man? Even if it wasn't intentional. Even if you didn't witness the carnage with your own two eyes. Who *wouldn't* it drive mad? The circle grew tighter until, just before you arrived and came after a job with the Home Guard, I almost didn't make it to my house one night. Six in the morning before I arrived home. Eight hours to drive fifteen miles."

A smell rose from the bar as a patron lit a cigar. We could hear each tinkle of each glass touching the next in the cabinet behind the publican. The silence in the absence of an air raid siren was blaring.

"It happened in the canteen car, too," Clive continued. "They were shorter drives. I returned to the station on the same routes we'd taken. I would sweat the whole time, convince myself on the way back to the station I would be able to see what I'd hit. Only on my way home, I couldn't get there. I kept getting into tighter loops."

"This all sounds scary, Clive," I said. "Surely you don't sound as if you've cracked. Your nerves are simply frayed."

"I've got a theory," Clive said. "I believe I've come to understand the cause of it all, what my mind's up to. What the world's up to. Zeno's paradox. I read philosophy at Oxford. Zeno was a Greek philosopher who held that if you looked at it using math, no physical mass could ever move. He used the example of a bow and arrow. In order for an arrow to hit its target, it's got to move through space—let's say ten feet. To get halfway to its target, it must go five feet. Each time the arrow moves across this smaller space, it must get halfway there. It's mathematically impossible for the arrow ever to get there. It'll divide in half infinite times without ever crossing the final infinitesimal divide.

"No one has ever been able to disprove the theory.

"Maybe I was testing the paradox. Get halfway there, turn around. Here we are now. Siren, all clear. It's been a year and no bomb has dropped on us. No smoke. No bang. No ash. No rubble." The men across the way erupted in laughter. My shoulders rose toward my ears. Obsessive Clive Pillsbury just sat there in the wash of his recitation of Zeno's paradox.

"I'll go refill our beer," I said.

Air had returned to the room. The publican pulled me a Watney's. Clive and I clacked beer glass and mug. Some coffee dumped out onto the table. We touched glasses. Those, at least, did meet.

5.

During the first weeks of autumn the bombs began to land on East Enders, but not yet on us. Explosions had left thousands homeless and streaming into the city—and left our neighbors with a false sense of stability. Shelters filled. Morrison ordered the tube stations in central London billeted. Communities arose in stations all over the Underground. Londoners were beginning an exodus into their homes, under the streets, which would later find them moving north and east until they were clear of mortal threat.

At night I walked to the park across from our flat; iron railings of the park's fence had been stripped during the salvage drive. In the middle of all that verdure, the call of rooks up in their plane trees, past dark, all the people were packed away in their air raid shelters in town or in their Anderson shelters out back. It was as if I had that city to myself. Where my outings to Prague had been comprised of the joy of thousands of people forever rushing at me—I learned that to live life is to lay oneself down to a wave, to feel as best one could the direction the current was flowing and then allow one's body to go slack and have the wisdom not to fight it lest one drown—London at night during that anxious period of the war was tensile as the thin frozen sheet atop a moving river.

The air was thick with the dust of debris. Nightly bombings kicked up soot. Where behind closed eyes I once saw each of the faces I'd known in the stones of Prague, now my eyes were abraded by astringent dust. The air was filled with frantic resolve, so that even on a night like this, all thoughts were suffused with mortality. What we were seeing as we drove through those streets was only the beginning of thirty thousand civilian casualties. I came to feel almost ashamed of the fact that still holding sway over my mind was the image of my mother, naked, with her suitor in my father's immense home. That when I woke at three in the morning with my mind churning, it was churning over that moment when I'd followed my instinct to leave Holland, not having thought of what it would mean to Françoise. What did such things mean now amid falling bombs in London and Rotterdam?

Well, everything. And nothing. And amid this, marked each day in the papers was not the notation of someone dying in a *bombing*, but of their having died *"very suddenly"*: "Thomas Brown of Lancashire died very suddenly Tuesday night"; "Sally Fargo died very suddenly earlier this week. She is survived by . . ."

There was no one to bury. How hard it is to believe a life has ended until one sees the body interred. Or the damage done.

It wasn't long before Clive Pillsbury and I saw our first bombings firsthand. While people were arriving from the East End, having hitched rides, the two of us took long rides about greater London, surveying the damage and feeding squaddies. In Aldersgate one afternoon, a week after the evening of Clive's confession, we passed a sandwich shop, its façade open like a cleft palate. A sign affixed to the door, left standing, while the rest of the front had been blown away, read MORE OPEN THAN USUAL.

"Let's not stare too long," Clive said.

It'd already been cleared of survivors.

Clive crossed arms over chest.

As I pulled away Clive turned to look at the building. Something more had been keeping my partner from looking. There was a mannered quality embedded deep in Clive which might have accounted both for his initial refusal to look at that building and the kind of obsessiveness that had led to his Zeno's paradox madness. It might not be polite to stare at a birth defect, but when I first saw a man with a port-wine stain on his jaw while on a trip to Prague, walking the streets of the city, I had to be taught by my mother to look away. Such tact didn't come innately. It had to be learned, and it struck me at times that men like Clive had learned the lesson perhaps too well.

Once we'd gone all the way past, Clive turned forward again. I was surprised to find that there seemed to be a new calm in him. Rather than ramping up his anxiety, seeing the damage firsthand had somehow eased the burden of expectation—as if the anticipation of fear was worse than danger itself.

"Be much work for a canteen truck now," he said. "We'd better get some sleep."

I watched to see if Clive futzed with his coffee less in the days to follow. Though I can't be certain—we were now so busy we rarely had a moment to sit for a drink—it seemed to me that he did.

6.

Nighttime was a mad dash through black streets. Every night we were out until sunup, plying squaddies with drink and food as they dealt with bombed-out buildings. We skirted brick and broken glass, or some hoary old man in the street who had resolved not to be kept inside by something so trivial as a falling bomb, lucky not to have been hit, either.

"The fire's over near London Wall, Poxl," Clive would say, relaying word from our dispatcher, and then, "Didn't we just pass our left?" and finally say, "I'm just certain that was the left-hand turn you wanted, Poxl," and I would proceed as best I could. Bombs were dropping by the dozen. All across London the men of the rescue squads and fire brigades were rushing about, awaiting word from their dispatchers. We had come to wish we were on those teams who arrived first at the bombings.

Our work was plagued by a distinct lack of heroism, a distinct lack of action. We followed the squaddies and the firemen, always five or ten minutes behind, ready to provide tea and coffee.

At home the bombings brought great strain to my cousins. Johana no longer made schnitzel or *smazeny syr*. She didn't cook for us, and hardly seemed to eat at all. She hadn't heard word from her husband in so long, we all assumed he was gone, though we didn't say it aloud. Hers had been a marriage of convenience, and Johana had never valued fidelity, but even as she met other men in London, she grew more and more distant to Niny and me. To this day I don't understand what emotions drove her then. What distance had been closed in those nights of our holding hands out back in our Anderson shelter began to grow again between us. I came home in late September to find her sitting on the sofa, staring out the window. Something was wrong in the flat. It took a moment to discern: Streetlight shone on her little ceramic spitz.

"You must keep the curtains closed!" I said. Only months before it had been she who implored me to act in just such a way. I rushed over to close the blackout curtains. "It is imperative we provide no targets for their bombers."

"What does it matter?" Johana said. Her bangs stitched her forehead like straw over the vats in our fathers' leather yard. "Bombs will fall or they won't." She made no move to open the curtains again. She made no move to clear her face of her hair. Had Françoise reacted so blithely in the moments before bombs began to fall on Rotterdam? Even having to think of it tightened the muscles in my neck. I pushed the thought out of mind. I had nothing to say to her.

I found Niny in her room. She had a low light on, reading Dickens.

"You've heard her talk about Scott Pritchard," Niny said. I had no idea what she was talking about. Whatever closeness we'd come to feel out in that Anderson shelter, Johana didn't share with me details of her love life. "Johana has fallen in love with an East Ender." Niny took the novel she was reading and placed it on her bedside table. "His house took a direct hit yesterday. Killed instantly."

I walked from Niny's room to the small bedroom my cousins kept set up for me, and kept clear of Johana in the coming days.

Steering clear of Johana wasn't hard, as soon word came of a massive fire in Knightsbridge. Clive's face evinced a rare agitation. "Let us follow my directions, if just this once, then, Poxl," he said.

Up one alleyway and back down the wide avenue, we raced north through the city, when suddenly I was jarred forward. My head smacked windshield, and for a moment I couldn't tell if the darkness before my eyes was the backs of eyelids, or if it was night.

"Are you all right, Clive?" I said. I reached to turn on the overhead light. I struck a match and saw that Clive was fine. The refractory glint of glass particles floated in the air between us. Petrol vapors rose from the cab of the truck. The match burned down to my fingers. We were at rest.

"You've a trickle of blood on your forehead," Clive said. He swabbed at it. A flash of white heat jumped above my left eye.

"I'll be fine," I said.

We had driven into a bomb crater. That was the end of our Chevy. Its nose was accordioned, and the vehicle tipped at a forty-five-degree angle to the street. Clive had a look of bewilderment. It was the last time I saw him influenced by the weight of outward events.

When we returned across the river by foot—we had been dispatched from Corbett's Passage, at the end of London Bridge—there wasn't much to be said except that the canteen truck had met its demise. Someone would have to clean it up. There was little time for reprimand, for the necessary bodies had to be put to work in the required capacities.

With our truck permanently removed from service and new needs facing London, Clive and I were shifted to a rescue squad. We spent our first week getting outfitted and then trained. Our squaddie uniforms bespoke pragmatism and officialdom. We wore black tin helmets with a bright white *R* on front. In the mid-autumn sun they would grow hot to the touch. Mine was heavy on my head, held on by a thin leather strap. We were provided with large blue coveralls, which we wore over our street clothes. In a matter of days we were provided full blue battle dress. I was no longer a disheveled Czechoslovak, alien to the land he'd set foot upon; instead I was a patriotic Briton. We were not on the offensive as were the boys of the Home Guard—but it was a step forward.

Each rescue squad truck had four rescuers, a driver, and a team leader. I was driver. Clive was team leader. Along with us was a rotating cast of four more men. There were three trucks like mine at Corbett's Passage—tin-lined mortuary vans fitted with stretchers on their roof racks, with ample room inside for the six of us, equipped with shovels, pickaxes, ropes. Shifts started at eight in the morning. At a newsstand on our first day we watched as a small man Clive and I had often noted for his good humor was out chalking up a new message:

GERMANS CLAIM 1,000 TONS OF BOMBS ON LONDON. SO WHAT?

In the following days we were given the end of our first-aid training. By November I passed my exam. We worked twenty-four-hour shifts, riding about the city, waiting for the control center to call out an address. Fire wardens on rooftops all over the city spied blazes, then set off air raid sirens. A call would go to the control center, where they would send an incident officer out to coordinate the efforts of the fire brigade, whose job it was to tend to those who were trapped in the upper floors of the damaged buildings and then to put out the fires. Then we squaddies came to find any people trapped there.

As the autumn grew cold the Luftwaffe began a new campaign, dropping incendiary bombs, making it ever more important for us to reach bomb sites quickly, before the burning phosphorus gained purchase and set buildings—and bodies— ablaze.

7.

Winter descended on London like someone had flipped a switch. One cannot remember until the bone chill of winter has come how frigid air feels—how fifteen degrees Fahrenheit feels when it radiates past your top coat, your skin, into your bones.

That one must feel to remember.

We'd been granted moments of autumnal respite: false quiet

in the first week of November, days of autumn rain when cloud cover was too dense for Luftwaffe sorties, the quiet of each afternoon before the blackout would go into effect and people retreated into their flats or shelters. I was reminded every day how absent love was in my life on those evenings. Something like that same muscle memory Françoise had told me about overtook the parts of my mind that could love: My hand longed to make a chord on the neck of the guitar, but there was no guitar. And I was the one who'd pawned it, my actions having left me without instrument. Time spent thinking about it was time spent alone, turning over in my mind the moment I'd boarded that ship. But always within a few days the bombs would come at night and drive time for such thoughts from my mind, put off until the years that followed allowed all the time I needed to dwell on such things.

December brought the heaviest damage to the city yet. Buildings burned for nights on end. We worked following up the fire brigades everywhere we went. Days we assisted with the massive cleanup following each air raid. We were bombed every day for three months by five-hundred-pound explosives, which dropped more frequently than footfalls.

Christmas week brought a lull. There were few children for people to shop for; they'd been sent north. Shops on Oxford Street made a good show of it anyway. I'd never experienced Christmas in London. Mostly I kept quiet about my Judaism amid the goyim I worked alongside. Given the distinct loneliness and isolation that fact could elicit, in December I went to Johana and Niny's to celebrate Hanukkah. I'd been spending most nights—after the bombing started in earnest—sleeping at Corbett's Passage. Once a week I would return to the flat, hoping to see Niny, but even when she was home, she and I were exhausted from our work for the war effort. Our skin prickled from lack of sleep and yearning for Leitmeritz. We seldom talked. When we did, it was formalities on the way to our beds on the few nights I slept there, too exhausted to return to Corbett's Passage. I would sit before the radio, listening to news of home or Holland, news that could never satisfy the building remorse I felt at having left Françoise behind.

The first night of Hanukkah, Johana was absent, off sitting her private shiva for Scott Prichard, allowing Niny and me to spend some time alone. Though it was the Festival of Lights, the room in the flat where we celebrated our holiday was dark. Winter was here. Day ended early. With blackout curtains drawn we were cast in darkness. Niny lit the shamas. She covered her eyes while she touched match to candle and chanted three *baruchas*. I hummed along, unafraid of looking straight at the cool, soothing light. Hannukah fire still put me at ease. When the candles were lit, Niny uncovered her eyes. We sat together and played dreidel. It was the first I'd played since my childhood in Leitmeritz.

"This was in a pile down in the city," I said. I handed Niny a small box. She unwrapped it to find a pair of silver earrings inlaid with amethyst. I'd found them at the edge of a pile of rubble near Fleet Street. On rescue missions I would sometimes pick up an unclaimed trinket to take home. I'd given her some singed magazines—never anything anyone would miss, only something I'd caught glinting in the morning sun. I would leave those things in Niny's bedroom. The earrings I'd found a couple of weeks prior were the first thing someone might have missed, but—but Niny deserved them.

"Oh, thank you, Poxl, thank you," Niny said. She put her arms around my neck and kissed my cheek. It was the first time I'd been touched in a long time, and something jumped in my bones, then settled. I helped her thread them into the delicate holes in her earlobes. The skin of her lobes drew taut. Four small creases appeared at top when the metal pulled down on them. My mind was given over to flashes of home, early memories of my mother, of a ride back north to Leitmeritz from Prague not a decade earlier, the rush of the Elbe calling up into my ears. And of course of Françoise. Had her American, who had promised to be with her and then left her, as I was beginning to see I, too, had, gifted her a necklace, spent quiet time with her? Thinking of her that way returned me to the very jealousy that had driven me from her. Every thought of Françoise was just that complicated: regret and Iago's green-eyed monster, in lockstep.

Niny and I felt no need to turn the radio on that night, only sat and watched as the candles in the *hanukiah* burned down, wax puddling on the table. When it was cold, and again hard, we picked at it. Wax lodged under our fingernails. It was a good pain, wax pushing at the space between finger and nail. We both picked as we could, let it sink in until we no longer spoke at all.

8.

Three days had passed since Christmas. Back in Corbett's Passage I slept on a thin, hard bunk. An ominous lull impelled the days after the holiday. Each evening we waited for the sirens and kept our shades tight.

Then it was the end of December, and we'd almost made it to 1941 on a week without bombing. The night of the twenty-ninth, Clive and I left when dark fell. After receiving four separate calls from dispatch all at once, we were to hit whichever fire we could reach safely on the bombed-out streets. We took the truck around Southwark. The two of us sat up front. In the back was the rest of our crew, the squaddies we'd been working with the past month—Townshend, Highbridge, Clampton, and Gingham. We'd become a unit.

The night was obscure under dark clouds. We heard the grinding of passing planes and watched as ack-acks were aimed. Spotlights searched the sky, but the low ceiling of clouds rendered them useless. Air raid sirens sounded. Looking out over the city we saw three, four, ten bright yellow tracers. I imagined they had come down with a narrow *thwoop*ing sound, though we instead heard the low rumble of the rescue squad's truck and the wail of sirens and the heavy mechanical churning of the Luftwaffe planes we'd grown to expect: a sound like every radio and truck on the Continent all thrown in a straight grinding line above the city, like electricity itself traveling through the space above our heads.

I stopped the truck and got out. A huge spray of sparks spilled up from a single glowing rod like an enormous novelty sparkler. Sparks sprayed off. They landed, white-hot, on the pavement. The rest of the crew held back near the truck until Townshend called out, "We're off to the Underground shelter to wait it out." Clive motioned that we'd be along.

Phosphorous at the center of the sparks was so white we couldn't look at it straight on. If an incendiary touched you it could burn through to bone. The bomb sat in the road like something not entirely sure of itself. It threw shadows across the buildings around us—we were just south of the Thames, where long rows of dun brick buildings rose into the night. Here, near the river, were cobblestones laid with the perfect precision of an expert mason's hand. Buildings around us were beginning to show the scarring from months of bombing. The restorative darkness of night left them glowing, shadows brushing over the flat stones. Bottoms of lampposts along the curb reflected a white glow back at the light.

If you lit so much as a match in the streets after the sirens sounded, a Home Guardsman would demand you put it out. But in the quiet dark of this night, here was a foot-long quiddity of light melting into the macadam and no one to chastise us. In the sky, a thin layer of clouds glowed like the exposed intestine of some primordial beast.

"Suppose we ought to find shelter ourselves, then," Clive said.

We'd been advised, ahead of the dropping of these incendiaries, not to pour water on a bomb, but to put sand on it, or cover it in woolens, as the white-hot phosphorous at its center would explode when doused. They were harmless if you didn't set them off with water, and if they didn't find their way to fuel: wood, paper, buildings. Before we could begin to put the bomb out, hundreds more incendiaries were falling. The sky lit up and seemed to flex over our heads.

We found a shelter at the end of the block with the rest of our crew. Heavy bombs rocked buildings all around. At last the high solid tone of the all-clear came. When we turned back, the truck was in the middle of the street, where we had first seen the bomb. We got to the end of the block where now there must have been two or three dozen incendiary bombs littered all the way up to the bridge—there were far too many to try putting them out. Sparks up by the bridge lit the dim lip of the river-bank where the water receded, slimy black in the bright light of the incendiaries. Rooftops glowed, seared through by the incendiary bombs sliding hot and deadly through the roofs, instinctively seeking fuel to continue their insuperable burning.

I drove on. Clive said, "I think you've meant to take a right a ways back." He wasn't looking at me but up at the sky, which reflected the hundreds of small white lights battering up to the clouds. We passed London Wall. No new siren, only incendiary after incendiary smoldering on the macadam. Searchlights traced the underbelly of the sky, ack-acks seeking viable targets.

We whizzed up streets almost entirely devoid of people. Almost every man and woman had taken to the country for Christmas, enjoying a true holiday for the first time since the bombing had begun.

Another air raid siren sounded.

I pulled off and we ducked into the nearest Underground station. We stood midway down the steps. Explosive bombs began to fall again alongside the rain of incendiaries somewhere to the north of the city. That jarring bolt was much more familiar than the odd silence accompanying the incendiary strikes. As soon as the all-clear sounded we were all back out to the truck.

We reached Fleet Street. A couple hundred yards ahead, a fire truck pulled up alongside the narrow entrance to Gough Square. A tendril of smoke lifted toward the lighted sky from inside the column on the other side of the buildings. A fireman was getting out of his truck and gearing up.

"A fire by Dr. Johnson's," the fireman said. In Gough Square was the house where Samuel Johnson had lived. "You'd do best to find shelter until this ends," he said, pointing up around us. Every third building was afire.

"We're rescue squad," I said.

"Do your work and leave me to mine, then," the fireman said.

We put on our coveralls and helmets. Fire burned on the top floor of Dr. Johnson's House, and another across the way. The wind died and a great cloud of smoke obscured our view. There were four firemen standing outside the house—throughout the war, AFS firemen were billeted at Dr. Johnson's house, and there were still a few back at the station. Our attention went to the two small factories opposite. A bomb had landed in the middle of these two ten-story factory buildings. A second had landed on the façade of a residence on the far row across from where we had entered the courtyard, between these factories and Dr. Johnson's House.

While the rest of our crew went to help the firemen, Clive went at the front of the smoldering mess with his pickax. Another air raid siren sounded and along with it the noise of Messerschmitts and Spitfires dogfighting overhead. Capricious winds from the two factories carried noxious chemical fumes that burned our eyes.

"What do you suppose it is?" I said.

"Don't know," Clive said. "Looks like a chemical factory. Who knows what's burning." Clive continued to work at the rubble. The macadam was so hot the rubber soles of my shoes sucked with each step. A long beam fell inside the front of the building, casting a line across Clive's leg. Red embers blew all around his head, tracers that now combined with red-hot bullets like those I would watch years later as they emitted from the machine guns on the Messerschmitts that tracked our Lancaster down over the Ruhr Valley.

"Suppose we'll need to get up there with some sandbags, then," the fireman who had led us into Gough Square yelled to them. Another large beam collapsed. It opened a large hole in the first floor, floorboards sucked down.

"We'll just leave it for tomorrow's cleanup," Clive said.

We were ready to rejoin the rest of our crew over at Dr. Johnson's when we heard a voice so small amid the cacophony of the men at work we shouldn't have heard it at all. Even with the greatest city in the world burning, one's ears heard first the sound of a human voice coursing through the night like electricity through wire.

Clive called out. From the open front of the building came a more insistent voice. Clive called to me to go back to the truck, where there was another coil of rope.

Fleet Street was twice as bright as when we'd entered Gough Square—fires burned so bright I was forced to shield my eyes. I was coming back with the rope when two nurses came up the block.

"In here, in Gough Square," I said. "We've found someone in need of help." I led the nurses into the square. Clive crouched close to the burning building. Firemen had doused the place and the flames had been subdued.

"His legs're pinned by a beam," Clive said. There was a life in his eyes I hadn't seen in all the time we had worked on rescues together.

"Must be in pain," the taller of the two nurses said. Clive just looked at her. "Well, ask him!"

Clive called down into the gaping hole. "He thinks one of his legs is broken."

"You'll get down there and see if you can get him out, but first we'll make him comfortable."

An air raid siren started up again but no one made a further move to seek shelter. The concussion of heavy explosives just blocks away shook the ground. Wind shifted and chemical smoke exhaled its noxious breath. The smaller nurse, who hadn't yet said a word, walked a step or two away and vomited.

"You'd best be off," the taller nurse said. "Won't be much help to anyone in this state."

The shorter nurse hurried to Fleet Street and the taller nurse turned to me.

"If you'll tie that around me," she said. She pointed to the rope in my hand. "I'll go down to make sure he's comfortable."

I pulled it around the nurse's thin waist. It was the closest I'd been to a woman's thin waist since Rotterdam. Since Françoise. I put my hands on her hips and she said, "That's a bit familiar, then, isn't it?"

"We should make sure you're going to get back up."

"I'd like that," the nurse said.

Her face bore a constellation of brown freckles alternately hidden and picked out by the light of the growing fires. Clouds stood bright as daylight in the night sky.

"Watch your head on the way down there," Clive yelled. Before the nurse took another step, Clive said, "I suppose before we lower you into a building we'd best know your name."

She said her name was Glynnis. We helped her to the front of the gaping hole at the face of the house. She stepped over three or four solid joists to the edge of the building. We lowered her down. Glynnis held three syringes of morphine in her right hand and the rope with the left and just before leaving our eyeshot, she said, "Remember, two tugs means hoist me up."

The rope stayed taut a long time. Then Clive began pulling. Glynnis's hand came up at the edge of the floor and while Clive held her straight with the rope I jumped in front of him and pulled her up. Her uniform was stained the color of dishwater from the dripping line. Her hair was mussed, its tendrils plastered flat against her face, hiding some of the brown spots I'd observed upon it. She was gaunt-cheeked, slender-nosed, and beautiful.

"He's sedated," Glynnis said. "The leg's trapped by a large beam."

She lifted her arms. I untied the rope. Then Glynnis tied the rope around Clive's stomach. His hands were calm at his sides when he tested it. Just then a new groaning emitted from the building. A spray of sparks flew up against the window. Then we heard the tinkle of the glass as it broke with the heat.

"On with it, then," Clive said. We let him down into the open face of the building. A few minutes later, we had him up, the victim with him.

9.

Now it was almost ten o'clock. Streets asphyxiated with smoke. On our way toward Ludgate Hill we passed a tall thin man covered in black soot. He might have been a Giacometti sculpture, drawn and spindly and given life like Hermione. He might have been my father, who in his peripatetic bolt from the Nazi takeover in Czechoslovakia might have been anywhere or no-where in the world. We pushed on.

Clive was determined to see for himself what was intact in central London. By the time we reached St. Paul's, every build-ing around the churchyard was in flames. A light rain had be-gun to fall. Christopher Wren's masterpiece appeared to have been set ablaze. *Si monumentum requiris, circumspice,* the inscrip-tion in the cathedral reads: "If you seek his monument, look around." A look around us suggested it must be doomed.

It is hard to overstate the sense of defeat that came in those moments when we thought we saw St. Paul's burning. At times symbols really were symbols, and to see that church burn to the ground might have felt like a particular kind of defeat. Frankly, the effect it would've had on all of London the next morning might have been the kind of sight that turned the whole war. But that feeling no sooner gripped us than it passed when we came close and saw the cathedral was essentially unscathed, merely reflecting the orange and red of the fires all around it, seeming to rise up to the low-slung clouds.

Again we were speeding up the boulevard until, on our way to Newgate Street, the three of us were jolted forward. We'd hit erupted pavement in the street. I got out and Clive turned around to be certain Glynnis was unharmed, but she was a nurse and instinctively was trying to do the same for the two of us.

"Cover your eyes," she said. "If you get an ember in there—" Clive grabbed her arm and pulled her to a stop.

"Too late," Clive said. He had an ember under his eyelid, and the air about us filled with so much smoke, Glynnis and I could see nothing.

We kept on by foot into the smoke storm. The only thing we

could see were the burning buildings. We'd gone what I felt certain was a block or two when I began to feel the first bilious churnings in my stomach, which coincided with a shift in the direction of the wind. The breeze lifted the smoke and revealed the way before us to be a block where the fires were only intermittent. Up ahead a fire truck had parked and four men from the brigade were trying to subdue a raging fire in a tall building with a first-floor storefront just ahead.

"You can't help here," one fireman said when we reached them.

Another air raid siren. It was clear we'd better go wait it out in the Underground.

10.

Inside Leicester Station we discovered an alternate city to the one we'd just left above. All down the platform people went about their evening business, doing their best not to acknowledge the firestorm overhead. Stations had been hit by bombs and had caved in, crushing everyone within, but there was no circle below to descend to. Two young men were engaged in a game of cards, each of them seated on a wooden crate. An older man stood bare-backed, his head craned out over the tracks as if awaiting a train, brushing his teeth. The only sound was the contralto of voices reverberating up and down the tunnel. People looked up without acknowledging our presence, or our bodies, which were covered in black soot and streaks of sweat. Our clothes were soiled and carried the toxic reek of burning chemicals.

"What is it?" I said.

"Looks like you've been through some kind of inferno," the man with the toothbrush said. He turned and spit the paste, then walked over a long row of bodies. It was ten minutes before we found an open space, during which time bombs shook the place each time they landed. Wails of infants echoed through the chamber. Clive couldn't open his eyes. Glynnis and I did our best to get him through the crowd.

"Like walking on a tightrope," I said to Clive.

Sight serves as tyrant to the senses, a fact made so clear now that Clive had temporarily lost the use of his. Joseph Conrad, like me an East European displaced to Anglophone lands, said his job as a writer was "to render with the greatest accuracy possible the visible world." I have always held an affinity for that idea. Our path was made arduous as we attempted to lead blind Clive about. When we set down, we all began to recognize our fatigue, but the adrenaline of the night was pumping still.

Next to Glynnis's nose was a large cake of wood ash. I reached to wipe it off. She jerked back, but I put my other hand behind her neck and held her head steady.

"You might as well do the rest if you can," she said.

The fabric keeping Clive's eyes shut tight was not so sullied by the soot as to need to be removed, so I asked him if I could borrow it. Glynnis sat still as I dabbed at her face. With this revelation of her features there arose in me a feeling long forgotten, one that hadn't been at the surface since the onset of the bombing in September. I looked at Glynnis's clear flat skin, pores small and youthfully taut to shut out even the heavy black mud that covered her face.

There hadn't been another siren for some time. The groans of downy sleep, death's counterfeit, resounded through the crowded tunnel. Glynnis wiped away the remaining grime. She sat with Clive's head cradled in her lap, lightly rubbing the area around his eyes. Would that it were my head in her lap. As I've come to know far too well, sometimes jealousy is the most sensitive detector of love. The rhythmic breath of the tunnel was canceled out by the adrenaline coursing through my veins. At the end of an hour, Clive opened his eyes.

"How is it," I said.

"Bloody hurts."

"Maybe you ought to keep them closed."

He looked down to where Glynnis had her eyes closed. It was the first time he had properly seen her.

"Lovely," Clive said.

"Isn't she."

"I can't say I'll want to stay down here much longer myself," Glynnis said. She didn't open her eyes. I tried to look away from her but found I couldn't, and when my eyes returned to her they found what I'm certain was a smile on her face.

It was a good deal easier getting back out of the station than getting in, with Clive's eyes returning to him enough for him to walk under his own power. A different kind of tempest was roiling above. Smoke had been driven off by the wind. We walked a couple blocks into a pocket of cooler air. Just then we heard the long high cry of the siren, another air raid, and ducked back into the Leicester Square station until the all clear came again.

It was the last of the night. The bombing had ended.

The only sound was the tympanic crackle of fires burning and the low bass of their more distant roar. It had begun to rain, a gentle spitting from the clouds—the red, bloodred, and orange clouds were still giving off light, as if the entire sky had become a nearby star, its swirling hot core just above St. Paul's Cathedral—and I took off my helmet. What damage had occurred was for the most part done, and what people there were in those buildings were saved or not saved. We were near delirium, and it was only after walking for a half hour that Glynnis said, "Fleet Street once more. We're walking in circles."

We were all quite lucky to be alive. Next to St. Bride's Church, down that little alleyway, the voices of firemen came loud and cheerful out of a pub whose windows had been blown out. At two o'clock in the morning, on this night that our whole city was in flames, this public house was open for business.

"Here comes another rope and tackle team," a fireman seated near the front of the pub said. "Friend—pull three more." The publican stood us round after round, and joined us. We discussed what we'd seen with these men from the fire brigade— they were eager to learn that we'd been in Gough Square, not far from where they'd been.

"Let us all drink a round to Samuel Johnson!" the first fireman called out. An old woman walked into the bar carrying a large bag. She walked up to the firemen behind us and pulled out three turkey sandwiches with thick wedges of rationed cheddar. The old woman looked as if there was nothing more in the world she would like to see than for them to eat her sandwiches, so they took and ate them without a moment's hesitation.

Clive got up to buy us another much-needed round. While

he was gone, Glynnis turned and not looking me in the eyes said, "Guy's Hospital. That's where I am if you want to call on me." Her eyes met mine for just long enough. Then she said we had better join the crowd. Outside, the city was burning.

11.

"A life is made up of a great number of small incidents and a small number of great ones," Roald Dahl, himself a former RAF pilot, once said. The period that followed the Blitz, those early days of 1941 into 1942, returns to me in the piecemeal memory of small incidents. Those early days during the Blitz, there were moments through the winter when we continued at our rescue work as squaddies and weeks when cloud cover was too thick for flight; nights with Clive at the pub and nights at home with Johana and Niny. Air raid sirens sounded and ack-acks fired and I rode my bike less and then more around London.

Glynnis dropped by to see me.

Clive came by to see me and then to see Niny, until soon he ceased looking for me as much and really only sought out my cousin, and during this period my thoughts of joining the Royal Air Force would be waylaid.

Glynnis needed my help. Her mother had taken ill. Glynnis had been raised in Knightsbridge. Her mother still maintained a home there, but in the early days of the Blitz she had traveled out of London to a town to the north and west of Stanhope, the Goldring family's ancestral home. The Goldrings had lived in Kent since the late fourteenth century. They could trace their lineage to a vassal whose work on that land could still be seen

in certain stone fences that wended deep into the deciduous for-
ests native to that land. There was a famous story of a church
deep in a wood where an imp had been carved into the corner-
stone, an attempt to replicate something similar found in Lincolnshire. Glynnis felt pride that her forebears had been
responsible for it. But none of that was the reason for Mrs. Goldring's having absconded to Kent at the start of the air war, as I
was soon to discover. Her mother was living in a cave, she'd told
me. I didn't know even what to expect when we saw her.

We both secured weekend leave, and on a Saturday mid-
March we found ourselves aboard a train east, staring off into
the verdant hillsides of the area east of London. It bore the occasional mark of Luftwaffe attack. Every dozen miles we might
see space in the far horizon where earth had been upturned, a
brown gash in the grass. Sometimes there was water lying in the
fields. Glynnis pointed out where a flock of brown geese had
stopped to wet their feathers.

We stood by a window smoking. My arms and chest felt filled
by some kind of acid in the first moments of this solitude—the
anxiety that had underlain my thoughts all those days of falling
Luftwaffe bombs now seeking exit. That reprieve was granted
only in my looking at Glynnis's face as standing water and sway-
ing rushes passed outside our window. Tendrils of cigarette
smoke surrounded her lovely plump face.

Not thirty miles later we detrained. The air was fecund and
still and the distinct lack of carbonite in my nose felt a presence
for its absence. Glynnis and I walked for what felt like an hour
until the straw-thatched houses gave way to deciduous forest,
maple leaves like palm fronds overhead. Soon the road took on
steep declivities.

There was nothing before us but granite boulders lifting up from the ground like bunkers, covered in flat, wide leaves. I followed Glynnis into the woods. With each step it felt I was somehow moving further back into time. This was evident at the very least from the clouds of black midges, which grew in density as the vegetation thickened until they seemed to envelop our heads. We had no such dense forest anywhere near Leitmeritz. Alongside the Elbe trees might offer protection, but I was used to the swish of tall grasses. I don't believe I'd taken in so many smells in years, if I'd ever smelled so much before—deep rich loam kicked up beneath our feet, the tickle of spores from toadstools lifting up sharp like mustard. I'd been looking at my feet so long—the breaking of toadstools, the overturning of thick leaves, all of this so different from that rigid cobblestone order of my youth and memory—I didn't realize Glynnis had stopped.

"We're here," she said. We went in through the mouth of the cave. It was far smaller than what I'd imagined. Having never seen people living in a cave before, I don't know that I'd imagined much of anything. Glynnis stooped down and I stooped behind her. We squeezed through a dank passageway, alongside which walls jabbed at my hips, until I heard a sound ahead. At first I thought it was the babbling of a brook, but as we walked farther in, I saw light flitting in the distance. By then we were standing, and the babbling of the creek was the sound of voices, voices growing louder until I could see the back of Glynnis's brown hair and ovoid shapes materialized alongside voices, and then we were in a room with a cave ceiling twenty feet above our heads. Ahead of me were hundreds of people, all sitting on stools of stalactites and blankets dark and shadowy amid light produced by candles and an occasional kerosene lamp.

"It will take us some time before we're able to find my mother," Glynnis said. "I'll ask around."

She went forward to find a familiar face. I wandered. When they were children, Glynnis told me some time later, she and her brother had come to see their grandmother, and they came to spelunk in these caves. What we'd seen at the Leicester Square station only weeks before was nothing compared with this small village belowground. In a far recess of this enormous cavern, in the soft darkness of the cave's shadow, men stood before large cauldrons, cooking for the masses. It was almost impossible to see where door openings led off into the farther recesses of the cave. For a moment panic gripped me as I couldn't see where I was going and I felt I heard someone calling my name, and then a hand was on my arm.

"It's confusing in here until you've learned your way," Glynnis said. "Stick with me."

"You've found your mother?"

"She doesn't like to be kept waiting."

We walked from the few light sources until I could feel cool moisture lifting off cave walls. We were squeezing again through a passageway just wide enough to let others past. Bodies pressed against me without a word of apology. Someone was breathing heavily behind me and soon he was pressed up against me. I thought to turn and say something when light came before us again and we were in a smaller cavern, this one with ethereal white planes covering the ground ahead.

"This is where Mother sleeps," Glynnis said. She took me by

the hand. We crouched alongside a mattress nested on the cave floor. Mrs. Goldring was lying prone. When Glynnis announced our presence, her mother did her best to prop up on one hand.

"Mother, this is—" Glynnis said. But she stopped there as I'd already begun speaking.

"My name is Poxl Weisberg, Mrs. Goldring," I said. "It's a pleasure to meet you."

The English and the accent I'd acquired in the previous months were a source of pride for me.

"Wherever are you from?" Glynnis's mother asked.

It was impossible to tell if she was looking at me, as a bright kerosene lamp cast light behind her, obscuring her face in deep shadow. I told her I lived near Bermondsey now, in Corbett's Passage, where I worked as a squaddie.

"Not what I meant," she said.

"Well, Mother, I told you that Poxl is Czech, come to help with the war effort," Glynnis said. She had, she had, Mrs. Goldring said. She was sorry; she'd forgotten.

Glynnis's mother was suffering from the very earliest stages of dementia. At first the frankness of her ramblings caused me great discomfort. While Glynnis worked to set up her linens and to see what needed to go back with us to London for cleaning, I did my best to engage her mother. At times she rambled about poisonous snakes she believed were populating the latrine cavern, or old Mr. Lovelace whom she knew from childhood and whom she feared might take liberties with her in her sleep. But soon a kind of honesty arose amid her bellyaching.

"It's about impossible to sleep in this cave," Mrs. Goldring said. Before I could ask her why, she continued. "Isn't a single flat spot anywhere in this whole room. I've put my bed down everywhere I could and one space is bad as the next."

"What's so bad?"

"Ever slept on uneven ground?"

It was a simple question, but one that took me some time to answer.

"No," I said.

"For a time you might settle into it," Mrs. Goldring said.

My eyes had adjusted to the dark now. Deep creases drew down from the prim line of Mrs. Goldring's white mouth. She wasn't looking at me—she looked up at the ceiling, off at the sleeping men behind her. She didn't look me in the eyes.

"Without fail, every night, I jump upright, gripping the sides of my mattress. Even the slightest tilt, the slightest dip to one side or the other, and there's no way but to feel you're falling off the ends of the earth. As if the whole world has tipped, invested in shaking you from it."

I didn't know what to say. More than anything it was nice to hear someone complaining about something so mundane. For so long it had been the stiff upper lip of the Britons—and only that stiff upper lip. How good it could feel to hear someone complain. I asked Mrs. Goldring if she didn't find some entertainment here. Had she made friends? She looked at me a bit oddly and then with no small fanfare pulled out from beside her pallet a large book. It was wrapped in oilskin, and so had no water damage from that damp floor.

"I read at a play each night, and that keeps me going," Mrs. Goldring said. In her hands she held a complete edition of Shakespeare, a portable edition in soft cover she'd brought with her.

We'd been assigned a German translation of *Romeo and Juliet* in the gymnasium back in Leitmeritz, but if I'd paid any attention, not a word or character or idea had stuck.

Now something stirred in Mrs. Goldring—and in me. I don't know if it was the plays, or the company, or the simple fact of our having a respite from the Blitz, but I focused completely on listening to Glynnis's mother. Where in the moments before—and in so many of the days to come—Mrs. Goldring's oncoming dementia had brought her from complaint to compliance, from cohesion to chaos, when she began to speak of the madness of Lear, suddenly precise thoughts coalesced. She told me much about these characters I'd never heard of. Her favorite, Mrs. Goldring explained, was Cordelia. The love for a father should always be so strong and clear, she said, and she could only hope that her Glynnis loved *her* quite so much. When I told her I didn't know this play, for the first time Mrs. Goldring stood.

"Don't know the greatest achievement of Western culture, Mr. Weisberg!" she said. "Only one way to remedy such a grave offense."

She opened the volume to *King Lear*. Before I knew it, we were taking turns, she as Cordelia and I as Lear, she as Goneril and I as Edmund. There we were in a cave in the countryside east of London, dividing up ancient England over the mistaken response of a daughter who loved her father. We felt as if France and Albany were standing in the nooks of our cave, listening in as we unwisely divided the kingdom; our anger at Goneril and Regan was as great in those moments as it was for the Messerschmitt pilots over London. The pages of that edition were all very clean, not a mark on any one of them.

Near the end of Act 2, Glynnis returned to us. She told her

mother we would be back, that we'd come see her when we had
a leave.

"We," she said.

"Poxl and me," Glynnis said.

"Upon your return, we will find our way into Act 3, my boy,"
Mrs. Goldring said.

Kerosene light danced on the ceiling ten yards above our
heads, about the deep-lined face of Glynnis's mother. She looked
right at me for the first time.

"I could do with that," Mrs. Goldring said.

On our long walk back to the train, Glynnis asked what had
allowed her mother to seem so lucid at some moments after
weeks and months of decrepitude. I told her I didn't know. I'd
only just met this woman and wouldn't purport to know.

"But we read *King Lear* together the whole time you were
gone," I said.

I suspected there might eventually be more to say on the matter, but I left it at that.

12.

In the months ahead, when we were granted weekend leave,
Glynnis and I went to see her mother. While Glynnis went off
to procure whatever her mother needed, I stayed and read. First
we read *Lear*, and then the rest, from *Timon of Athens* to *Titus
Andronicus*, from *All's Well That Ends Well* all the way to *The
Merchant of Venice*, where we paused as Shylock asks, so pained,
If you prick us, do we not bleed? If you wrong us, shall we not
revenge?

When Glynnis grew tired and returned, I would survey the cave myself, while Glynnis and her mother talked, or read from the plays as well, though having grown up with them, Glynnis surely didn't have the same patience for her mother's proclivities that I did. I wouldn't say I came to know its every recess, but the cave itself came to be a kind of holiday home for us.

And without our quite knowing when it had happened so fully, Glynnis and I had taken to each other. We made love quietly on weeknights when we could. While her face bore that constellation of freckles, when her shirt came off, I found that every inch of her skin not touched by the sun was wholly white. I liked to turn on a lamp in the corner of her small room near the hospital when we undressed. In the quiet after we'd disentangled I heard about her childhood. She'd grown up on a dairy farm, her family one of modest means. After watching her parents' husbandry of their cattle—"I'd seen more pink bleating calves pulled from their mothers by the age of ten than one should see in a lifetime," Glynnis said—she came to decide that medicine attracted her. Not just medicine but also the birthing process. She began her training as a midwife soon after leaving her parents' home. But then the war threatened, and now she was a handful of years into working as a nurse.

"It's a funny transition, innit?" Glynnis said. I told her I didn't follow her meaning. "I wanted to be in a hospital helping to bring new life into the world. Here were are in London watching it taken."

"You're doing exactly what you should be doing now," I said. "The war will end one day, and you'll go back to it."

"I suppose. And you, Poxl West? What will you do when the war you're so certain will end does end?"

I didn't want to tell her that I didn't know, so I gave her an answer somewhere in between.

"*Before* this war is over, Glynnis Goldring, I will fly for the RAF." It wasn't the first she'd heard of this desire, but I suppose it was the most clearly she'd heard it.

"And what will become of me while you're off flying?" she said.

"The same thing that becomes of you now. Or you'll come with me, come work for the Women's Auxiliary."

"I don't want to leave here," Glynnis said. And for a time we left it at that. We stopped speaking and held each other tight. After hours on Mrs. Goldring's pallet there was something almost too ordered about Glynnis's bed—there was no sense of being thrown off by the gravity of the shifting world, no feeling of the disruption that a dim cave can bring.

So more often than not we found ourselves back in that cave on every weekend pass we could procure. I liked to carry a lamp with us on those weekends when we went to see Mrs. Goldring and observe every cave room there was. I learned after the war that as many as eight thousand Britons had set up camp there, and by springtime they'd moved beyond a dining room and sleeping areas. Deep in the paths water had borne through the rock over many thousands of years, through a passageway so tight one felt one might be stuck until one starved to death, a ballroom had been constructed. Some boy small enough to pass through the crevice along with a small chandelier had brought tools as well, and near the top of the cave ceiling, he had installed that glimmering glass. An old Victrola was powered by a hand crank in a far corner of the room.

It took some convincing to get Glynnis in there with me. She wasn't much of a dancer and neither was I, but when Glenn Miller came on I took her hand and we did the best we could.

One night for a fast dance someone put on one of those old Decca Records recordings of Bill and Charlie Monroe doing "You Won't Be Satisfied That Way." For just a second I hesitated when Glynnis came to me, my mind thrust away from that place, but I did my best to regain myself. Glynnis took my hands, and she and I danced hard to it. I had her hands gripped in mine, and I didn't let go. The low-slung rock of the cave's ceiling seemed to push down toward my head, and as if against my desire, constructed images of Françoise stuck under the beams of a bomb-imploded house entered my mind. I didn't picture Rotterdam: I pictured that building in Gough Square where Glynnis and I had first met, only now Françoise was there. I can only guess that as I held her there, Glynnis thought I was simply a young man in love—with her. And that wasn't inaccurate. But there was more on my mind. My palms grew sweaty as I considered that this empathy for Glynnis, considering her thoughts, was more move to empathy than I'd given Françoise even after I left her, even after I arrived in London.

Something must have crossed my face. Glynnis said, "Poxl, what is it? I've never seen you look so sad. Or happy. I don't know which."

"I don't either," I said. I'd never spoken to her of Françoise before, and I wasn't going to start. "But let's forget it." Presently the song changed, and it was past, and we went back to dancing slowly. I'm sure my behavior seemed odd, but neither of us made mention of it again. The cave was so broad and wide most of the sound was lost in the room anyway, or it echoed so that it was as if you were hearing both what was being played and what had been played seconds before, the two lines crossing until it was no longer clear which was which: past or present.

Glynnis's hands were in mine. We were dancing slowly. I had to say something, even as the melancholy of my thoughts sat as a residue on my mind.

"I'm glad you brought me to this place," I told Glynnis.

"My mother's taken to you."

"It's a wise child who knows her mother," I said, and she held me close.

13.

All this life east of the city, amid the protective womb of the cave, might have kept me wholly in its thrall had it not been for the fact that no matter how I'd taken to Glynnis—and I was, I truly was in love with her—roiling under my conscious thoughts I still longed for nothing but to effect change myself. In battle. That nagging didn't ever leave me. With each passing day, in fact, it grew. While Mrs. Goldring and I read of Macduff headed off for Dunsinane, or found Hamlet taking up arms to avenge the death of his father, I still thought subconsciously of those RAF pilots who were at that very moment dropping bombs on the Reich. While we were away in the east, dancing the fox-trot in the relative dark of a cave ballroom, I was able to push out of my conscious thoughts that London was being bombed, potentially to her ruin.

But as I said, those were just days between the long weeks when Clive and I still scoured the streets for bombed buildings. When I went to visit her, Niny was beginning to bear signs of fatigue. I would find her in her room for entire evenings, just reading and unwilling to talk. Johana's grief at the loss of Scott Prichard had negated even the existence of her husband, Vaclav, whom Niny told me had now not written in a year himself; we were beginning quietly to feel certain he hadn't survived his stint on the eastern front. And Johana's grief at the loss of the man she'd seen more recently seemed only to grow with time.

In addition to the effect of those bombs falling upon us, word came of deportations of Jews all across Eastern Europe. On one long hiatus from both work and the cave, a letter arrived from the longtime foreman of Brüder Weisberg, whom Niny had written. He'd been kept on after the factory was wrested from my father. The letter was addressed to the three of us.

I do not see reason to reproduce verbatim this morbid letter here. I'd never heard back from anyone in Rotterdam. Now I was hearing from Leitmeritz instead. The foreman at our fathers' factory stated quite directly that my mother had been sent to Terezin. She was sent on from there to her death, as we later learned, in the slow brown fields somewhere in western Poland. My father had been taken along with his brother Rudy—father to Johana and Niny—to Terezin, as well. The camp was just three miles south of my hometown of Leitmeritz. It was all too easy for the SS officers to liquidate the population of that small city.

I will not attempt to reproduce the conversation between my cousins and me in the hours and days after the arrival of that letter. Each of us read it and left it on the dining room table as evidence for the others that it had been read.

I walked out to the park across from our flat and sat on a bench. I watched the sparrows fly up into their eaves. I didn't know I was crying until I saw on the faces of those who passed a mixture of concern and distaste—everyone in London during that period was suffering losses.

The thing was to press on.

Knowing my mother was gone came, in the days to follow, to feel like the loss of the very *need* for love. Like never wanting intimacy again. Like those Londoners I'd been observing amid falling bombs, it was my desire to withdraw. What was I doing reading books with some other Mother when my Mother had ended? My parents were the firmament in which the sun sat, and I could see now that was true whether they glowed as one or in separate vectors. I'd been angry upon finding her with my father's cuckold, sure—but some part of me assumed I'd see her again. That there would be time for reckoning, time for the airing of emotions and grievances. I didn't know until this moment I'd felt that way. Now it was clear. There was something petulant in my flight from Leitmeritz. I could now see that there was something *more* than petulant in my flight from Rotterdam, from Françoise. I'd learned to run when problems arose, rather than meeting them head-on. Now there would be no reckoning—not in Leitmeritz, nor anywhere else. Knowing my mother had met her end was like imagining every star in the sky blotted out by some small boy with a pin whose touch extinguishes each light.

She now existed only in memory.

So picture me later that week as I received the foreman's letter—instead of on a train east with Glynnis, whose calls I refused, riding aboard a bus bound for Piccadilly Circus, riding amid the burgeoning rubble of central London, inching up to an old woman and peering at her head: Would I suffer the disappointment of seeing her ear not pierced, bearing no amber

earrings, wrinkled and foreign? Or might I have the glory of
seeing that after seventy years of life, forty of them during
which her ear bore the weight of heavy jewelry, she might have
that same slit I'd once fondled in my mother's lobe? He who
chanced upon me staring at his large work-stained hands and
seeking my father in them—what do you think he thought of
me? He scowled and looked away, that father with a thousand
Polonius faces. He did not know that like the Bard himself
seeking his damaged father in every glove maker in the London to which he'd just arrived, I sought my Czechoslovak father and evidence of his leather work.

Soon something began to change in me.

I called on Glynnis again. When I saw her I did not mention
news of my mother. She and I made love in the same quiet way
we always had, but now some small part of me was held in abey-
ance. There was an odd comfort in being with Glynnis now, perhaps a greater comfort than I'd ever felt with a woman, for where
once I found need in being with her, now I felt only the physical pleasure that passes like top waters over the current drawing down in the depths. Now I did not feel the desire to read
plays in caves in rural areas. I did not seek a weekend pass to
return to the caves. I can see looking back on it that digging my
heels in, meeting my problems head-on, might have led me to
stay in London, remain by Glynnis's side. But in those days after that letter, it meant something different to me. It meant meeting the German advance head-on. It meant no longer rescuing
those who'd been wronged—but acting to stop from their needing rescue to begin with.

I returned again and again to the RAF recruitment office in
Southwark.

So, maybe I've got it wrong. Perhaps the loss of my parents was like living in a city for many long years and never leaving. You have lived a rural life as a child, and walked off into the woods to stare up at the sky. It wouldn't make sense to say you loved or didn't love the stars, only that you knew nothing would change them.

They were stars.

Now you live in the city. War has driven you there, war and your own capriciousness. Every night you go about your business: drink, succeed, fail; take in live music—save lives volunteering in a war effort. You do everything that might fulfill one with even the noblest ambitions. But you never again leave the city. Overhead is an eternal pink glow, light that never dims past a point, a phenomenon some might call light pollution but which is the only thing that sustains you. At four in the morning, you have left a pub. You are, quite frankly, drunk. Have been for days. To placate you, above: pink sky, never not pink.

Then one day, rather than taking some leisure in the woods to the east, rather than the ease of a woman's bed, you take to the sky in an aeroplane. You are airborne, it is night, below you the glowing white clouds—and above, where once there were stars all across the firmament, now there is only blackness. That void carries a memory of stars, of the way you once felt them guide you . . . perhaps you even remember, before it has happened, a time when, lost in the night's sky on a training run, you feared you would not survive your flight, and only upon finding the Dipper, its pointing you to the North Star, were you able to make it back to base. Only now the night is black, and all along, that pink urban shelter you were confined to kept you from knowing that for all those years, the stars were fading from the sky. And you remember a time when you dropped bombs on cities, destroying them beyond resurrection, and all you could see below you were clouds. While you might have known but not understood that you were destroying what lay below you, now there aren't even stars above.

14.

Here's one thing I learned from reading with Mrs. Goldring before I took my leave of her daughter: When Hamlet asks Yorick how long a body lies in the ground before it rots, the first clown replies, ". . . eight year or nine year. A tanner will last you nine year." When Hamlet asks, "Why he more than another?" the response comes this way: "Why, sir, his hide is so tanned with his trade that it will keep out water a great while, and your water is a sore decayer of your whoreson dead body."

Was my father a difficult Jew to kill, to bury, to cremate? Had his skin so toughened that even once the life was snuffed from him, he wouldn't cede his toehold on this craggy wall, his thick, tanned hide failing to succumb to the flames of the crematorium where he was kilned? Was his death different if he proved a tough Jew to burn?

After the war I read many of the books that were written during those times. I was later to gain mastery over the Shakespeare plays I had only begun to read with Mrs. Goldring in those days before I left for flight training, enough to teach those plays to interested students. Before that I read the histories of our times, the modernist literature produced during my youth. T. S. Eliot, as I say, had himself been a fire watcher during those days of the Blitz, and I read every word of his "Little Gidding," which will always evoke those days for me.

After the war ended—long after I'd decided to drop bombs of my own on Germany, to fight a war thrust upon me that the side I was on was now winning—I learned that John Milton's bones were vaporized on the last major Luftwaffe offensive of 1940, the night Clive Pillsbury and I met Glynnis Goldring. We never saw those bones, just as I never saw my parents' remains or the obsequies for them. I didn't even know what had become of Françoise. But that very same night Milton's bones were done away with, before that final pub where Clive and I went with Glynnis, we had just passed a cemetery when I felt compelled to return to it. I wanted to make sure I'd seen what I thought I'd seen. I got down on one knee and picked it up. Shaken loose of its rest, and lying upon the grass, was a dirt-encrusted bone. A femur. A human femur.

If you wrong us, shall we not revenge?

The Germans were going to kill even our dead unless we were to do something about it.

15.

Those late days of the Blitz, my hunger to engage German soldiers gained full purchase over my mind. Glynnis and I would meet in the evenings and engage in a particular kind of intimacy—and even for the pleasure she brought me, even knowing I was in love with her, it was as if that love appeared to me through a newfound scrim. I longed to join up more than before.

"What is it, Poxl?" Glynnis would say as we lay in the half-light of her kerosene lamp.

"What is it?"

"Yes! Yes. You aren't looking at me. You don't look at me."

I stared at the ceiling. Then I did look at her.

"It's what I've said before," I said. "It's fine being a squaddie. But they need to put me to use. If I could just get in a plane, I could be of use."

Glynnis lay back and she did not say aloud that my joining up, should it happen, would mean we would see each other less—and who knew the consequence beyond that. If ever there was a moment to tell her about Françoise, about my parents, this was it, and looking back now I can see it might have changed things, might at least have given her a sense of what was on my mind. I cannot say exactly why I did not tell her. I can only say that I didn't. No matter what had changed in me, when I looked at her, in that moment, I couldn't deny she was wonderful to look at. The way her plump cheeks pressed up against mine was almost enough to draw from me a confession of my letter from that Czech foreman. An explanation of my keeping from taking trips to the cave. A confession of nights out alone drinking. A divulgence of my time in Rotterdam that could have helped me see what I'd done in leaving.

Almost.

Regardless, when Glynnis asked me to go to the cave with her I now refused—for reasons that actually had nothing to do with her and everything to do with her mother, I did not make another trip east with her. I did not talk to her about my parents, and I would not. At Corbett's Passage, my bunk was too hard. Back in Bermondsey the ceiling was too low, too close to us. The tiptoe of shadow touched and lifted up there.

"It's nothing," I said when she asked, over and over again, what was wrong, and I made her believe me.

16.

Every day I went to Southwark to attempt to enlist in the RAF.

Luftwaffe bomb on Rotterdam; I was gone.

Luftwaffe bomb in the East End; cousin Johana's Briton had been done in.

What was there to do?

What there was for me to do was to fly a plane and take out the Luftwaffe myself.

I tried to impress upon the recruiters at RAF reception that even given the faults they perceived in my English, I had experience flying planes with my father at his aero club outside of Prague. I was twenty-one and desperate; I was a Jew looking to kill Nazis. I would be most effective killing Nazis in an aeroplane fitted with Browning guns and blockbuster bombs. Early on, I received only a strong endorsement of my work in the rescue squad (more pat on the head than pat on the back) and a nebulous invitation to try back sometime later.

Then Clive was inducted into the RAF. It was early fall, fully a year since the Blitz had begun. By this time he was seeing my cousin Niny only once every couple weeks. Although Clive wasn't deemed fit to have joined early on in the war, we began to hear on the radio that Bomber Harris was ramping up a full-scale retaliation for the Blitz, that Bomber Command was building bombers and fighters faster than they could sign up young men to crash them. Clive arrived at Niny's flat to say he was to enter pilot training the following day. He and Niny hadn't consummated their relationship, hadn't brought it past a flirtation, the early stages of courtship.

Now it was a courtship ended.

He didn't even look at her as he left the flat—his obsessive personality was focused on his new path. This was how relationships might begin and end at that point in our lives: One kind of man might, in the moment before he was to leave for assignment, motor around the countryside with his woman, and though they'd only known each other for a matter of months, ask her to marry him.

Clive was very much not that kind of man.

Two months later, a change at 10 Downing in the laws pertaining to the employment of nonnaturalized citizens flying for the Royal Air Force made it so I was accepted as well. Should I be shot down over the Reich, I wouldn't be long for the world. I wouldn't be protected by any POW laws, a Czechoslovak Jew flying for the RAF.

"So, young chap, keeping this name Leopold Weisberg on your passport won't do," the inception officer told me. What name should I take instead? "Peter West is more appropriately a British name for a pilot in the RAF, don't you guess?"

So though I would never in my life have anyone call me Peter, I took West as my new surname. If they had to call me Poxl West—if this would allow me to pilot Spitfires and engage in battle with Luftwaffe Junkers and Messerschmitts—then this is what they would call me.

With a new name and my knowledge of planes from my time

with my father in an airstrip outside of Prague, I enlisted. I went
down to Guy's Hospital to tell Glynnis of the news. I found her
at her bed checks.

"What is it, Poxl?" Glynnis said.

"I've finally gotten it," I said.

She tapped at a saline drip attached to a man's arm. On the
windowsill behind that bed was a single hollyhock stalk, with
three carmine blossoms pointing in three different directions.
Hollyhocks do not give off an aroma. Glynnis did not hold
my eyes with hers. The only smell in the room was the smell of
iodine.

I was so elated in that moment of being accepted to flight
training I'd not given real thought to how Glynnis would take
it. She looked up from the serum dripping through the line she
was fixing and I saw that tears wet her face. A black ant was
crawling around the green stalk behind that hollyhock bloom.

"Careful to fly well up there," Glynnis said. The ant crawled
around that hollyhock stalk. I couldn't bear to look at it. I raised
my eyes to the red blossom. "What will become of me down
here? You in the air. Me underground with Mother."

"You'll go about your nursing," I said. "London is safer now.
Perhaps Mrs. Goldring will even come home."

"That's not what I mean," she said.

I would be back on weekend leave when I could. I would write
letters. For so long I'd known only that I longed to leave. That
old muscle memory. Now in the moment of leaving it felt as if
some space had opened up beneath my feet. I must plant them
more firmly on the ground. With the carmine of that hollyhock
and my elation I felt the immediacy of a desire for Glynnis I'd
not felt in months.

"When I return," I said, "we'll talk of marriage."

For the first time Glynnis's eyes caught mine. Saline dripped in the intravenous line behind her. In my peripheral vision I saw the black ant crawl up until it achieved the very inside of that hollyhock blossom.

"I don't know if I need that much," Glynnis said. "Just."

Then she reached up and pressed those kiln-hot cheeks against mine until they baked into kisses.

Acknowledgment: Second Interlude

After years of my peace-loving life, now I was fifteen years old and interested only in war. It was the spring of 1986, barely a decade since the end of Vietnam. That one—and Korea, too—were between us and what we understood to be the morally unambiguous days of World War II. Dovish was really the only mode for us then, Bostonian or otherwise. Teenage or otherwise.

I spent hours in the library at our public school looking for books about the British military and Eastern Europe during the war—books I read, books I thumbed through, all to fill the void Poxl West had now left in my life. Military histories by John Keegan that were too dry and martial to keep my teenage interest. Narratives by Elie Wiesel and Primo Levi that elicited only bile from me at the time. These books contained stories, but not the stories my uncle Poxl had to tell. Somehow even they, in their dour precision and moribund facts, couldn't touch the tales of sexual impropriety and reckless aviation Poxl told. He hadn't been forced into victimhood, didn't need to be called survivor—he had flown his way right into the attack against that awful German force. More often than not I found myself flipping to the back to look at lists of names in their end pages: acknowledgments of relatives long dead, lists of names whose thick Ashkenazi sounds carried no meaning to me.

During that same time I found that the things that had once floated me on the weekdays between my outings with Poxl were somehow lacking in buoyancy in comparison with what little I could dredge up on his time at war. Now for the first time I had Poxl's book—but not Poxl. The absence was almost tangible. As I sat and watched the best team the Bruins had fielded in years win game after game, even on the most perfect full-ice pass from Ray Bourque to Cam Neely, I could hardly get excited. My team appeared good enough to head for the Stanley Cup for the second year in a row, but my uncle Poxl wasn't there to take me to the MFA or the opera, to distract me from the things I felt I loved more—so he distracted me from afar. He stole my concentration from anything that didn't pertain to him with his absence and his successes. He'd promised to send me a copy of his book, signed, and I still didn't have a copy personalized by him. He'd promised to take me down to New York City and show me something more, and I hadn't yet seen it. For years he'd had me, but he hadn't published the book he always longed to publish; now he'd published a book, and it was as if he'd flown from me, too. My football team had been to the Super Bowl, and even the prospect of a second championship for one of our town's teams that year didn't carry the same weight it once had. The Celtics, too, had fielded their strongest team in years, and the Red Sox, with Roger Clemens and Wade Boggs, seemed as if they might be bound for a World Series themselves. Never before were our teams so stacked with players: McHale and Parish, Rice and Evans, Fryar and Marion.

All I wanted was my uncle Poxl back.

At the time this desire felt wholly natural. Thinking of it now, listening to my own wistful voice and how it ached at Poxl's absence, it sounds like obsession.

Maybe it was.

But it carried with it the absence I would always feel of my grandfather, the one Poxl had come to fill here in town. Before I knew enough to know, Poxl West had been in my life. He'd chosen to be there, not because he was duty-bound, bound by blood. His attention to me was the conscious bestowal of a gift, one that was renewed every time we saw each other. There I was, fifteen—the gift had been given, and now it was not being given, at just the moment when its magnitude was revealed, clouds parting to display morning's spidery light. Was this what Françoise had felt when he left? Glynnis? His own mother? I'd lost a grandfather before I knew what it meant to have one, but in his place I had what every Ashkenazi kid in America needed without knowing he needed it: a Jewish war hero, at my side. When Poxl was around, he *did* fill in for my missing grandfather. Now it was like I'd lost two grandfathers in one sweep of Poxl West's international success. Does this sound like obsession? Do I lament looking back, magnifying what Poxl was then? I only know that's how it felt at the time. And that, if I'm honest, it's how I feel decades later.

One afternoon amid the unexpected blanching that had overtaken my days during that period, my father decided he would take up Poxl's absence and take me to Waltham, to a store called Mr. Big Toyland. The toy store advertised regularly on local television stations. My parents were friends with the owner's daughter—my father had helped them out with an audit years before, so we were treated well there. We got a small jolt from watching their kids thumbing their way through the Cabbage Patch Kids and G.I. Joes on those TV commercials—Ellen and Joseph, who'd been at my Bar Mitzvah, up there on television, enjoying some local fame. We knew them, and there they were on television, between episodes of *Diff'rent Strokes*. Fame feels larger when you're fifteen: It appears to be its own reward. I'm not sure what I wanted to be acknowledged for, what I did at the time that deserved attention, but the idea of being on television was mesmerizing.

In addition to toys, Mr. Big sold baseball cards, the best selection of old cards in town. My parents thought spending money on baseball cards was a kind of institutionalized insanity. Usually I had to beg my father to take me out there.

Today he'd offered unbidden.

On the way out we passed through the wealthy town where Larry Bird, the best player on the Celtics team, had bought a large house after being drafted. He was known to spend afternoons outside in his driveway shooting baskets. There was something intimate about it, its own gift, seeing through the window of a car what we normally had to see on the screen of our television sets. It could back traffic up for miles, drivers stopping to watch his mastery, the perfect shot executed by a man with mangled, broken fingers on each hand that somehow came together to make him the best shooter of his generation.

When we arrived in Waltham, Mr. Big wasn't there. One of the clerks—no one we knew—took out books of cards for us to look through.

"What about that Larry Bird Topps'?" my father said. It was twenty-five dollars, an exorbitant amount back then to spend on a card. "You were just talking about him."

I told my father I wasn't that into basketball cards, so we turned to the curio case that held baseball cards. There was a 1976 Topps Fred Lynn, statistics on the back documenting the year he won both Rookie of the Year and MVP. A Yastrzemski third year. Even a couple Mickey Mantles. Somehow they all seemed trivial compared to tales of Uncle Poxl's feats of war. My father must have noticed something in my face. He turned to the clerk and pointed to a card on the top level.

"Ted Williams," my father said. "'51 Bowman. You know he had to stop playing for more than two years, in his prime."

"He did?" I said.

"Yeah, he enlisted in the army."

"Really?"

"They say he gave up the best years of his career, the height of his hitting powers, to fight in the war."

My father looked over the cards in the case where we were standing. I was a card collector and a Sox fan, and I'm sure I had to have heard this story before, but somehow it had never registered with me. It hadn't stuck. Now I looked down at the cartoon depiction of Williams's handsome face twisted upward, the bat swung back around his body at the end of a perfect cut.

"You want it?" my father said.

On the plastic case the card was held in, a white sticker read "$140."

"Are you serious?" I said. My mother hated my baseball-card collecting, thought the money we spent on it was money wasted. Did I think at the time this was strange, my father overcompensating for Poxl's absence? Because in remembering it now, I see it for what it was. I'd grown dour on a level that must have begun to concern him. Here we were, attempting to rectify it. If this fact registered subconsciously, it was quickly forgotten in the excitement of what we were about to do. I was getting a thing I wanted and never dreamed I could have.

"They say these will be a good investment in the long term," my father said. "Like a relic of history. You'll have to keep it in good shape—not take it out to show friends or anything."

For weeks I'd wanted something I could put my hands on, something that had been denied to me: Poxl had promised to send books and he hadn't, and though my father had bought us copies, that hadn't sated me. But he'd recognized need in me, and here he'd pulled off an emotional sleight of hand: He'd gifted me something I didn't know I wanted. We don't eat because there is food. We eat because there is hunger. It didn't occur to me then what Poxl West had been doing all along, filling in for my grandfather. He was attempting to plug an emotional hole, not to acknowledge it as one. Perhaps that's what left me wanting in those days since his absence; and perhaps it was obsession, but not obsession with what I thought I was obsessed. It was a doubling down on absence. Wasn't this the fissure I didn't see then, what Poxl's heroism did for me as well? Shouldn't I have seen what Poxl didn't see himself—that his bombing Nazi Germany didn't undo his parents' deaths, the morbid facts I was attempting to sidestep in putting down Wiesel in favor of West?

Should, shouldn't. We can't undo the past. The fact was I didn't see it. It looks so clear now saying it, but that's not what I saw. I saw Ted Williams's handsome, expensive face staring up at me, and I saw Poxl West's handsome face, and I felt sated. Who could blame my father for wanting to give it to me, and who could blame Poxl.

I didn't feel any of that when I was fifteen years old and in possession of a baseball card so valuable I would never have thought I'd own it. On the ride home I clutched the paper bag the clerk had put the card in and looked out the window, thinking of someone other than my uncle for the first time in weeks.

The shift my father had helped make in my mind didn't last long. I read about Ted Williams's war heroism, but soon after I also read about his personality. Williams was known to be a surly figure— wouldn't talk to fans, refused to sign autographs.

My uncle had sat and signed books for anyone who'd wanted one signed.

We went one weekend to visit my mother's great-aunt Leah at her apartment in Quincy, the only one in her family who lived here in Massachusetts. She was by far the most Bostonian Bostonian in my mother's family, and she subscribed to NESN so she could watch every game now that she was too old to travel from Quincy to Fenway. She told me about how she had once been on an airplane with Williams, in the mid-seventies.

"Wouldn't so much as make eye contact with me when I went up to tell him I was a fan," my great-great aunt Leah said. "I was wearing a Sox cap at the time and everything. Written the man off ever since."

When I got home that day I put the Williams card in a drawer. I pulled out *Skylock* for another read and it felt like some buzzing at the back of my head had been silenced. I didn't have Poxl near, but that couldn't negate the fact that I had read his book. I found what I could on the RAF in our school library. But now when Rabbi Ben brought up Poxl in Hebrew class, I would find some way to deflect the conversation, not wanting to talk again about the idea of Poxl's coming to visit us—not wanting to admit I hadn't spent time with him in months, and I hadn't asked if he'd come see us. I could talk about *Skylock*, but not its author.

"So what's the deal with Kabbalah, anyway?" I said one Monday evening when conversation had drifted away from Hebrew and I feared it might drift toward me. But there was real need in my voice, and whether it was for an absent uncle or an unknowable God, everyone in the room could hear it. Rachel Rothstein rolled her eyes and I immediately wished I hadn't said a word, but Rabbi Ben sat up straight.

"You never seemed all that interested before," he said. But before I had time to respond, he said, "Shit, I wrote my dissertation at Yeshiva on Moses de Léon. He was the thirteenth-century Spaniard who wrote the Zohar, the central text of Jewish mysticism. Check it out, guys—he believed that God was in everything around us. The world started in *ein sof*, he said. Who can translate that term, *Ein Sof*?"

Our Hebrew had gotten us only so far that Rachel could say she knew the first word, *Ein*. It meant "one."

"It means 'nothingness.' One endless nothingness. The world started in nothing, and even though God made something—Adam, Eve, a garden, Zion, later us—the original state of our souls, of our existence, was nothingness. The Zohar says we need to return to that state if we want to touch the Godhead."

"I want to touch some kind of head," Zach Swartz said.

Everyone cracked up.

"What's that, dude?" Rabbi Ben said. Now everyone just looked down at their feet. "Well, look, Eli, if you want to hear more about Kabbalah, let's definitely find some time to rap outside of class. I'll give you some Gershom Scholem. You'd like *Major Trends in Jewish Mysticism.*"

I didn't know what to say. I told him that was fine, and everyone in class looked at me like I'd lost my mind. But I hadn't lost my mind. I just was missing my uncle, and while he wasn't my uncle, Rabbi Ben was here.

After class that night I went into his office, where he walked around his overloaded bookshelves and showed me the major texts of the modern study of Kabbalah. Some part of me had come to think that the elders at our shul read only books about the atrocities of World War II, and all at once my eyes were opened to the fact that mostly on Rabbi Ben's shelves were texts of Talmudic study, midrash, and Kabbalah. We only see what we want when we're in need, and for months I'd seen only one history. Now I was seeing something else. Here was one thing Poxl West hadn't talked about, but which was always lingering: God.

We were sitting now, me in the chair in front of Rabbi Ben's cluttered desk, him behind it. I was ready to hear what he had to say. Receptive.

"So I finally had a chance to read *Skylock,* dude," Rabbi Ben said. This was unexpected. It threw me for a moment, made me more comfortable than I could have anticipated. Here I was, ready to ask him about the Zohar, all that he'd wanted to talk about for months, and instead he was bringing up Poxl West's memoir.

"And?" I said.

"And!" Rabbi Ben said. "Your uncle's a majorly good writer, and *mein Gott,* the experiences he's had. I can totally see why you've been so into that book. And him."

"Well, he is my uncle," I said. Talking to Rabbi Ben, in that moment, all my regret and sense of absence was gone. It was almost as if Poxl were back with us. "I did kind of play a part in helping him get his manuscript together."

"It occurs to me that some of what goes on in there isn't so different from what draws me to the Zohar. I mean, when he describes flying in his plane, he describes looking into the face of the whirlwind. That's what Job did, right? Look right into the face of the Behemoth. For me that's why I care about thinking about God. Not just to say, 'What stories do we read in the Torah?' But to say, 'What would it look like to meet face-to-face with the deity?'"

When Rabbi Ben had brought this up in class, we were too uncomfortable to discuss it. But sitting in his office, I remember I gave it real thought. What had Poxl West seen up in those skies? And more important: What occurred in my daily life that could bring me face-to-face with *Ein Sof*? Rabbi Ben gave me a handful of books to take home. I shoved them into my book bag and thanked him.

I wish I could say now that I'd read them.

But once they sat down on the shelf next to *Skylock,* their gray cloth covers just seemed so gray. There was a book full of stories of heroism and emotional drama; here was some unintelligible drawing of Hebrew letters adding up to a rudimentary picture of a body that might be our Lord. And there I was, a teenager, confused. I wanted to think about mysticism, but it grew ever more intangible the more I thought about how tangible Poxl West's story was. That it had come almost to replace the human himself for me. I liked Rabbi Ben and I liked Gershom Scholem, but for me, then, with Poxl gone and only his book to consult, it was still *Skylock* to which I'd be turning in my moments of confusion.

Finally in May, I turned in a final report in history class on Uncle Poxl's memoir, which by then I'd read five times. Each time I reread I watched as Poxl again left his mother in Leitmeritz, again left Françoise, again left Glynnis for training. As much as it hurt, as much as it tore the scab off my not having spent time with him, what I fell back on was his heroism, and what came after. I cited more than a dozen sources on the Royal Air Force in the report, sources on military actions in Britain during the war. I quoted from two other memoirs, and I even learned to make the citations properly.

Interspersed within those quotations and summaries, I wrote florid reminiscences of my trips into Boston with Poxl, memories that made it feel almost as if he were back again, taking me to see Shakespeare, to eat sundaes. Almost. As I wrote, I overplayed my role in giving him someone to talk to while he was drafting the book. I won't lie: No matter what ended up in it, I still feel some pride now thinking of how hard I worked on that report. No matter what was to come, no matter what lay beneath any of my motivations during that period, Poxl West had brought to life in me a curiosity I wouldn't otherwise have had. One I retain to this day.

When I got the report back a week later, my teacher had written on the last page, "Impressive research, impressive topic, impressive writing, impressive, impressive, impressive. And above all, impressive company you've been keeping. Meticulous work: A–. Keep up the good work."

ACT THREE

I.

My first few weeks after enlisting in the RAF were taken up with logistics. I was given an examination in math, which I passed with ease. I was issued a respirator and identity disks, eating utensils, and a whole new set of vaccinations should I be shot down over North Africa. An officer in his RAF blues gave me and three other recruits a lecture about how short we should keep our hair, how it was imperative that a pilot shower after each run, and bathe himself every other day on any account.

"If you meet some young thing in the NAAFI, you're to use protection," this officer said. The idea of meeting any "young thing" was far from my mind at that moment. This officer was tall, and broader across the chest than the Elbe near Brüder Weisberg, and of a British type who, frankly, scared me. "We don't need any more of our crew walking around with balls swollen with disease, if you see what I'm bloody saying."

We saw.

The walls grew brighter and my palms began to sweat, thinking what diseases I myself might have acquired, having spent more than a year sleeping with Françoise and now Glynnis. It was as if the world before me was succumbing to splashes of color, and a kind of spasm shook my eyeballs so that I could not focus. I could think now of what diseases I might have, but had I thought before of what the experience was to them? I didn't even know what Françoise's fate was, let alone what she might be thinking now.

In a room with dun-colored floors, which smelled antiseptic and vaguely of man sweat, an officer shouted that I was to take off my clothing. Soon he hit me with a painful spray from a hose to assure I was rid of any bugs. From there I was whisked off to a Nissen hut where I was to spend the night, before moving along to begin my training.

Next day I rode by train down to the southern coast, where I was plied further with a trainee's gear at the Initial Training Wing to which I was assigned. It was the same train Glynnis and I had ridden to visit Mrs. Goldring not three months earlier. Water still lay in the fields, and now the fields, which only rarely had been scarred by bombs, were torn up, as if plagued by some infernal vermin. I pulled down my rucksack to inventory my new possessions. Everything seemed to come in threes: three navy blue sweaters, three pairs of heavy socks ("You'll need those up there, it's cold as hell at thirty thousand feet"), three service collars, and three service shirts, stiff and itchy on those first days I donned them. I'd received fork and knife, and to-day a heavy navy blue wool sweater with a cable-knit collar, which I would later learn was named after the British isle of Guernsey. Again hygiene was a major concern, and while I found the treatment of the RAF officer rather lax compared to those conventional views one is given of the rigor of military life, I received bristled items of all varieties—one for my clothing, one for my boots, even one to keep the buttons of my uniform clean.

After that train ride east—after our path departed from those tracks Glynnis and I had once traveled on and dipped farther south—my memory consists only of the chaos of orientation and more lectures on basic personal comportment before I was soon on a train headed north, this time to RAF Cranwell. There I was stationed in yet another Nissen hut. During the days I rose at seven and was in the classroom in yet *another* Nissen hut where starting at eight every morning I was plied with a deluge of English words—*nacelles, ailerons, throttles, glycol; cumulus, stratus, cirrus*—and where I earned mediocre scores at gunnery (I never got comfortable with the Browning automatic) and in my use of the Morse buzzer, which in the end was of far greater use to the navigator than it was to me.

From there I was sent back even farther north to Lincolnshire, where my training group practiced flying Tiger Moths. Did I think of that story Glynnis Goldring had told of her ancestor who had centuries earlier seen an imp carved in stone in some Anglican church in this very Lincolnshire where I was now to be stationed? Was a certain compassion not evoked in me, a sense that the hope for love I'd left to the south might outweigh what was ahead of me here in the north? If such clarity of emotion was available to you when you were twenty-one years old, I can only convey to you my most sincere, ardent jealousy. No matter the upheavals of my most recent years, I was still a young man bent on moving forward. When I returned to London after my service, perhaps I would fulfill the suggestion that Glynnis and I could marry. I would write her letters.

For now my mind drew northward.

As for my arrival there, I can say only that these Tiger Moths we were soon to train on were quite familiar from my time flying in Czechoslovakia. This was an updated model, but it was very similar to my father's. I felt I knew what I was doing. Soon enough I was faced only with the formality of recording two hundred hours in the little blue logbook.

In a matter of months, I wasn't far from taking to the air for battle.

In the classrooms and briefing rooms where we were to study the visual differences between Messerschmitt 109's and Junker Ju 88's and Dorniers and Focke-Wulfs, I looked up when our training officers would place long pieces of yarn on large maps of Western Europe to show us routes we might take in flying over the Channel and into the Ruhr Valley. What I would see there were flight paths traversing the airspace over much of England; over the North Sea; directly over Rotterdam and over German soil. I was ready to take flight.

2.

Near the end of my training, my time to strike against the Nazis would be delayed. I had nearly logged my two hundred hours on that Tiger Moth to take the Pilot Navigator Test. There had been much talk of who would pilot bombers and who fighters, who would go up with half a dozen of their fellow fliers to drop bombs on those German cities from four-engine Lancasters and Manchesters—and those who would engage the Luftwaffe in Spitfires. But this decision so important to my fate wasn't mine to make. My experience flying solo was noted in my blue logbook by my superiors. I was to fly a Spitfire.

At that aerodrome in Lincolnshire, I took one of those sleek machines skyward, just twenty hours short of fulfilling my training. Below me were fields, one of which might still provide feed for the very cattle that Glynnis had once fed when she was a girl, pushing her along her own path to medicine. An early fog fought the high sun all morning. The low clouds we'd been taught to fear hadn't abated by late afternoon. Training in these fighters was limited to night flying, as we would be escorting bombers to their targets over Germany. At 2100 hours I readied for takeoff, through darkness and clouds. As the flight progressed and I began to run low on petrol and prepared to return, clouds near what I thought was our aerodrome were so thick they wholly obscured the ground. Even as I sank below ten thousand feet, I passed through opaque clouds, and soon found myself hopelessly lost. The coordinates I was meant to follow had me nowhere near the aerodrome, but deeper and deeper into the dark sky above western England. I would have to guess my way back to base.

I got on the radio, calling, "Hello, darky," "Hello, darky," seeking an operator.

The night was a blank, unyielding future. I had come to see my destiny as a line stitched in a glove: bending and bobbing above and below leather—but always by design. The night's darkness and the clouds' opacity seemed, if anything, a benefit. On occasion a light would brighten a section of cloud below, but a single flash of light is not enough to sustain a life.

Soon I was down to my last ten minutes of petrol. Faltering on the wind, with only my ailerons and the growing certainty of my hand to reach my destination, the aqueous, impermanent world washed away from me and then back. There was a particular switch that always gave me trouble, and I found it easier to remove my right glove to flip it. In the cold of that cockpit, I bared skin to metal. Off in the distance, to match the flashing lights behind my eyelids, I espied two spotlights: a runway, and at its end a red flare not unlike the markers the Pathfinders would use later in the war to mark my bombing targets in the Ruhr Valley.

I was out of petrol and forced to land with only the wind to propel me. So I landed heavy. My underbelly scraped hard, calling sparks up from the pavement below. The control column drove into my ribs. My entire chest was imploding, and before me every dream and desire I'd harbored for now months and even years was growing diffuse, distant. Before I was even debriefed I was taken to a hospital, where after a number of days I was diagnosed with pleurisy, which I was now suffering from as a result of an infection that developed from my injuries.

During the months following this landing, I had a great deal of time for thinking, and I thought often of how different the experience of physical pain as an adult was than it had been when I was a boy. When I was eight and broke my wrist, physical pain still contained that singular didactic ability to transform action. So much of life is defined by the acceptance of pain. When I was four I put my hand on a teapot and burned my fingers. The raised red imprints are still seared onto my pinkie and ring fingers, and at the heel of my left palm. I was still learning from pain, conditioned to understand what to touch, what not, how to proceed as a human.

Pain had a single lesson: Some things must be avoided. One

kind of pain was the pain you received when you burned your hand; another kind of pain was the pain of bad decisions rued for years to follow. What pain do I feel now, decades later, when I think of that day I left Rotterdam? What pain did I feel when I lay in that hospital bed, trying to imagine Françoise now in life or in death? It was Glynnis I should have been thinking of, but something in the indeterminacy of what I'd left in Rotterdam kept my mind returning to it much as my mind returned to that day I'd gripped the teapot.

This inauguration into the experience of human-being had not yet ended when I was thirteen and traversing Prague with my mother, when the sometimes unbearable sexual desire I'd coupled with my experiences then arose in me. I wonder even now at what point in our development pain becomes something one endures, at times something one comes even to learn to enjoy—if only to test one's stamina, if only to remember once more that the routine of one's days has brought about in one the forgetfulness of death. Forgetfulness at the mind meeting each coming moment. Being itself becomes an attempt to skirt pain at all costs—when from the start that experience has been the siren informing us we are interacting with the world in the first place. And isn't that the experience of new love: knowing that once again it may end in just the pain it ended in the last time? No matter what I'd felt in leaving Françoise, when I saw Glynnis, some part of me was prepared to believe it would end better. Or that I would see Françoise again. Who could predict the line one's life would follow? Was I the child fearing the reprisal he had experienced when blisters formed on his fingers, or a masochist drawn into the web whose creator awaits

with numbing, fatal venom? Surely it was this that tracked me
in the moments when I strapped on my safety belt in that plane,
tracked me that first night I saw Glynnis Goldring's pale, beautiful face in the half-light of a tube station, tracked me when I
met Françoise and even when I left her. Surely.

3.

I was confined to six months in an army hospital outside London. Clive and my cousins were able to visit on weekend passes
from their respective areas of service—Johana and Niny had
joined the WAAF, each working the radios at RAF Turnbull.
Niny herself had visited three or four times before I'd recovered enough—frankly, before I was weaned from morphine
enough to converse coherently—to wonder aloud about the most
conspicuous absence of that time: Glynnis's having failed to
come see me.

"Poxl," Niny said. "Poxl. I've been waiting until you were
lucid."

A Luftwaffe bomb had struck Glynnis's hospital, she said.
Just three weeks prior. Papers reported three nurses had died,
all of them "very suddenly."

Glynnis.

The sill of the window by my bed bore no flowers. I was glad.
It was the only thing that made me glad. Creeping up at the edges
of my mind were those hollyhock blossoms the last moments
when I saw Glynnis, the black ant crawling about them. I had
told her that day that when I returned from my service I might
marry her. I don't know if I meant it then, and I don't know what

I would have done had she survived the war. Now I was not even well enough to attend her wake.

Niny left me that afternoon. I was alone for days with my thoughts of Glynnis, thoughts of my dreams both of her and of flying a Spitfire dashed. During the night I beckoned the nurse to increase my morphine. Like my mother, Glynnis was gone. Like those women I'd known in Rotterdam, Glynnis was gone. No occasion marked her passing. In the nighttime's opiated haze, the cold, wet air that lifted off cave walls touched my cheeks again. During the days I did my best to achieve coherence. On one of her many visits, on a day of decreased morphine, Niny brought me my own edition of the Shakespeare plays Mrs. Goldring and I had read aloud to each other on so many occasions, and while the book itself held the same words as Mrs. Goldring's copy, this version was somehow inferior. Still I read. Now Niny herself took up the parts opposite mine. That seemed appropriate.

What I can tell you from that period is that when I was lucid, each time I watched Hamlet fail to express his love before Ophelia's horrid act; each time Niny read to me the last lines we hear from Desdemona before Othello's green-eyed monster overtakes him; even in those moments when Jessica is courted on the periphery as her father is forced to give up his pound of flesh—each time I began to have an image return to me, one that grew stronger at night. In the cobblestones of memory, cobblestones that had been relegated to that part of memory where image cannot gain purchase, swimming images began to return, and chief among them was Françoise's face. My thoughts were so given over to what I'd lost in Glynnis's death, it took me some time to realize that when Niny left and the sun settled below

the horizon outside and I absconded to the half-life of my morphine drip, it was not only Glynnis Goldring's face that arose
in mind. There was another face that came, too, returned to me
with the atavistic pull of a love that won't leave. Perhaps it seems
indiscreet to say that it was not only Glynnis's face I saw then,
in the days just after her death—when I should most have been
mourning—or too honest. Cold even.

But nothing bears truth so wholly as the truth love tells. And
as Françoise's face arose in my memory the gravity of my leaving her in Rotterdam began to pull me deep into its grasp. I'd
had few moments since I arrived in London to sit with my
thoughts. Now that I was confined to a hospital bed, I had nothing but them. *Regret, remorse*—these are not the right words here.
But Glynnis was gone and I'd left Françoise without so much
as a good-bye. Gravity is a funny word here, as the gravity of it
began to push so hard, it seemed it might grind me to dust as
I lay in that bed.

4.

My lungs took a long time to come around. Once they did I was
forced to endure a painfully slow convalescence. It would be
many months before I could fly. By then, war had advanced
under its own ineluctable motion. News of bombing successes
came by radio every evening. Soon Bomber Command had entered what would come to be known as the Battle of the Ruhr.
RAF bombers opened the western border of Germany in what
we all prayed was the prelude to a land invasion. The United

States joined the war. I was only half-conscious of this moment when we could begin to feel all that hunkering down in London, living in Underground stations and driving the battered streets seeking survivors, fleeing to the east to live like our ancestors in caves paid proper recompense.

Once I was back on my feet I was posted again to 100 Squadron. Our aerodrome had been relocated to a small town not far to the north of the very port at Grimsby where I first arrived in England. Within my first months of returning to the cockpit I began my training on a four-engine Lancaster. This required me to log months more air time—flying a bomber was very different from piloting a Spitfire. It was a bit unusual, this move from a fighter to a bomber, but the focus of the air campaign had shifted in those months I'd spent in convalescence. Bomber Harris had grown obsessed with a blanket-bombing attack on virtually every German city, and the RAF needed all the bomber pilots it could muster. Soon enough, my initial disappointment at not returning to a fighter was quickly erased by my relief to be flying again.

Soon I came to know the crew members with whom I'd be flying. Our rear gunner, Parkington, was from Manchester. He took the first afternoon of my arrival to show me our surroundings—the Nissen hut where I was to sleep, a billeted country house we used as mess—and that evening Parkington took me along to a pub called the Rooster's Peck, where lately we would often find ourselves in those languid days just after I'd accrued my next hundred hours in the air, awaiting flight briefings.

After we'd had a few, our navigator and flight engineer, a pair of Londoners both with the last name Smith, who had been educated together and had known each other for many years, arrived.

"So this is our new Polish Yid pilot," Navigator Smith said. This Smith was a gangly agglomeration of limbs and teeth and appeared as if his only reason for not going for pilot was the sheer length of his legs. He sat in front of a warm Watney's, elbows on knees.

I told him I would be second pilot on the first couple of runs, until I'd come to know the Lancaster enough to have a crew under my tutelage. I wasn't a Polack but a Czechoslovak—Poxl West, a young Jew from Leitmeritz, arrived via Rotterdam to London in the interest of killing Germans.

"Tutelage!" Navigator Smith said. "Big word for a Polack."

"But I'm not Polish. I'm Czech."

The rest of the crew had arrived already besotted from having been to a pub down in Grimsby. My complaint was lost amid their din. On this first night I wasn't able to discern the names of every man I was to fly with—a dozen officers from other crews in our wing had arrived along with the rest of ours. While Navigator Smith might have enjoyed poking fun, when drunken Brits got to talking I found myself swept away in a sluice of words. I receded into my warm pint and observations of these men in their dark blue uniforms.

Next morning we went to the mess for a light load before briefing for that night's run, at 1300 hours. This being my first run, I listened to the chatter of the crewmen around me. We were to take a quick run over the Channel, to the small Hanseatic city of Bremen. Other than Bremen's being near the northern coast of the country, this destination meant little to me. As my crew departed I came to try to get some sense of the significance of this path.

"Our plan," Navigator Smith said when I asked about our mission, he being navigator and so the most obvious person to ask about a flight path, "is to fly in an aeroplane and drop some four-thousand-pound blockbusters on Jerry's head. What more do you need to know?"

I said nothing, finding Navigator Smith unlikely to be my ally, and was ready to depart when another of our crew came up alongside us.

"Ease up, Percy," he said. This new face belonged to our bomb aimer—and also the front gunner, as that crew member did double duty on a Lancaster. He was a troll at just under five feet, a Canadian called John Gallsworthy. Within moments of meeting him I came to see he would be the antidote to the absence in my routine of Clive Pillsbury. Gallsworthy was an oafish, pigeon-toed nineteen-year-old who acted and spoke with the benefit of an education far beyond his years. Not long after we met we would find we had in common a great love of the classical and contemporary painters my mother had introduced me to when I was a boy. Gallsworthy had taken two years of courses in the history of art at McGill before the war. He stashed by his bed half a dozen books full of the paintings of Constable, Géricault, David, and Delacroix, and I came by a redoubled education in the history of British and French painting from my acquaintance with this thick-bodied pug.

We returned to our Nissen hut to begin flight preparations.

"To start," Gallsworthy said, "you should know that not only is our navigator Percival Smith a difficult case, but the pilot you're replacing was his closest friend all the way back to their days at Eton. He's predisposed to a certain acrimony toward you. A number of the boys in One Hundred Squadron were with them in a first-year class at King's College, and after training they were left to pick crews. They all chose to stay together— but you and I and the Aussie, Ford, were forced upon them."

As he would be every time I saw him, Gallsworthy was smoking. He took a deep drag. In my memory I see a middle-aged man drawing upon his ancient cigarette, though Gallsworthy wasn't yet twenty.

"Losing Binghamton has been very hard on Percy Smith. Don't take what you get from him to heart. But, still, you might prepare to be at the center of his sights for the coming weeks."

All the men in the crew, with the exception of their pilot, had been flying together for the past year. They were the only Lancaster crew to have remained intact since the beginning of the bombing of the Ruhr Valley, having spent better than four months flying in Lancaster S859, S-Sugar. Having lost Binghamton only a week before had undone their imperturbable sense of identity—as flies to wanton boys we are to the gods. They kill us for their sport.

I was to be the new face in this bunch, a group that before my arrival had been on one of the first bombers in the now-famous Thousand Bomber Raid on Cologne—the greatest success of the bombing campaign to date. There was a level of upheaval from having lost one of theirs, and a pride for their successes.

In addition to providing this reading of Navigator Smith, Gallsworthy proceeded to run through the unofficial flight preparation with me, reminding me of what I'd learned more than a year ago in elementary training: One must shave to maintain a proper seal on the oxygen mask he would need above five

THE LAST FLIGHT OF POXL WEST

thousand feet. Most of the gunners wore three pairs of socks, and I might consider doing the same. Above all, one had to know where his parachute was at all times and where his Mae West— what we called the inflatable jacket for a water landing—was, for as S-Sugar had been flying patched up but intact for dozens of runs, its luck was bound to shift.

Gallsworthy interpreted apprehension on my face and finished by saying, "Tonight is to be an easy run."

I took this as a great relief, and I said so.

"Don't go taking it as that," Gallsworthy said. "Just hold yourself together. We always draw an easy run before a serious one, to boost morale."

5.

At 1700 hours Gallsworthy and I jumped a truck to the airfield. Navigator Smith was focused, along with Flight Engineer Smith, on securing something under the nacelle on our side of the plane. Erks performed a check of escape hatches, panels, tires. We climbed into the waist of the plane. I moved up to the cockpit, where I took my place next to the pilot I would soon take over from, the Aussie, Mark Ford, who was to become an officer and would move on to training new pilots. He had huge hands, was notorious for demanding silence from his crew, and I was to learn before long that as much enmity as I'd experienced from the rest of his crew, doing away with him would come as a kind of welcome departure for many men in S-Sugar.

We taxied behind another Lancaster. As we began to roll

there was a great noise from the engines and into our headsets Ford said, "Six oh five," and I looked at my watch and repeated it. Ford said, "Check the oil" and I said, "Oil okay," and he said, "Flaps twenty-five degrees," and I repeated it, and he said, "Radiator shutters automatic," and I repeated that. We taxied farther and a flash of light came from the flight tower, and while Ford pushed the throttle forward with his right hand, I took it palm-up with my left and pushed it full again, an activity I found easiest done with my right glove off, just as I had for that switch back in my Spitfire.

Our path to the North Sea was conducted in Ford's officious silence, save for the moment when we rose past five thousand feet and he called for us to put on oxygen masks. We'd lifted off with the sun at our backs. As we passed over the verdant landscape on our way southeast again, my memory was granted a new layer: In odd-shaped green field after odd-shaped green field were the dark borders of a Cézanne, whose paintings Gallsworthy had lingered upon in his books. Forever the face of each crew member is reconstituted in my mind now in the image of those plots of land. As we traversed the easternmost airspace over England, Navigator Smith called out our coordinates at each turning point and Ford and I made our turns until we were over the North Sea.

Gallsworthy had made clear after the briefing that defenses would be densest over Cuxhaven. We were to be on the alert.

We rendezvoused with a squadron of Spitfires to our starboard, who waggled their wings in greeting and joined us as we came into formation with the rest of our bomber squadron. Our wings were not ten yards from theirs. At altitude, I replaced my glove. It was cold up there. I buttoned the fur collar of my jacket and every few minutes I thought to waggle my toes like the Spit-fires' wings. Gallsworthy had warned me the night before of pi-lots who had been taken off flights for weeks because of frostbite they'd received at thirty thousand feet. I'd been in hospital enough and wasn't going to take any chances.

"Open eyes and clear minds," Ford said. "Coming up, Cuxhaven."

Thirty seconds later, orange bursts lighted within clouds be-low. The closer we came in our approach to Cuxhaven, the more we heard the explosion of flak, until for the first time I felt our plane concuss—Ford banked left. We were so tight in forma-tion we nearly clipped the wing of a bomber not ten feet from the Perspex of our cockpit.

McSorely came over the interphone: "Jerry—port quarter—two o'clock—closing."

Messerschmitt 110's arose in echelons so close I could see each pilot's face and they opened their guns: a fluid expansion of night against dark crepuscular sky. In the brown light, flak explosions lit the double-finned tails of three Me110's. Red and orange tracers corkscrewed and bullets plinked our side. I dropped my right glove again. I was about to jam hard against the control column and bolt to the airspace below, far out of for-mation, when a Spitfire came hard on that Me110's starboard. A contrail of smoke leaked from its back. It turned straight down on a perpendicular vector in the half-lit evening sky to-ward the dark earth.

"Got those fuckers!" Gallsworthy called.

Ford admonished him to keep off the phones unless there was imminent news—I thought to argue that my friend the front gunner's comment *was* news, and imminent at that, but now I was caught in reverie at how we would soon enough be plummeting toward German soil just as that Me110 had. I rode the rest of the way to our target in a state of tense readiness, having for the first time been hit by Luftwaffe fire. In my months of desire to join the RAF, I'd thought of nothing but the chance to kill Nazis who had sent my parents to their deaths, who had dropped the bomb that had killed Glynnis, and the one I felt must have killed Françoise. But there was no German here, no Nazi—just aeroplanes and flak as likely to destroy us as we were them, and the darkening evening. Amid this trance I was barely even cognizant of the moment Gallsworthy called out over the interphone, "Bombs away!" and we gained altitude, my feet pushing down ever so slightly in my boots, our Lancaster relieved of six four-thousand-pound blockbusters and dozens of incendiaries.

I looked behind me as fire rose from the ground now choked by smoke and aglow as we banked left for our return flight. Ford tolerated more banter over the interphone now that the bombs were away, and as it had been decided we would take a northern route back to our airfield to avoid Cuxhaven, there was less concern about flak and Luftwaffe convoys. My eyes were fixed on the now-black night as we entered the wee hours of the morning until at some point I became aware of a kind of whining in my ear, which was in fact a voice saying over and over again, "You alive, West? West?"

"Yes, yes, sorry," I said.

It was the voice of Navigator Smith over the interphone, employing that new surname I hadn't grown accustomed to yet. "So you've seen your first flak now, haven't you, Polack?"

I began to explain over the interphone that I wasn't Polish, but a Czechoslovak, when I heard Gallsworthy say, "He's done his job, hasn't he?" Navigator Smith cut him off to ask what it was that kept me from answering him when he called after me the first dozen times. Luckily for me, Ford said he'd heard enough until we were back at base.

"Would you like to land us, West?" Ford said.

We descended through the clouds now built up below. I landed and we were taken to debriefing and then to sleep. Late the next day, I awoke to Gallsworthy's declaration that the crew was going to the Rooster's Peck for a pint of mild.

At the pub, I'd barely sat down before Navigator Smith raised a glass.

"To the greatest pilot S-Sugar will ever have," he said. He looked me in the eyes, then looked back over the faces of the crew. "Vance Binghamton."

They all raised their glasses. I raised mine.

"What are you raising your bloody glass for?" Navigator Smith said.

"I was joining your toast."

"Because you knew Vance Binghamton?"

"I didn't."

"Because you're fit to fly his Lancaster?" I didn't say anything. "Then don't raise your cunt glass. We've all lost our pilot. What've you lost, Pilsudski?"

I looked around and found the whole crew awaiting an answer, or looking down into their drinks. The lights grew bright and my neck was all sweaty.

"There was a girl killed by the Germans," I said. "Françoise." By which I of course meant Glynnis. But I didn't have time to correct myself. Now my whole crew was just sitting there looking at me. For a moment I perceived only seriousness in their faces, until my nemesis spoke up.

"Well, if you're grieving, at least we won't have to hear about you biting the nipples off WAAFs," Navigator Smith said. At last the focus shifted from me as the table swelled with laughter. Even mid-upper gunner Pinehurst, who had only treated me with respect, was laughing, if nervously.

Gallsworthy came to sit in the chair next to mine. He explained this vulgar comment by Navigator Smith. In our wing, there was an infamous Polish crew known for their sexual exploits, but whose reputation among the WAAFs had taken a turn when a story was passed around about a teen from Warsaw who was so aggressive he had bitten the nipple off a girl from Coventry.

"But," I said to Gallsworthy, "I'm not Polish. I'm a Czechoslovak."

McSorely overheard our conversation and said it didn't matter to Smith—and it didn't matter to him, either. As the silence after this comment grew, Gallsworthy suggested McSorely might like to play a game of darts. I hadn't ever played. Gallsworthy asked if I'd like to learn.

Navigator Smith said, "Oh, we'll teach you."

Smith and McSorely formed one pair, Gallsworthy and I another, and we played a game called Cricket. Throwing the darts was difficult, a skill I'd never encountered. These Brits were so practiced at it I'd never catch up. Gallsworthy had played at a pub near his home before he enlisted, and he was quite good. After a half hour the score was close. Navigator Smith took his throws and missed all three of his shots at the nineteen he and McSorely needed to close out. He'd just missed his mark with the first two darts, but the third clanked off the wood of the board and bounced back to the floor near him. It stuck upright in a floorboard.

"Bloody hell!" Smith yelled.

As with many men who are for some reason or another constitutionally angry, he was as hard on himself as he was on everyone else.

I went to retrieve the two darts stuck in the board.

Suddenly pain pinched my right shoulder.

"What the hell're you thinking!" Gallsworthy shouted.

He came over and pulled out the dart that had punctured my shoulder. We both looked at Navigator Smith. Even McSorely was staring at him. Smith colored at his neck. The blush overtook his face.

"It slipped," Navigator Smith said. "Or I didn't see him there. Or something."

It was clear from his pinched, stoic face that he knew exactly what he'd done, and it was clear what he'd intended. Gallsworthy took me off to the infirmary, where a WAAF nurse sewed the wound up with just a couple of stitches and discarded my bloodied undershirt. After that, I steered clear of Navigator Smith when I could.

6.

Our aerodrome was quiet for the next week as we lived most of early July under the misty scrim of northeast fog. Each morning we woke for another day of refresher classes in aircraft recognition. The puncture wound in my shoulder scabbed over and the stitches were removed. Navigator Smith and I ceased to make eye contact. The S-Sugar crew awaited word of our next major attack. It was during this time I began to settle into the kind of routine that makes one's endeavor feel as if it is in fact his life. Finally, it was announced that we would be sent over a defenseless Belgian town near the German border, and after that flight came off without any trouble, Flight Officer Ford informed me I would take over as pilot of S-Sugar on the following night's raid. I was to bring my crew for debriefing at 1300 hours.

There was talk all day about how our Belgian run was a cheesecake mission to give us rest for one more serious. We were a scrub yet again that evening due to the density of the mid-July cloud cover.

Thursday, we were due at a briefing midafternoon. Our wing commander got up and read some saber-rattling from Bomber Harris about how the mission we were about to undertake was the most important of the bombing campaign to date.

Our target was Hamburg.

All of Hamburg.

In addition to being the site of the Krupps factory, where many of the ball bearings necessary to the Nazi war machine were manufactured, and the biggest U-boat factory in all of Germany, Hamburg was a populous city deep within German borders. We were to hit either or both factories. We were to damage German morale. Bomber Harris made it clear this attack could turn the momentum of the war. This was our opportunity to take out specific targets, to drive German morale to a nadir.

It wasn't lost on any one of us that part of our mission was not to kill Nazis this time. It was to kill Germans, Nazis or otherwise.

Wing Commander Pennington turned to a map detailing our flight path from the aerodrome deep into German airspace. We would be going deep enough that we couldn't alter our direction—Manchesters flying with us, with smaller fuel tanks than the Lancasters', would continue on all the way to North Africa—and the approach would place us not over Cuxhaven, but over the Kiel Canal and Lübeck, both of which were notorious for the intensity of Luftwaffe aerodromes, which sent up hundreds of fighters each time they spotted us.

"No way we'll get past all those Me110's," Navigator Smith said.

Wing Commander Pennington assured Smith and the rest of us that there was something new awaiting the Luftwaffe that night to protect us.

We had a temporary second pilot on this flight, along to observe before taking over his own bomber. He turned out to be an acquaintance of Gallsworthy from his Initial Training Wing, a Liverpudlian called Rowlandson. He was charged with loading S-Sugar with this new weapon we were to use against the Germans. After our briefing he and Gallsworthy, who as the bomb aimer would deliver our secret weapon, went off to discuss it.

I went back to our Nissen hut, where I shaved once again. While I was shaving, Navigator Smith came into the latrine. I hesitated for a moment, but it was too late to turn around to leave. I was shirtless, and I still had a large gauze bandage on my right shoulder protecting my wound. Smith looked up and saw the patch. He didn't acknowledge me.

I harbored some hope he might provide me a bit of a wider berth given that there were just the two of us. No matter how acerbic a man might be, it has been my experience that if one finds himself alone with him, just two men without any further audience, an interaction might grow easier.

Navigator Smith proved an exception to this rule.

I wondered aloud if there hadn't been some concern among our crew that we would be dropping bombs not just on selected targets in Hamburg, but that we would be bombing the city as a whole.

"What of it," Smith said.

"We would be killing civilians," I said. "We might be knowingly killing civilians."

"What do you know of killing civilians?"

I told him that before arriving in London I'd lived for a year in Rotterdam, and the people there I knew had most likely been killed by Luftwaffe bombs.

Now Smith just looked at me.

"So that's your girl you were talking about?"

I tried to explain that I'd been meaning to speak of a Briton named Glynnis, to whom I'd briefly been engaged and who'd died in central London. Instead, though I'd not meant it, I'd referred to a woman I'd known in a Dutch brothel.

"I don't need your whole damn family tree. I'll just tell you the same thing I told you last time," Smith said. "We're here to drop bombs on the heads of some Nazi bastards. This is total war. Look—you're going to have to adopt a press-on attitude,

Pilsudski. That's your mantra from here on out: Press. On. Regardless. Isn't it what you're here for?"

I didn't respond.

"Let me pose a question, then," Smith said. "You think your pain for this Glynnis or Françoise or whatever is so unique. What makes you think all the boys in our squadron haven't lost girls of their own? Aren't thinking about their girls back in London?"

Navigator Smith wiped his face of shaving cream. He studied himself in the mirror. I thought to say something more, but there was nothing more to say. I'd lost Glynnis to the Luftwaffe attack. I'd left Rotterdam. I'd left Niny and Johana, and Johana had lost her paramour and most likely her husband, and my parents had been taken from their home. And I'd lost Françoise, left her thinking only of what it meant to me—never what it meant to her. I could still hardly conceive of what she'd thought I'd done.

In those moments with Navigator Smith, there wasn't anything to explain, nothing to talk about. He left the latrine.

I donned my RAF deep blues and dressed in layer after layer now that I knew intimately the cold of thirty thousand feet. My crew convened on the airstrip near S-Sugar at 1800 hours to await the call for takeoff. Gallsworthy had conferred upon himself a kill for one of the Messerschmitts that went down over Cuxhaven. He was only now painting a swastika on the side of our Lancaster by way of commemoration. I asked after the secret weapon the wing commander had mentioned at the briefing.

Gallsworthy showed me a dozen large paper-covered

packages sitting below the waist of the plane. Rowlandson had left them there to be loaded. He would drop these packages as we entered German airspace. Neither he nor any of us knew then how it was to work, but the effect of the dropping of these packages was meant to clear our flight path. Gallsworthy paused in his painting and picked up a package. He turned it over in his hand, as skeptical as I was that a paper-covered package would effect much of anything in the midst of that "total war."

The aerodrome was a din of engines starting, flight engineers checking bombers. The sun was moving ever closer to a dense stand of trees in the western sky that brought to mind my first trip to the cave with Glynnis. Water had been lying still in the fields then. Though we hadn't seen much damage, the first time a huge brown crater revealed itself out there, Glynnis had gasped. I hadn't realized I was clenching my fists until I heard her. We'd both grown so accustomed to the ruin of buildings all across London. But seeing earth torn up like that—no human harmed, no building destroyed; no real danger, only the ability of a two-ton bomb to move solid grass-covered earth—had some new effect on us.

I just said, "Navigator Smith was after me again."

Gallsworthy suggested I begin keeping clear of Smith—I was providing him too much ammunition with which to antagonize me.

"These are nineteen- and twenty-year-old men you're talking to," Gallsworthy said. "Boys like you, but who haven't been through what you have."

Just then word came from Wing Commander Pennington:

Cloud cover over Germany was too dense. We were a scrub yet again.

That night there was an NAAFI dance downriver at Grimsby. While the rest of the crew went out I hoped to give the night over to a long letter to Niny. But Iago that he was, Navigator Smith knew the business of roiling emotions well. I stayed in our Nissen hut and spent the night instead writing a posthumous letter to my mother. I wrote her of the Tiger Moths and the vacuous chill of the air at thirty thousand feet, where nightly now we flew to drop huge bombs on the very villains who had sent her to her death, and to move ourselves ever closer to the heaven where she now resided.

I wrote and wrote and wrote.

I wrote her things I couldn't quite admit aloud to anyone but her: I'd never made it back to see Glynnis, and I'd never told Glynnis about my mother's death. The weight of that guilt, knowing she was now dead. Even when she and I were quietly making love I would sometimes close my eyes and think of Françoise. That anger had sent me fleeing from Rotterdam when I honestly still to this very day didn't know that I'd wanted to leave Françoise—but I had, and now I didn't know her fate. And now I'd begun to picture myself there, to imagine what half-bombed Rotterdam looked like and what I, Poxl, as a villain looked like to the woman I'd left without a word of my leaving. Somehow I felt that if anyone would understand this unnamable emotion it was my mother. I told her how many times I'd wished I hadn't walked out of our house without saying good-bye to her, too, the first of my flights beginning that moment I left her home, the one that imbued my

muscles with the memory of leaving that allowed me to depart
Rotterdam, and that I never truly thought I wouldn't get another chance, how I wished I could see her. How I wished I
could see her. How I would always for the rest of my life have
wished I could see her again.

When I'd finished I sealed the envelope and placed it in my
footlocker, where over the days to come, as this letter writing
would become something of a habit, I would accrue quite a collection of undeliverables.

7.

Saturday night we were briefed again, this time by Wing Commander Pennington himself. We arrived at the airfield at 2100
hours. At 2315 we took off. Clear skies, a rarefied night absent
moon or cloud. Three hundred miles from the English coast we
joined our wing in formation over the North Sea. We were in
rear right. This was the most dreaded position, most exposed
to flanking attacks. Still I was grateful to have to worry only
about the bomber to my left. Maintaining formation could be
the difference between living and dying.

As I moved in, Navigator Smith came on the interphone.

"Press on regardless, Captain West." I said certainly, but suggested that perhaps we should keep quiet, as we had for our former captain, Flight Officer Ford. This didn't keep Smith from
bugging Gallsworthy and McSorely about the WAAFs he was
sure they'd been with the night before. He ran on until we
reached the German border. Contrails of Stirlings strung out
thousands of feet below. At that height I was reminded of

Goethe's description of blindness: "Everything near becomes distant." Though I knew intellectually those fighters were a thousand, two thousand feet away, that distance might have been all distances, or none, in the enormous Prussian sky.

Our rendezvous point, position A, was less than an hour from Hamburg. Now Gallsworthy was to begin dropping his mysterious packages. Over the interphone the only sound was of his timing the drops: "One Lancaster, two Lancaster, three Lancaster," all the way to sixty, then another drop. Frigid air filled the cockpit each time he opened the window. When he reset his count we looked behind to where thousands of silver swimming minnows filled dark air, reflecting the lights of bombers. Yellow flares marked the path before us. As we approached the Kiel Canal the previously cloudless sky filled with brown clouds of flak smoke.

Gallsworthy called out that he'd seen a Lancaster far off to our starboard. All seven men of its crew bailed out.

Then we were through it without incident.

Another half hour and Navigator Smith came over the interphone: We had achieved our final turning point at Kellinghausen. What we saw before us then made procedure unnecessary.

Hamburg was already glowing, an earthbound star. Lancaster squadrons all across the midnight horizon were lit by individual auras against the dark summer sky. By the time we made our approach, no green or yellow flare was discernible. They'd mixed together with the blockbusters each squadron had already dropped, four-thousand-pound bombs and four-pound incendiaries landing again and again as our bombers dropped their loads, blooming like enormous sunflowers thousands of feet down.

Gallsworthy came on the interphone: What was there to drop on? Bombs atop bombs? I thought of my mother. I thought of my father, and of Françoise, and though I chose not to speak, I might have said, "Bomb until there is nothing left to bomb."

Navigator Smith came after: "Press on," he said.

I felt the lightening of our plane as our bombload went down and we went up and below us was the obfuscating cloud of dense smoke.

I banked left.

Already we were on our return path. We encountered not a single Luftwaffe fighter. Those silvery minnows Gallsworthy had dropped had fooled German radar into thinking there were thousands of bombers all across the vector on which the minnows flew. Bombers before and after us had dropped the packages, too, and the Luftwaffe fighters hadn't had enough fuel to stay skyward long enough to engage us. We'd approached Hamburg on the driest night of the summer and hardly faced any resistance.

Hamburg was given over to flame.

With the city burning behind us the night was no longer dark. Western suburbs of Hamburg burned phosphorescent, glowing out to their fuzzy lighted edges. There, glinting amid the dark earth below us on the path back to base, was the Elbe. The river flowed northward from below my father's tannery, through Hamburg and on to the North Sea on the other side of which I was now stationed. For the first time since arriving at RAF Grimsby I caught a whiff of days swimming with Johana and Niny, gnats buzzing in the low Bohemian evening. Below us the shrapnel of a bomb found its way into the Elbe, floating upstream and out to the North Sea. River water carrying it had

flowed from Leitmeritz and from Schalholstice, where it cooled
in vats of tanning leather at my father's business. Through
Poland. Through the city I had just set ablaze during the dimming July night.

Hamburg's flames lit our backs for miles, dimming in our
wake until the ruined city ebbed to a match tip on the far
horizon.

Soon we were clear of Hamburg. And in those moments after I'd exacted revenge on German soil, a face arose in mind so
lucidly I couldn't imagine shaking it, perhaps ever—a face I'd
hoped to forget since I left her but which clearly I couldn't shake:
Françoise's.

8.

Debriefing back at base at almost 0500 hours was joyous. The
first moment of true happiness I'd felt since discovering I would
be accepted into flight training. It allowed for a true forgetfulness of all else: This bombing was our whole world in the moments after we returned. Morale soared after our unqualified
success. Navigator Smith recounted perfect turns his pilot—the
Eastern European Jew now called Poxl West—had executed at
each turning point. A low black course of stubble had cropped
up on his jutting chin, and the deep furrow of his dark Etonian
brow brought a feckless look to his flat face. McSorely described
the night sky and the Catherine wheels raised by each blockbuster bomb as it landed on central Hamburg, one after the next,
stoking flames so high we couldn't see the city itself.

Even taciturn Flight Engineer Smith disregarded unspoken

protocol and told the WAAFs who questioned us about our perfect run. There was such good cheer in the Nissen hut, I wondered if rest would come that night for the crew of the S-Sugar. But we all fell immediately to sleep, and then, late that morning, I was awakened by Navigator Smith's cries. They were half-human, a macaw's squawk, which stirred no man among us but me, all the rest wholly overtaken by exhaustion. I dropped from my bed. I held his thrashing arms. He woke only long enough to dart upright. He looked me in the eyes. He steeled his body. He had long, sinewy arms and a thicket of dark, dark hair along them to match his brown brow. I could feel the sisal sharpness of his arm hair in my palms as he thrashed. Sweat covered his face and his eyes flashed.

Then he grew still. He recognized me and returned to himself.

"Wizard flying, young Yid," he said. "Now let me sleep."

The evening following our run, there was revelry. We went to the Rooster's Peck, where Gallsworthy and I played a game of darts. Our crew congratulated me on a perfectly executed run. Any reservations I'd had before dissolved in the warmth of drink. Even McSorely stood me a pint, and from behind his acne-covered face—he was only nineteen, after all, and looked like a schoolboy—I could see a softening of his features. After darts Gallsworthy returned to our table, where he hoisted a warm Harp and said, "To our pilot, Poxl West—a hebe who does some fine flying!" Laughter erupted among the men of S-Sugar. Reconnaissance reported severe damage to the Hamburg Krupps factory. We'd hit our targets. We'd done in Hamburg.

On our meander back to our hut, Gallsworthy held me

back until we were a good thousand feet behind the rest of S-Squadron.

"Poxl," he said. "Poxl, I know you know all about women." He was slurring his words, and while I should have been thinking of Glynnis, I was thinking about Françoise. "You had Glynnis back in London and you have your cousins. But me . . ." His weight shifted all the way to his right foot, then to his left, almost tipping him each time. "Me, I've never even kissed a girl, if you can believe it." Gallsworthy was a squat five feet tall, maybe a few inches more, and, even despite his training, nearly two hundred pounds.

I could believe it.

He continued.

"If I could meet a WAAF or some girl in town," he said.

My kind slovenly friend Gallsworthy needed my help finding love. Even for him a taste of death over Hamburg had touched off a longing for love. I told him that when we were back in London he would come with me and meet my cousin Niny.

"Let's have the picture of her," Gallsworthy said. We were back to our Nissen hut by now and though he'd seen the photograph a thousand times, I went to my footlocker and picked out the photo of Niny, Johana, and me along the Elbe in Schalholstice, just outside Brüder Weisberg. We stood beside one another, not touching, and behind us the very vats were sunk into the ground, inside of which my father's men submerged the hides in need of tanning.

Gallsworthy was the drunkest I'd ever seen him. Now he was lying back on his bed. I took him the photo and he held it very close to his face and said, "Niny, Niny, Niny," an incantation, until his arms bent back and the picture sat against his chest.

He passed out dreaming of my cousin and of the image of my Elbe, which he knew only from that photograph, and which no amount of killing or distance could ever rob from my memory.

9.

Next few days we awoke to fog so thick it was as if we were back up among the clouds. By Wednesday there was an even heavier cover, morning announced only by a subtle glowing change in hue. The Americans were grounded during the day, just as we were at night. It was Thursday before another run could be attempted. Some kind of electricity ran through the crewmen in the briefing room—our turning points were changed, but the destination remained:

We were to make a second run on Hamburg.

All the other bombers in our squadron had flown a second run on the city Tuesday, but we'd been grounded. Upon takeoff we had lost oil pressure and were forced to return to base. They reported what we had: a clear, safe run to the city. There was an edge to their stories. They'd experienced a parallel success to ours, but now they described flying into a column of smoke so thick they could taste soot from the city in their oxygen masks. We had fuzzy heads the days after our victorious run. We had time on our hands from the failed takeoff and the fog. Idle, we began to consider what we'd done.

"How many you suspect we killed on that run?" Gallsworthy said at breakfast. "Thousand? Two?"

"More, I'd think," McSorely said.

"More than two thousand," Gallsworthy said. "That's a lot

of civilians." He paused and took a bite of his sausage. "That's a lot of anything."

"Well, sure," McSorely said. "But it's a huge city. There're plenty more who survived."

Again from the edges of my memory came that image: cobblestones rising to mind; Glynnis's pale skin. Françoise's broad nose.

Wing Commander Pennington arrived and briefed us on our run. Flight Officer Rowlandson was to fly with S-Sugar on one more run before taking over his own commission.

Soon we lifted off again into a light mist. We weren't far from base before it grew apparent this was to be a more challenging run. S-Sugar was among the lead bombers. No matter how high we rose through the clouds it felt we would never overcome them. Over the North Sea we finally broke from cloud cover to witness a blanket of undulating gray below. A bomber's moon provided some light. It wasn't a help for long. Navigator Smith called out coordinates for our upcoming turning point. We were miles out over the sea, passing above Heligoland, when before us was a billowing column of black pumice. My first thought was that this was what we'd wrought in Hamburg.

We'd ignited Germany. Here, rising nearly 35,000 feet above the ground, was the evidence. Then the swelling and dying of dozens of white explosions ran through the great black mass. It was hard to know how so much flak could be thrown into the air. Perhaps we were witnessing some unprecedented new Nazi weapon, some horrible counterpunch to the silver strips we'd dropped to disrupt Nazi radar and which had allowed us to light such a monumental conflagration.

"Flak ahead," Navigator Smith called out. "Or . . . something."

Gallsworthy came on the interphone next:

"Not flak," he said. "Lightning."

Before us was the largest cloud ever amassed in the air above Nazi Germany. As we passed over the German coast south of Cuxhaven, the great mass undulated. All through the cloud, branches of white fire spread and retreated like the passing of axons to synapses in the great black brain of the Reich.

Gallsworthy came over the interphone again:

"Perhaps we might consider turning back, Captain West."

No sooner had the words escaped his mouth than Navigator Smith followed: "I'm not going out with an LMF"—lacking in moral fiber, the worst kind of discharge from the service. "You're certain to get one, too, Captain West. How will that look for a citizen of a Nazi protectorate?"

We stayed in formation.

The bombers ahead pushed headlong into the cloud. Silence saturated our bomber. The only sound was the low, anxious rumble of nearby thunder. For once something wrought by the Lord had quieted Navigator Smith's constant chatter. At last the sky grew as angry as I was at the loss of my parents, of Françoise, of Glynnis. Like a tumid-eyed pup seeking his mother's teat, we edged around the crevasses comprising the outer realm of that great black cur, which lit up so frequently it was difficult to know just what we were seeing.

We would fly directly into the cloud.

First came the winds. A current of cold air swept S-Sugar's wings, rocking us until we banked right and then left. Soon we were alone amid dense cloud. No other bombers from our wing were visible.

Nothing was visible.

We pushed on, and then a flash—for a second I was blind. When I regained my sight, a deep blue glow enshrouded the cockpit. The de-icing tube on the other side of the perspex bore a halo of blue flame. Blue tendrils shot back and forth between Browning guns of the front turret Gallsworthy manned. All around the propellers to our left and right, blue auras outlined the blur of blades.

"I can see a kind of blue light between my guns," Gallsworthy said over the interphone.

Navigator Smith said, "All over the instruments back here as well."

Five seconds passed. The world again flashed so bright I was blind. This time when I regained my sight, the world was wholly suffused with corporeal blue. It was so cold I could not tell if I was experiencing electricity or air. Again the dark world flashed white so bright my sight was gone as if for good. A kind of mania gripped us in those moments as we looked in the eye of the lightning from a cloud in which we were sitting.

A pounding began on the fuselage. Gallsworthy came again over the interphone:

"We're hit! We're hit!"

Then Navigator Smith: "I don't see Jerry—does anyone see Jerry?—where's Jerry?" No sooner had they spoken than we all saw it. The propellers were throwing off ice in chunks the size of shingles. Navigator Smith said he could see the ailerons icing over. In a matter of seconds we would freeze into a block and plummet like a bomb into the sea. I had my hand on the throttle, which pushed hard back against me. My grip slipped, then slipped again.

I took off my right glove.

I was in need of traction.

Now I pushed the column in hard. We dropped a couple hundred feet. The ailerons were icing worse. I knew if I were to try to fly higher, we'd never make it. I pulled back horizontal and desynchronized the engines. We shook like we were inside a paint mixer until I synchronized the engines again. No sound came over the interphone.

We were free of the ice. In the brief moment we seemed free I began to feel spider legs of trepidation slide over my hands. Then another flash stole my sight, then a third. When I regained sight we were bathed in blue flame so thin I could see where on my hand minute blue effluvia sank canines into skin. I could feel it all around my molars, blue maws of flame stabbing their fangs into enamel. I tried to put my hand to my lap for my glove but my muscles all tensed. They wouldn't untense. My jaw clenched tight and a jolt stole through me and atop my head I felt a burst of hot pain.

A great blue flash.

Eyes failed.

Then: nothing.

10.

The world returned in electric blue flames. No sooner had I regained consciousness than my brain made me believe I heard the voice of my cousin Niny saying in her native Czech, "Oh, I think he might be waking," and "Keep your eyes closed, Poxl."

I didn't understand what Niny was doing in the cockpit of a Lancaster over Lübeck. Some large part of me felt as if from the time I'd first entered that cockpit I had been living some other, borrowed, life. One I knew well enough, but one that wasn't mine. Soon enough my hand came to my face to feel the soft cloth covering my eyes.

Niny said again, "It's all right, Poxl. You've survived and they've just got you here in Grimsby at the hospital and you're all right."

A doctor admonished her to speak to me in English so he and his nurses could understand her, and for her to tell me by some miracle I'd survived a lightning strike on S-Sugar. My only thought then was to tell her how I'd wanted her to meet John Gallsworthy, the best chap I'd yet come to know in my squadron.

But I wasn't able to say anything at all.

Following the moment I was struck by lightning, Rowlandson had Gallsworthy drop his bombload, turned S-Sugar around, and brought her back to base. Somehow amid the orange spiraling bullets of Me110's they encountered on their return, the men of the Lancaster S-Sugar survived yet another run, only to lose the commission of their pilot to an electrical storm.

There were losses and there were losses, and my loss was of a particular variety: the loss of my commission to many months' more rehabilitation in hospital. I'd suffered a rupture of my tympanic membrane as blue fires surged through my body. I could just make out the words Niny spoke at my bedside. My

doctors came through and observed spreading ferns of Lich-
tenberg figures across my left arm. These red patterns across
my skin were evidence of the lightning that had entered my body,
bursting veins and capillaries along its path.

Only when I'd just regained my sight was I able to witness
the ferns' remnants. The eruption at the top of my head, where
the electricity had singed my scalp, burrowed its path and exited back into the cloud over Lübeck, had mostly healed by the
time I'd regained my hearing and had been weaned off the morphine that got me through those initial weeks, almost exactly
as it had after my bout of pleurisy. I was left with a small patch
of scalp atop my head where no hair would ever grow again.

But I was alive.

It would be a month before I was able to see. In those words
of Goethe's, "*Alles Nähe werde fern*": "Everything near becomes
distant." Even when my hearing returned, the physical world
stayed far from me until I could again see. I lay in bed for days,
relegated to a chamber in a cave. The world around me grew to
the likeness of those caverns where Mrs. Wilma Goldring, who
felt me a suitable partner for her daughter Glynnis, who sparked
in me a lifelong love of Shakespeare, had lived out the Blitz so
as not to succumb to the bombs that took her daughter. Only
in my cave, there were no other humans to join in my isolation.
Around the shadows and in the corners of those visions I had
in the weeks I lay alone convalescing I would see faces: at times
Glynnis's or Suse's or my cousins' or my mother's, but as time
progressed, only one face came to me: Françoise's.

Now an idée fixe that had long been developing gained purchase: How did I know Françoise might not still be alive? So
many others had died and I knew it. What if Françoise hadn't

been killed in the bombing of Rotterdam? This thought gained its toehold, and then more images: a carmine hollyhock blossom on the sill of a window to the east of London; purple tamarisks by the side of the Elbe in Leitmeritz; a bloom of purple tulip on the sill of a window in Delfshaven. I began to imagine Françoise alive and with a kind of electric shock I truly began to wonder what she would be thinking of me, what thoughts would pass her mind should the name Poxl appear there. The man, the boy really, who had come and fallen in love with her and then left without a word. Without a word. I let my mind drift back to the purple tulip, much easier. All these images again intertwined and I returned to fever dreams like when I was a child, an odd negative and positive switch: black and white, white then black, growing ever more menacing.

As I grew more and more calm, as the world began to return to my eyes and sound to my ears, things practical returned to mind. I saw the Leathersellers College, where I longed to return to work. I saw cousin Johana's little ceramic spitz—I longed to see that little dog, and the flat I'd now absented for so long.

II.

Niny visited on the weekends when she was granted a pass to come see me in hospital. On one of her visits, just as I was beginning to regain the use of my eyes, I asked after my good friend Clive Pillsbury, whom I'd not seen in the brief period during which I was able to fly just five runs in a Lancaster bomber—I would never now come close to approaching the thirty-two necessary to complete my tour—and whom I was surprised to find had not yet come to visit.

"I'd hoped to put it off," Niny said. "I don't know how to say it, save for just saying it. Clive's Spitfire went down over North Africa. He's missing."

It was almost a verbatim recurrence of that moment when I learned of Glynnis's fate. Even without the proper use of my eyes to take in what I'm sure was the harrowed look on my cousin's face, I knew in what way Clive Pillsbury had gone "missing." Niny was a WAAF working the radio north of London. In taking communications from pilots for a year now, she had developed into an accurate detector for those kites that went down with a chance of their crews surviving, and those whose crews would stay missing until the Messiah again visited the Mount of Olives.

I would soon learn of the fate of my crewmates from S-Sugar, as well, which would come only a month after I was struck by lightning: John Gallsworthy went down along with all the crewmen on that Lancaster, S-Sugar, over Essen, on yet another of Bomber Harris's raids of the Ruhr Valley.

Some might suggest there was capital *P* Providence in my having been taken out of my bomber on the last night of the Battle of Hamburg. But mine is not so benevolent a God. Mine is the Elohim of the Pentateuch, whose ways are the ways of punishment, not reprieve. God of Sodom's destruction, not Lazarus's resurrection. God of Job's misery. No other cheek turned, no sin granted absolution. Were I to have stayed on my commission, I would most certainly have found myself missing along with those men. But my fate had long been discrete from the fates of my fellow travelers.

I learned long after the war that well more than half of the
men who'd joined the RAF during the war died in service. It's
become a commonplace, the millions of Jews who died along
with my parents back in Czechoslovakia. Those destinies were
distinct from mine—the numbers of those lost trying simply to
survive, the numbers of those lost in the reckless action of attempting to fight back from the air. Instead, I lay in hospital
until I was able to leave under my own recognizance. With my
mind increasingly focused on a return to Rotterdam, I boarded
a train south to London along with those few belongings shipped
to me from my bunk up north of Grimsby.

I was going home.

12.

Soon after my return to the little flat near Bermondsey I
found that while I'd not fully recovered from the effects of
the tempest, and didn't have energy enough yet to travel far
from the flat, neither was I constitutionally suited to spending my time in idle convalescence. The period after my stint
in the Royal Air Force I longed for Mother, Elbe, Father, Radobyl, youth. I didn't talk to many people: What life I'd created for myself in London before I left for the RAF was
almost entirely gone. Glynnis, Clive, even John Gallsworthy—
nothing of it was left.

Only Françoise might possibly have survived.

The Nazis had started a harrowing ground and air war on
London, indiscriminately firing V-2 rockets at Allied targets.
Although the Luftwaffe didn't send their planes overhead to

bomb in those days as they had in the Blitz, for a period there was an even greater fear of annihilation. People had ceased going out to pubs, even to their work.

Then, as suddenly as they'd started, the Luftwaffe attacks stopped. We didn't hear V-2's tearing across London. Quiet blanketed the city. Throughout April, we heard radio reports that the Reich would give up. One day people even began hasty celebrations, only to learn from the Beeb that it was a false hope. The continuation of the war after that felt somehow even worse for the brief reprieve.

One afternoon during that period, when I found my energy returned in the afternoons and I was up to traveling greater distances, I purchased a train ticket and rode east out of the city toward Kent. Outside my window I saw the same water in the fields. The ground was torn up to a far greater extent than even the last time I'd gone past. V-2's had flown indiscriminately from Holland, and while many of the rockets had found their way to London, many had bored their way into the ground here. I did my best to focus on those patches where the grass was still green, saved from arbitrary destruction.

When I arrived I walked deep into the woods. It was a drier season than the last time I'd been to visit Mrs. Goldring. Midges were scarcer. The walk felt longer than it had those days with Glynnis. Soon enough I was at the mouth of the cave. I did not hear the murmur of voices until I was upon them. In the big chamber at the front of the cave, there were maybe two dozen people milling about. I didn't want to talk to any of them and so proceeded deep into the cave, hoping only to achieve the room I sought.

Back in the living area where I'd once sat with Glynnis Goldring's mother I found the one thing I would hope *not* to find,
again and again, in the coming months and years:

Nothing.

The room had been vacated. No pallets on the floor. No white
bedding for Mrs. Goldring to lie upon. There was no one there
even to ask. I realized that perhaps I'd find no evidence of Glynnis's mother, either.

For the next hour I walked around that huge cave. In some
rooms I would find groups talking in a low hush. At each I inquired after Mrs. Wilma Goldring, the old woman who suffered dementia, whom I'd come to visit those months before.

No one seemed to know of her. Soon enough I found myself
quite lost. After maybe half an hour, I heard voices again—I'd
come upon that same group I'd first encountered before finding Mrs. Goldring's room empty. I was leaving when I saw
someone new had joined their group, an old man who looked
familiar, though it was very hard to say—there had been thousands of denizens of that cave in the days when I last visited it.
Each face as it passed me then was obscured by shadow. I asked
this old man if he knew of Mrs. Goldring.

"Wilma Goldring," he said. In the cold, damp dark, all that
was visible of his face were just the wisps of a white beard poking from his cheeks. "I've known that name since I was a much
younger man than you." This was the elder brother of old Mr.
Lovelace, whom Mrs. Goldring had spoken of when I first met
her, fearing that he might "take liberties" with her deep in that
cave. The coincidence of meeting him here felt providential. But
he followed with the news:

Mrs. Goldring had passed a couple months earlier.

"Her daughter succumbed to the Blitz, you know," he said. He looked at me. "But yes, of course you knew." He told me Mrs. Goldring had taken it hard when she lost Glynnis. Living in those damp caves can't have helped. It seemed once again there would be no ceremony to accompany a loss. But as I turned to depart, the old man said, "Are you the Czech boy she used to speak of? Floxin or something."

I told him that I was, in fact. Poxl. Poxl West. Weisberg. West.

He asked me to wait there a moment. He absconded somewhere deep within the cave. Minutes later he returned. In his hand was Mrs. Goldring's copy of Shakespeare. It was still covered in that oilcloth that protected it from the cave's damp. It was more worn than when I'd last read from it, but I recognized the book as I would have her daughter's face.

For the first time during that period, some remnant of loss had been left behind.

"She wanted you to have it," he said. I thanked Mr. Lovelace's brother and departed.

When I returned to the light outside that cave I sat down. Mrs. Goldring had not inscribed the book as I'd hoped she might have. I thumbed through the thin, crinkling pages and saw she'd taken notes in her last days. I opened to *King Lear.* There I saw where she'd penned in our parts:

Next to each Lear speech, she'd written in "Pocksall," and next to each of Cordelia's, "Me."

I cannot describe the hope seeing these inscriptions instilled in me. For the first time since I'd left Rotterdam, some evidence remained of someone I'd lost. She'd been thinking of me, recording my name in the margins. This edition of the plays would come to supplant the one Niny had gifted me when I was in hospital. It was the edition I would read for the rest of my days.

13.

At the end of the first week in May, on what has come to be known as V-E Day, the streets filled with people. The youth in our neighborhood took to the streets, hung out their windows and threw ripped paper onto one another.

I stayed inside and drew the blackout curtains. Only one of those people I'd come to love in those years since I first left my father's house in Leitmeritz might still be alive. I had to find out.

The war in Europe was over.

My war was far from over.

One day not long after that, I overheard Johana ask Niny when she thought I would find my own living arrangement. After the intimacy of our Hanukkahs and the Elbe-swimming days of our youth, I had come to expect Niny to support me no matter the circumstances, and at first I took her lack of immediate response as an affront. After listening further I came to see that Niny did have my best interests in mind. She suggested she would speak with me. When she knocked on my door late the following afternoon and suggested we take a walk, I found our conversation was not primarily to concern the state of my affairs.

Over the previous six months, Niny explained as we walked past the open façades of buildings and scarred plane trees, she had been seeing a Spitfire pilot she met at an NAAFI function in a country house near Wiltshire, where she and her fellow WAAFs were billeted. This man was named Thomas Paxton. He was twenty-five, raised in West London.

"On our first weekend pass in common, we drove all the way to Dover," Niny said, "where he walked me along the edge of those cliffs and asked after our home." She explained she had never before had the odd feeling she had for this Thomas Paxton. He was an avid and well-versed student of European history. Inquiring after her accent, he discovered she had been raised in Leitmeritz. He had traveled to Prague on several occasions, had traveled across Bohemia. On their first outing together, he described in detail the oxbow that bent around Czesky Krumlov, the medieval castle that rose majestic above its river; trips he'd made down to the spas at Karlovy Vary; the gray stone of the Charles Bridge passing over the Vltava. He had gone swimming in the Elbe, and appeared to understand those feelings we'd experienced as children.

"It has been six years since I've set foot in my house in Leitmeritz," Niny said. "It has been six years since I've seen Prazsky Hrad, since I've even thought of a weekend trip to Krumlov, heading down to the Elbe. But here now is a well-traveled Briton who can talk me back to that place."

A quiet breeze touched us as Niny spoke. This was the first time in as long as I could remember that I had listened to someone else talk. It was as if, for the first time since S-Sugar had entered that cloud above Lübeck, I'd returned to myself. I'd spent all that time alone in my bed near Grimsby. Now I could see the dark moles on Niny's face, and it was as if I'd found a home again in the visible world.

"When I'm with him," Niny continued, "even as the mist blows off the North Sea, moistening my face along those cliffs, I feel as if I'm not with him at all, but in Prague. We'll lie together in the grass, and with eyes closed, we will be in Prague together."

Niny and I reached the park near our flat, where I walked when I'd first arrived. The wrought-iron fence around the commons had long since been stripped and melted down for matériel. Someone had made a slapdash bench of some rubble and boards. Niny and I sat on it.

In the clear late-afternoon air, we stared up at the rooks in their plane trees, and past them to the eaves of buildings along the park. In beds lining that space where once there had been a neatly kept privet hedge, lilac bushes, and boxwood, now spills of earth overturned by bombs lay in piles. Flowers withered brown in the thin light. As we sat there, Niny described Thom's home, where she'd met his parents and his spaniels. He'd been raised in one of those immense four-story town houses in Bloomsbury we coveted. This home at once reminded her of our grandmother Traute's house in Zizkov. It began to feel, my cousin confessed, as if every aspect of this Thomas Paxton drove her into the past.

"I find myself dreaming of our classmates from the gymnasium. During the day I'm forced to record dozens of missing bombers and fighters. I interact with officers at social events, and the most interesting women I've ever met among my fellow WAAFs. At night my dreams are populated only by the children we once knew. Last week I dreamed I was in the R/T tower, taking a distress call from a Spitfire, and it became clear the pilot on the line was Frantisek Pessl from fourth-form math."

Niny didn't seem to know where to look. The confessional denuding of memory kept her eyes from mine. This was something different from muscle memory—it acted longer and more carefully. For a moment we were left to observe the clouds. Sparrows batted up against the sky. Birds were abundant in the months since the Blitz, having found new nesting places in eviscerated buildings. I picked a single bird to study as I waited for Niny to continue. This pale sparrow flapped her wings once and found a current from the square. She glided. All around us, the air smelled of the stale carbonite exhaust of spent bombs.

"This past weekend, I called on Thom to tell him I couldn't see him anymore," Niny said.

"A rash decision," I said. "What could have driven you from a man who knows such happiness?" Right in front of her, my cousin had love! A love she could taste and touch, exactly what I was missing. "You should go to him and profess your love," I said. "Not leave him."

"Maybe that's it, Poxl. For weeks I watched you in hospital, murmuring about your mother with some painter, and your father, and Radobyl, and over and over about Françoise." I had no memory of such murmurings. "I know you didn't know you'd been speaking, Poxl. I kept Johana away so she wouldn't hear you. I told the doctors to let you alone. But I need to tell you now."

The sparrow I'd been following dipped and then arose again.

Another caught its path midair. One flew off to my right, the other to the left. For a moment I could follow them both, but then they were too far apart.

"If you love this Thomas Paxton," I told Niny, "you should take up with him in earnest." Niny's eyes caught mine for the first time since we'd sat down on the bench. There was something in them I'd never before seen. A young couple walked by. Both Niny and I looked down. Our eyes sought ground, boards, broken macadam. When the couple had passed, Niny looked back up at me. She looked directly into my eyes.

"This isn't where I want to live, Poxl. Life in an elaborate memory? What kind of love is there to find with a man whose main asset to me is his ability to evoke the past? This is living one's life in a history classroom."

A crease had developed in the space between Niny's eyebrows. Where her brown eyes had once been open wide, I could see at their sides they were down-turned. While I could see all over Niny's face the kind of writhing uncertainty Thomas had left her in, I could no longer parse its meaning. The crease between Niny's eyes drew even deeper. For the first time since I'd returned from 100 Squadron, I felt myself removed from my memories, if only for a second—separated from those events like a man who has lived a life and told a tale, only to find the two have diverged in some confusing fashion, lost their cohesion. I was listening to Niny. I thought to comfort her, to remind her I was her confidant.

Instead Niny took my hand in hers.

"Johana wants you to find your own flat," she said.

By now I didn't care. I tried to change the subject, but we'd lost the earlier thread.

"I don't want you to go, Poxl," Niny said. "But maybe the time *has* come for you to start thinking about what's next." I pulled my hand away, and Niny turned her eyes back to the sky.

14.

One afternoon the second week in May, I went to talk to a superior officer at RAF headquarters in central London. I pushed for an updated physical evaluation. Soldiers and airmen wanted above all to return home, but I had no home to return to—not my real home, anyway. I was declared fit to serve. I was more than willing to take on the work of establishing order after the fighting had ended. I was assigned to the administration of a refugee internment camp and airfield in the Rhine Valley, a camp for Germans and Nazi collaborators who had been captured at the end of the war.

A move south.

A move toward Rotterdam.

I was the RAF's ideal postwar tool—raised with Czech and German and with five years' travel across Europe, I spoke Dutch, French, and English. Within weeks I was to head southeast over the North Sea again.

Niny accompanied me to the transit station. A bus would take me to the aerodrome. On our ride into the city, Niny tried to talk to me a bit about what was ahead. Even if Françoise was still alive, there was good reason to suspect she might no longer be in Rotterdam. She was right. But I had to find out.

"You should return to Thomas Paxton," I told Niny. "When you do, ask him not to speak of Prague again. You cannot live your life with this man talking only of the past." Niny searched my face. "My experience is not your experience. There may come a time when Thomas can indulge in the memory of your life in Leitmeritz. It's up to you to forge a relationship with the present."

The bus's wheels cried out against their brakes.

"And one day when we see each other again, Poxl, maybe we'll speak of our parents," Niny said.

The bus driver was closing his doors. I called out to him not to leave, and then I held Niny as hard and long as a cousin might properly hold on to his cousin, without any desire to let go.

15.

My assignment was at a camp in Wunstorf, just west of Hannover. I'll note briefly that I use the German spellings of these cities' names to demonstrate the seriousness with which I took the diplomatic demands of my new commission, no matter where my allegiances and vituperation might lie in regard to the past years' events. This camp was populated by captured Luftwaffe pilots and airmen, along with an RAF wing that was to oversee their work. In the year after my arrival, the POWs' number would swell to more than ten thousand. It was our charge over the coming months to enlist these POWs in enhancing the aerodrome there. It would serve as a principal supply station for Berlin in the days after the armistice.

Within a month of my posting, I was placed in charge of a

fifty-man detail. These men were demoralized, eyes forever
down-turned, not even knowing where in their enormous country they were. I gathered them and spoke frankly. They would
work to get this airfield in shape. Some complained the Geneva
Convention said they couldn't be forced to work. What would
they rather do? I asked. Sit in prison? I said it in German. I said
it in Czech. I said it in Dutch. I said it in English.

In the weeks to come I took up with the fraternity of men who
had been my dread enemies. In addition to overseeing my crew,
I reregistered dozens of men a day as they were directed from
their bases across northern Germany. While many of the men
at this camp had flown Messerschmitts or Junkers or had even
served among the brownshirts, a good number were not soldiers
at all, but railroad workers, janitors, ticket takers—anyone in
uniform had been picked up by Allied troops.

One afternoon while we had begun leveling a large swath of
earth that was to become one of Wunstorf's new runways, we
were besieged by the kind of wet cold that fights through to your
marrow and forever evokes in me those days at thirty thousand
feet in a Lancaster, when my very bones themselves felt as vul-
nerable to Luftwaffe attack as John Milton's, or Yorick's. During the lunch hour I was part of a game of contract bridge. The
men under my command were out with shovels and mattocks.
When I returned from making water beyond the confines of the
tent, the door to my office was open. Another officer was sitting
at my desk.

"I heard there was some Polack working this camp," the officer said. "I had to see for myself."

Here before me was none other than Navigator Smith—Percy
Smith, as returned from the dead as Banquo's ghost or Her-

mione's statue, with apparently no charge but to torment me. I put my hand to my shoulder, which still bore a small scar from his dart.

"But you went down with our crew," I said.

"I took shrapnel from a flak burst in the leg on the last run before our kite went down," Navigator Smith said. For a microsecond the snarl on his face gave way to something less sinister. "You were a pilot of S-Sugar, West," Navigator Smith said. "Word reached me you were here in Wunstorf. I had to come see it for myself."

He rose to leave. While I awaited some further commentary, there was only his exit.

This visit from a wraith left me in a stupor for the rest of that day.

Smith was alive. Of Mrs. Goldring, I'd found only a relic: her annotated Shakespeare. But here, now, was a man I'd long thought dead, walking about a refugee camp in Germany.

16.

For weeks routine bore down upon the camp. Every day for more than a month we approached a piece of field that needed to be flattened by a backhoe, razed, and leveled, upon which we then put down a tarmac. We focused on work.

I passed Navigator Smith in the mess. We grew to have a friendship so real I might even call it warm. I joined the bridge game he played in. With each hand—with each comment I ventured—I awaited his derision, but the obstreperousness I knew from him in RAF Grimsby was gone. Each time I referred to him as Smith, he implored me to call him Percy. We treated each other as equals.

"Why wouldn't you want to just go back home?" he said. "I hear the girls in Prague are beautiful." That was no longer my home, I told him. My parents had been taken. He just looked down at his hands when I said it, but even softened, Smith wasn't one to let the melancholic in me take over for long.

"So why didn't you just stay in London?"

I looked at him long and hard.

"I'll tell you," I said. "But you have to listen. Can you?"

Navigator Smith came to show me that men are capable of change. Percival Smith changed. As I narrated my early days in Rotterdam, now a lifetime ago, about my love for Françoise, who was a prostitute but who I could now see was the first woman I ever truly loved, whom I was coming to believe I loved still, Smith listened. In the beginning of my narration, I saw him narrow his eyes at times as if to speak, perhaps to register some disagreement. Then he would just settle into listening again. He listened as I told him of my brief, nebulous engagement to Glynnis Goldring, and of my revelation that it was Françoise I thought of most in those days after we bombed Hamburg. And part of my story became a story of regret, a story of the wrongs I'd perpetrated—not on the battlefield, but in my personal life. I was beginning to see, I said, the villainy in my having left Rotterdam as I had. His face bore no judgment. He didn't even attempt a joke. When I'd finished telling him of my goals, I said, "Now, do you have anything you'd like to say?"

"I threw a dart at you once and hit you in the back," he said.

"I still have the scar." I pulled down my cotton shirt to reveal the gnarl of skin it had left behind, shiny and tight.

"I was an angry young man in those days," he said. "I'd just lost my best friend. I drank myself to sleep every night. Every morning I was raw, hungover, and grieving." He looked down at his hands. I was about to tell him I knew what it felt like to lose control of one's emotions at loss, but he spoke again. "And I was—well, there's no excuse. It was a terrible thing to do."

"It was."

"It was," he said.

I pulled out my pack of Woodbines and we smoked one together. We talked about nothing for a period. Then he went on his way. In those moments after he left me, after I had narrated the story of Françoise, and had received the first real apology I'd had from anyone for any of the misfortunes that had befallen me since I left Leitmeritz years earlier, I felt a kind of peace.

During this same period, the length of just one summer, something strange happened that came to confuse me far more than having become so close to my former enemy. The image of Françoise, while still present in its residue, began to muddy. The stones of Prague and the flashes of flak returned at night. Sometimes they carried the face of my love. Sometimes not. Now, even when these images came, they arrived with the ineffability of dreams. Sometimes instead I now saw Glynnis; at times Clive's face even returned to me, or John Gallsworthy's, or my mother's.

Then they disappeared.

In their place I had images of those verdant fields of central Britain, the same green as on my first flights south of Prague with my father. Images took no discernible form—memories dispersed to the margins of my mind. My palms sweated. My skin prickled. The top of my head grew hot to the touch, and somehow its heat seemed to radiate—rather than the memories of the events that had caused it—only memories of my mother sitting in her home at the top of a hill in Leitmeritz. I stopped sleeping and instead stared at the ceiling, took long walks to smoke and clear my mind.

Around this same time we came also to hear stories that cast a pallor over all of our thoughts. An officer in the mess told of an afternoon he had taken a group of Luftwaffe pilots on a trip to see a camp called Bergen-Belsen. It was only a couple dozen miles west of us there at Wunstorf. There at the camp, by his account, emaciated Jews had been discovered. They had avoided the crematoria. Many of the pilots he took that day wept when they saw what they'd been protecting, flying for the Luftwaffe. This officer talked incessantly about what he'd seen—he didn't know enough about me to know his audience. I'll provide no further detail, only to say that in the image of those soldiers of the Wehrmacht weeping when they saw the effect of the machine in which they'd been moving parts, I retained a certain truth that would later be of use to me.

17.

One warm day in mid-July, around the time my men were close to having laid their runway, Percy Smith came to see me. Normally he would have taken this as an opportunity to sit and offer a postmortem of the previous night's card game, but that day he spoke with a certain seriousness.

"Poxl," Smith said. "Didn't you tell me you met Françoise in Rotterdam?" I told him I had. "I've a chap on my detail says he was stationed in Rotterdam during the occupation. I'll send him over if you like."

Smith's eyes were flat, the corners of his lips not upturned as they once had been during his meddling and needling. In his face was a new kind of need: I was the last of his deceased crew. He who had been my enemy was now my friend. This was a lesson I would recognize often in the days to come. While in the pages of *Othello* we may feel we understand a character like Iago, when we meet him in life, he retains the capacity for change. He's not cut off from the obviation of his sins. If Othello had spared Desdemona and himself, surely he and Iago could have met in some new circumstance in their later years. There would have been memories to hash out, confessions to be made—the great dissembler would have had to try not to dissemble for once, to speak and be heard after his great sins had been unveiled. But couldn't they have been as Navigator Smith and I now were?

I told Navigator Smith I would talk to this boy.

A day passed, then another. Smith's man didn't arrive.

I was hardly able to get my men to complete their work for the distraction it caused me. A week after Navigator Smith came to see me in the mess, a man named Rheinholt, whom I'd come to know by his face but not until now by his name, dropped by my office. I offered him a Woodbine. He lit it.

A small detail of my men had just begun building a wooden frame for a radio tower. I suggested we walk to a nearby Nissen hut so that we might oversee their work. Where had I come from? Rheinholt wondered. My Czechoslovak accent, though it had grown diffuse over the years since my emigration, had given me away. I told him of a year I'd spent in Rotterdam and then about my time in London.

"I was stationed in Rotterdam in '40 and '41," Rheinholt said to me. "When I tell him this, Officer Smith tells me to come and see you."

The area where my neck met my shirt was febrile. I told him before the war I'd lived in Rotterdam. I mentioned there might still be some residents there who mattered to me. Had he known any of the undesirables in that city?

"Undesirables?" Rheinholt said.

We reached the hut where my men were working. The high-pitched buzz of saws and the hum of a generator rose. We took a step inside the hut.

"Yes, yes, undesirables," I said. "Those who worked in certain professions that might be considered unacceptable by polite society."

Rheinholt took a moment to decipher my meaning. Then his shoulders relaxed and the skin around his eyes pulled taut with a smile.

"Oh, of course," Rheinholt said. "We frequented all the better whorehouses"—the term raised the temperature of my blood another degree—"while we were in Amsterdam, so we did the same in Rotterdam."

My palms sweated. The scar atop my head throbbed. I rubbed it with my fingertips and found it hot to the touch. Did he remember the names or looks of any of those women?

"Oh, I took up with a rather large one," Rheinholt said. "Big-hipped . . . I could hardly keep her away. Very large breasts."

"Greta?" I asked.

"Greta!" Rheinholt said.

He seemed almost as elated as I was by the coincidence. I asked him if she played guitar and he said yes, yes, if he remembered correctly, he had seen one in the corner of the room. At that moment a waft of the spruce my men were sawing came across the Nissen hut to where we were standing, bringing back the wood smells of my father's office in Leitmeritz—bright, clean, citrusy wood shot light through my head. An image of my father's officious pose in his room above the Elbe in the Brüder Weisberg factory stuck in mind. My nose was filled with wood smell.

"Did you know any of her friends?" I asked. "Rosemary? Was there a half-Asian girl named Rosemary?"

"There were all kinds," Rheinholt said. "I'd lie if I said I could remember any other than Greta. Though that does sound familiar . . . sure," he said. "There might have been a Rosemary."

It was too much. Françoise's face appeared less and less in my mind, yet again she became a reality in our conversation as the wood smell overtook it.

"Françoise?" I asked him. "Was there a Françoise, tall and freckled? Played mandolin in a band, a sisters' band?"

"I couldn't say," Rheinholt said. I was so full of memory and rage, my fists and teeth were clenched. "I just don't remember this one."

"Well, then, what of Greta?" I said. "What of her as the war went on?"

"Oh," Rheinholt said. "Some of her kind we had to move out of the Netherlands once things got bad." His face displayed no emotion concomitant with the joy he had only moments before displayed. Some of these men were real men and became friends; others were as hateful as the cardboard version of those Nazi villains that has stuck in the world's memory in the days since. This man belonged to the latter.

I watched as Rheinholt crushed out his cigarette. I did not

move or look up as he walked away. There was no evidence of Françoise, but there was no evidence of her demise, either. I clung to the fact. That afternoon I took to the half-paved runway and found a draconian new strategy for getting the men in my charge to work.

"You, over there, Klemperer!" I shouted at a former Dornier pilot least in my favor. "Off the ground. Get to work!" Klemperer looked at me. I lifted this man by his grubby collar in the warm July evening and set him down to work next to his fellow men. "There will be no further laxity on this detail!" That night in the mess, I found my tongue loosed as if it had been given similar orders. Françoise! I only wanted to see her again, for her to see me—for the one person left whom I'd loved to help acknowledge my existence. She was my Mnemosyne. If she was alive, she bore memories of me, just like I had mine of her. If she bore memories of me, those memories were the wrong memories. Perhaps the past can be undone. At the least it can be unearthed, long-buried bones torn from the ground by aerial assault. I would find her again, no matter what state I found her in.

18.

News of V-J Day came from our superiors around the time we were nearing completion of the airstrip. The last of the Axis powers had given up.

The war was over.

A cheer arose across camp, a great electricity flowing through the men who'd seen more than their share of destruction. Even the POWs under our supervision were brighter that day, despite their nominal loss—not much of one, given how long it had been since Germany itself had capitulated. I managed to enjoy myself among my fellow Brits. I drank a glass of champagne with Percy Smith, who, upon news of the Japanese surrender, sought me out in the mess.

"Who would have thought of all those men in S-Sugar," he said, "it would be me and the injured Polack celebrating together?" He saw the old fierce look on my face. "Okay, yes, yes. I know, I know. The Czechoslovakian. The Czechoslovakian Jew, Poxl West—the man who flew me over Hamburg."

Smith put his arm around me. Over the coming weeks, as we proceeded apace in our work, he and I came to develop what would end up the most lasting of all my relationships of that period. Françoise wasn't the only friend I'd made who might still be alive; Smith himself was here. While we came to befriend a number of the others we'd now been at work with for close to a year here in Germany, it was mainly the two of us in each others' confidence.

My prevailing memory of that period, that stretch after the glee of our victory began to mature into a more nuanced emotion, came one day soon after. It was during another of our long card-playing evenings. Percy and I were big winners at whist. One of our fellow men, an officer called Berend, with whom Smith had had a close friendship, and who knew our history in S-Sugar, joked, "It's nice to see two former enemies fighting alongside each other."

Percy put his arm around me and said, "Former enemies is a little too harsh, don't you suspect, Poxl?"

I breasted my cards.

"You two were in the same squadron, isn't that right?" Berend said.

"We were stationed together north of Grimsby," I said. "We flew together in the Battle of Hamburg."

"Proper war heroes, at that!" Berend said.

Another officer with whom Percy had a long history and who knew about the bombings our wing undertook, Landsman, said, "Or something like that."

Berend inquired after his meaning.

"We heard all about it," Landsman said.

"All about what?" Percy said.

"The tens of thousands of German civilians killed in those bombings," Landsman said.

"There were people killed in all the bombings!" Percy said. "They were bloody bombings! What were you, some radio operator down on the ground, you bloody moralizer, sitting back in your armchair with the WAAFs on your lap, sitting in judgment of those who saved you!"

Percy lunged at Landsman. Had I not been nearby to grab him, he might have done some damage. I didn't know quite what had set him off. Perhaps Percy was unable to deal with the calm settling in after the final armistice. He was a career officer, one who seemed uncomfortable in the skin of civvy street, a prospect now arising for all of us. Regardless, with the help of this man Berend, I pulled him out of the Nissen hut. We took to a field nearby to smoke. Out among the fields, cicadas chirruped in the late-summer evening. Nightdew lifted off the Rhineland grass. Far above, the stars of Orion's belt blinked. We walked long enough to smoke two cigarettes before Percy spoke.

"Bloody Landsman," he said. He proceeded to explain that

this officer had always been an antagonizer, always taking up the counterargument. The more silence fell in around us, the more the noise of cicadas filled the air. We kept walking. What in Landsman's attitude had pushed Smith so far? I knew his stance on the need for a "press-on" attitude during our tour. He had little tolerance for the kind of self-doubt that could develop among pilots who weren't inculcated into the military thinking he deemed acceptable. But the war was over. We were standing on occupied German soil. What losses we'd suffered, we'd endured, and now we had to try to move forward. As the cicadas chirruped in the dark I awaited his attack on *my* moralizing.

He was silent. Night birds called out from a stand of pines beyond the fields.

"There's a lad on my detail," Percy said. "Twenty-year-old called Schlict. Always yammering. Never made pilot, never got on a Luftwaffe bomber, stuck with a job as a firefighter at home." Percy drew on his fourth cigarette since we'd left his altercation with Landsman. Only its red ember showed in the dark. "This boy talks. No matter how many times I've put him on the most menial duties, he cannot keep his Jerry mouth shut."

Percy stomped out his cigarette and lit another.

"Early this week, he started in on how the war is over but that he doesn't have a home. Started again about how he had been a firefighter. In Hamburg, he said. When it started the first night, he said, he took to a bomb shelter. Once the blockbusters finished falling, he went out into the firestorm."

A steady breeze picked up out in the field. It forced a cloud across the moon. Percy took a drag off his cigarette. With one fag already lit in his mouth, he took another from the packet and played it over, end over end, in his hand.

"The main waterline in the city was broken by one of our bombs early that night. Schlict and the other firefighters had to go to the river to begin pumping from the source itself. There they saw hundreds of people diving into the water. Directly before his crew were four women. They'd been hit by incendiaries. Phosphorous was burning their arms and backs.

"One of those women kept running into the water to douse her arms. When she emerged, the phosphorous was so hot—burning to the bone—it would light itself again. She kept jumping into the water. Each time she got out, her arms would set themselves afire again. The way this Schlict described it: these women running into the water, screaming, coming out, igniting again. Over and over, until he and the other firefighters were able to get ahold of them, wrap them in fire blankets, and take them back to the station."

Percy stopped. He took a long pull off his cigarette. The red ember at its end was dancing with the shaking of his hand.

"Phosphorous in those incendiaries could do that if it hit you," Percy said. A hitch crept into his voice. "I told this Schlict kid to get back to work. To stop with his propaganda. Normally he would have started at me again, yammering until he'd had everyone convinced. For the first time since the lad had started talking, he stopped. I saw his pale face. He hardly even believed himself, the horror of this story he'd witnessed with his own seeing, remembering eyes. I could see him thinking, Maybe it hadn't happened that way. So awful his mind allowed his memories to be undone."

Percy stopped talking. A taste of bile was rising in my throat. I would like to think now maybe it was all the cigarettes we'd

smoked. But maybe it was that up until that moment, no matter what we'd done, we'd assumed we were like the vast major-
ity of men—like Lear himself—self-judged to be more sinned
against than sinning. Now something was changing in both of
us the more Smith talked. As I say, if you met him in life, years
later, even Iago might have turned from his role. But it could
work the other way, as well, couldn't it? That line from *The Merchant of Venice* had crossed my mind many times in the years since
Glynnis's mother and I first read it: "If you wrong us, shall we
not revenge?" Somehow, I'd not thought quite clearly that this
line had been uttered by one of Shakespeare's great villains, not
one of his great heroes.

We looked at the dancing of that red ember at the end of Percy's cigarette.

"What I haven't told you about the days back when we were
in S-Sugar," I said, "was why I signed up for the RAF."

Percy didn't say anything. I did. I talked to him about Glynnis Goldring and her mother. I told him about Johana and Scott
Prichard. I told him about my parents and my long-since-passed
desire to run Brüder Weisberg, and that I'd fled from Leitmeritz without ever saying good-bye to either of my parents, not
knowing I would never again see them. If I had it in me in those
days to cry, I might have cried, but I only said that now—now—I
wanted to find Françoise as much as anything. I needed to know
if she was still alive.

"None of it changes much for us, does it?" Percy said.

"How so?"

"We dropped those incendiaries ourselves, Poxl."

I said I supposed we had. "But like you said in those moments

before we went on our run," I said. "We signed up to fight Nazis who had bombed us in London. We continued with 'pressing on,' as you put it. That's never changed. Has it?"

Percy's cigarette was bobbing. I reached out to steady his
hand. He almost didn't notice I'd touched him. In the darkness,
we couldn't see each other's faces. We were out among night-wet
grasses. Hardly a sound save for the swishing of our boots and
all those chest-plated bugs we couldn't see up in the treetops,
vibrating their internal coils. We walked for another fifteen minutes over the landing strips we'd built, over dusty fields unpaved
and past half-constructed radio towers and unused nacelles
and Merlin engines of decommissioned planes left piecemeal
at the base. Night smells of gathering dew and stoked fires
carried across the grasses. We kept as far as we could from the
lights and laughter in the Nissen huts without entering the
forest on the other side. We were again approaching the distant glow.

"You should go as soon as you can," Percy said. I looked at
him in the dark, but I couldn't quite make out his face. "Listen
to me, Poxl," he said. "You should go to Rotterdam."

I asked him what he meant.

"The war's over. I'll talk to the major. I'll get it set up. You
can take enough time there to see if you can't find Françoise, see
if she's still there. Still—well, still there's enough."

"And what if there's nothing to find?" I said.

"I'm sure there is," Percy Smith said. My eyes had adjusted
enough to the faint light cast from the Nissen huts across the
field that I could now see Percy's face. There was so much certainty in his eyes when he said it, like it was the surest he'd ever
been of anything he'd ever said.

He needed it to be true.

So did I.

And then Percy Smith said something else that I'd needed for so long I didn't even know I needed it.

"And Poxl," he said. "If you do find her—when you do find her, see if she'll forgive you for leaving."

I would have to press on until I was able to find Françoise, and if I did find her, I would have to tell her everything.

"But just go find her," Percy said. "Get a transfer, go AWOL. Return to civvy street and catch a flight from free London.

"Go."

19.

The night Percy Smith told me Schlict's Hamburg story was filled with the reality of Françoise. Yet again I had no image of her face. I had only the pervasive sense of her absence. Her memory was more present than ever, but her face hadn't arrived to accompany it.

That void couldn't remain. I stopped trying. In the moments that followed, in my lightest sleep, a new image came to me in my dreams. Three women were doing something strange a couple hundred yards off. These women were submerging themselves in the Elbe, walking out of the water and then running back in. It wasn't the German Elbe of Hamburg I'd seen from thirty thousand feet, but the Elbe of my childhood, running through Leitmeritz. Radobyl stood off in the near distance. I kept walking closer, lugubrious, as if my feet were plunged ankle-deep in wet sand. I was stuck to the ground. I had to pick my whole self up with the lassitude of each step. As I walked, those women ran into the water and out, stopped on the banks of the river and then went in again. When I got close, the three women acquired familiar faces.

The nearest was my mother. Each time she got out of the water, she looked down at her hands, looked back up, and then turned back into the water. The other two women were Glynnis and Françoise. Their faces were cachectic, wasted, ashen. Each time they emerged from the water, a blue halo encircled their wrists. They were saying something together I could not make out at first. It kept on, a concatenation, until I could hear. "You can go, but she won't see you," they said. "You can go, but she won't see you."

Once I understood what they were saying they stopped.

Françoise held her wrists skyward. When she comprehended the blue flames wrapped around them, she turned and ran back into the Elbe. Two contrails of smoke lifted higher and higher in the summer air. None of them saw me. None of them saw one another. They just ran into the Elbe and back out—cachectic, ashen, catching blue fire each time they came up for air.

When I read *Hamlet* in my thirties, studying it in earnest and reading it for the first time since I'd encountered it in the cave with Mrs. Goldring, I came to find that there is a disagreement among Shakespeare scholars over the nature of the ghost of his father, King Hamlet, who visits him throughout the play. Some believe it is meant to be staged as a physical manifestation: The supernatural has occurred. A ghost has set foot onstage. *The Tragedy of Hamlet*, in this staging, is the original ghost story. But other scholars believe that it is simply the manifestation of Hamlet's guilt, the most famous indecision in all of literature: the question of whether Hamlet will act. There is no such thing as a ghost; there is only such thing as Hamlet's hallucination. To tell a tale, Hamlet famously says, is to "hold a mirror up to nature," and in the mirror we will never see the face of the dead. It is only our own image we see.

Perhaps it's clearer that when Macbeth is visited by Banquo's ghost it is simply his own guilt that has called forth the apparition, as invented as the blood covering his wife's hands. When Glynnis and my mother appeared to me in dreams, I was no Hamlet. I will wish every day for the rest of my life that I was no Macbeth, without knowing for certain the truth. They were dead, Glynnis and my mother. When they haunted me they did not haunt me bodily, though they did not leave me, either. But in my dream, Françoise was there in that river with them, and now it was time for me to hold up the mirror to nature.

Acknowledgment: Caesura

Only two months after his reading in Boston, two months after the triumphant publication of *Skylock,* after my parents and I read his book and I'd talked to everyone I could about every aspect of the book I could think of, my uncle Poxl's memoir was publicly revealed as a fraud.

His defrocking came all at once. We all learned of his fate together over breakfast one Sunday morning less than five months after he came to our house all full of joy at the discovery of his neighbor's hundred-dollar-bill-bookmarked estate, all full of the hope and possibility that was to accompany his impending publication.

"Look at this, honey," my mother said. "Another picture of Poxl. This one's on the front page of the 'Arts' section."

My mother hadn't read the headline yet. She'd only seen Uncle Poxl's face again, an occurrence that had come to feel commonplace. My father barely responded. My uncle had received enough notices in the local press since the publication of his book that we'd quickly grown desensitized to seeing his picture.

But this piece was in a bigger paper—the biggest. Though we lived outside of Boston, my parents subscribed to *The New York Times.* On weekends they relaxed by reading aloud to each other from stories they knew the other would read in full only minutes later. Such redundancy drove me to distraction, but without Poxl to take me downtown anymore, I longed to hear what I could of him.

"Oh," my mother said. "Oh, Maxwell, seriously. You'd better come look at this."

My mother and father crouched over the paper. At first my father started reading aloud, as he always did when he saw a story worth noting: "'Poxl West's memoir of World War II heroism, *Skylock*, has been a surprise hit, both a critical and a popular success from the week of its publication,'" my father read. "'This month, scholars at UCLA and Tufts have alleged factual inaccuracies that threaten to discredit aspects of the best-selling book.'" My father's voice started out full, but quickly lowered to a pianissimo. "'Some have called for a statement from West's publisher addressing their allegations.'"

He read the rest of the article to himself. My mother was beside him. There was no place for me.

"Well?" I said. Neither of them responded. "Some bloodsuckers out for Uncle Poxl's money?"

My mother and father just continued to look down at the paper. I pretended not to care. Later that night instead of looking at Uncle Poxl's book, I found myself reading the crumpled "Arts" page my parents had left behind.

For a month, Uncle Poxl refused to comment on the allegations. Then, as summer was upon us and the season of *Skylock*'s release was not quite ended, a piece was published in *The Atlantic Monthly* that Poxl and his publisher were unable to ignore.

The writer of the piece said my uncle had never flown the sorties he claimed to have flown during the firebombing of Hamburg. He'd never been in a lightning cloud over Lübeck. The writer had gone up to the RAF Museum in Hendon and found no record of a Poxl West ever having flown sorties in the Lancaster bomber S-Sugar. There were solid records of the crew from that plane, and no Poxl West was on the ledger. Another man, albeit a man with the surprisingly Jewish-sounding name Herman Janowitz, was listed as the plane's pilot. When the reporter put this to Poxl, seeking a quote for his story, my uncle had broken down immediately.

The piece included a long, difficult description of Poxl's behavior—erratic outbursts over perfectly made and viscerally described Pimm's cups and cucumber sandwiches at his apartment in Manhattan. The writer had the gall to ask him to take off his trademark porkpie hat and show the lightning scar atop his head. Poxl demurred and was asked again, until finally he showed his bald pate, atop which was a measly dog bite he'd gotten as a kid. Finally, he gave a tearful confession. The reporter gave a great deal of emphasis to the fact that from the moment he uttered the name Herman Janowitz, something wholly changed in Poxl's disposition.

Whatever my uncle Poxl might have been through in the war, whatever experiences he'd had then, bombing Hamburg wasn't among them.

Poxl's publisher had defended the book in the days after the *Times* piece—the claim felt unsubstantiated, and Poxl had stood by the fundamental accuracy of the book and its aims. But the editors of *The Atlantic* promoted the story they'd published through all channels, and given the book's success, the attention it had garnered, its ascendancy toward the status of instant classic, now it wasn't just a book; it was a news story. The response to its fall was commensurate with the size of Poxl's growing fame. The book might not have been a pure critical success on its own terms, but the story of the author of a bestselling memoir, a Jewish RAF pilot, fabricating parts of his story, was. The reporter who'd written the piece made a name for himself with it—he went on NPR's *All Things Considered*, was interviewed on *60 Minutes*. This was 1986, and there was no CNN crawl. The only way to find information was to seek it out like a historian, or to wait to see what the newspaper or television told you. It was long before the days of a thousand talk shows, in which a story might blare on the sidelines, or an Internet, where it might be trending, news only to those who sought it as news.

When the story hit, it hit loudly enough that no one could ignore it. *Skylock*'s publisher made a complete mea culpa. Poxl West had admitted that he'd lied about having flown those sorties over Hamburg that were so central to his memoir and its reception. He refused to go on television himself. He would address the claims only through his publisher, who said they would remove the book from the shelves of all the Waldenbooks and small bookshops around the country. If readers wanted to have their money back, they could have their money back. The world wouldn't be hearing from Poxl West again anytime soon, and what they'd heard to date they were encouraged to forget.

I threw away my spiral-bound notebooks soon thereafter. Rabbi Ben's books on Kabbalah took up the space *Skylock* had occupied on my bookshelf. As painful as the allegations were, my uncle's admission was even more painful. Now when I read back over that *Atlantic* story instead of the book, I saw things about it that I hadn't before: There was, in fact, too much emphasis on sex in the book. The pathos of Poxl's need for Françoise drove the narrative, and somehow my focus on the war heroism hadn't allowed me to see the vacillation in his guilt at leaving her. The narrative did wander at times. The anonymous reviewer from *The Economist* had taken a good bit of the writing to task, and maybe his anonymous parsing of Poxl's prose wasn't so inaccurate. Maybe the book hadn't been the triumph I understood it to be when I first read it. Maybe I was a teenager sitting around pouting in his bedroom and doing an amateur job of what I would later teach my undergraduates is called "historiography."

Maybe it was my uncle who'd made me love that book so much, and not the book, after all. But then hadn't the *Times* called it an instant classic? It was a bestseller, and didn't being a bestseller mean something? Best. The epithet contained the word *best*.

It was the most confused I'd ever been in my young life. I don't know if I've been as confused in my life since.

I kept expecting we'd hear from Poxl—that he'd call to let us know he hadn't lied but had been pushed too hard, that he had cracked under interrogation, that the whole thing was some misunderstanding. Or that he'd lied and had an explanation. Or that they'd gotten it wrong, he'd gotten it wrong—anything, anything as long as it came from his mouth. Or even for him finally to send us those signed copies he'd promised.

But we heard nothing.

In history class the following fall, for the first time but not the last in my long career as a student, I had nothing to write about. We moved on to a unit on American history. I was happy to be granted a reprieve from having to think about World War II. I tried writing a research paper on the Volstead Act. The comment from my teacher was written in letters just the tiniest bit longer and taller than before:

"A bit diffuse. Research feels thin. B–."

My parents didn't talk to me about my uncle at first, just after we learned of his ignominy. Before bed one night, I heard them at the dinner table.

"Does the kid seem like a mess to you?" My father asked this without my mother having said anything further. "I'd be a mess. We did this. He looked up to Poxl so much even before his success. How many times do you think he's read that book? It's all he talks about."

My mother said she didn't know. She didn't know what to say, she said.

I thought that would be all, until I heard her footsteps on the stairs. I was on my stomach on my bed. I tried to wipe the tears off my face, but it was no use.

She put her hand on my back. I put my face back into my pillow.

"I know how much you care for your uncle," my mother said. She was known as a taskmaster around our house, a hospital administrator at our city's biggest hospital and a home administrator, too. I was last among my friends to get to watch R-rated movies, and she didn't allow any sugary foods in our kitchen. Where my uncle Poxl had shown me the outsized sweep of the arts and culture in Boston, she had taught me the discipline that would serve me when I was older, but which felt only like an obstacle when I was a kid. But when she touched my back, she was the softest, easiest person on the planet. Her hand on my back was like Pentothal in my veins.

"How on earth could I have believed him all the way?" I said. "Every word. I ate up every word. And he didn't even fly those planes."

"You didn't have any reason not to believe him, Eli," my mom said. "Like we've said all along, your uncle is a complicated character. He suffered such grave losses throughout his life. And he's been so long alone, since the last of them—one loss too many. I think he just lost his way."

I started to say something back, all the things her soft hand on my back unleashed, but at that point I'd simply crumpled. For months I'd been going around telling everyone not only that my uncle Poxl's book had been a bestseller—but that I'd been a part of its creation somehow. I was the one who'd sat at Cabot's and over sundaes listened as he'd spun nimbus clouds around his head—and mine—narrating his bombing of Hamburg. I saw all in one stroke that Poxl West was less like an Elie Wiesel or a Primo Levi, and more like Prospero, conjuring an unknown world with the pen he'd only now abjured when public spectacle forced him to. So what did that make me? Some Caliban he'd given language to, slave and accomplice to his rough magic? Even if I was so lucky as simply to be his Ariel, a fairy out in the world doing his bidding, the task hadn't been what I'd understood it to be. It wasn't reporting; it was world building.

I put my face into my pillow and my mother rubbed my back until I fell asleep.

Later that night, after she left my room, I woke up in the dirty evening dark. Some light crept in under my closed door. My clothes were still on. I got up and put the light on to undress for my night's sleep. But before I did, I put my copy of *Skylock* on my bookshelf between a couple of *X-Men* collections.

The pain of a response like the one the world had to my uncle Poxl's lies brings with it an imperceptible vacuum. Descent from fame bares no bluster to match the bluster of its ascent.

There is only nothing.

As I say, my parents didn't hear from Poxl in the weeks after the revelation of his improprieties, his confession. He didn't call on us. He'd come to our house unannounced during the Super Bowl only months earlier, and that was how my uncle Poxl so often came.

Unannounced.

There is no announcement of absence. It's just that: absence. Days passed. All events were nonevents. I didn't go to see musicals at the Wang Center. I had nothing to write poetry about. At Brandeis there was a performance of *King Lear*. I didn't even think of attending. Occasionally I would see advertisements in the *Globe* for a performance of *Tosca* or the Bach solo cello suite performed by Yo-Yo Ma—my parents swore off their subscription to the *Times* around the time they swore off my uncle, or he swore them off; I didn't know which—and a strange open feeling would buzz and whir in the balls of my feet.

But there was no one to take me to any of these events. When he wasn't working on the weekends billing his hours, my father and I made trips out to Mr. Big Toyland for baseball cards, or I played flag football in the backyard with my friends, but it didn't feel like a replacement. It wasn't a replacement for what was missing. Just some other thing.

Truth was, I didn't think I cared much back then for the opera or Shakespeare or the symphony. I would much better have liked a trip to Fenway or Foxboro.

I just liked going to Cabot's for sundaes with my big, handsome, red uncle Poxl.

What I did have were my Hebrew lessons at Beth-El, which continued even into the summer, though class met less frequently. A few weeks after *The New York Times* article appeared, I sought Rabbi Ben out in the hour before our class. He'd long had a standing period before his class that he called "Rap Time," a time when his students could come talk with him about anything they wanted.

I may have been the first student ever to go see him—and now for the second time. He had on huge headphones like the guy in the Maxell cassette advertisements. I had to say his name three times before he turned around.

"Oh shit," he said. "I mean, oh." He took off the headphones and pointed to the burlap-upholstered chair in front of his desk. "Have a seat, my man," he said.

Even when I'd come to see him that previous time, after class, I hadn't really looked around his office. I'd been so focused on Poxl, I hadn't seen anything in front of me for months. Now here I was. On the wall behind his desk he had both a Grateful Dead poster (Oakland Coliseum, 1976) and a photo of an unremarkable bald old Ashkenazi Jew with oversized ears and large dark eyes. He saw me looking at both. "The show was the first I ever went to," Rabbi Ben said. "Sick Jerry solo on 'Dark Star' that night." I just looked at him. "The dude on the right, that's Gershom Scholem. Wrote my dissertation on Kabbalah on him, you know."

I knew.

"I know you know," Rabbi Ben said. "Just didn't want to assume. Did you ever get a chance to check out those books I sent you home with last time?"

"I didn't," I said. Where in the past I might have lied, found a way to say something broad about them, this was a new time in my life as a teenager. There were many things I wanted, and to tell so much as a single white lie was not one of them.

We both sat in silence for a second.

"So now I will do some assuming. You're not here to talk about Kabbalah. You're not here to talk about those books I lent you. You're not even here to talk about your crush on Rachel Rothstein." What was there to say to that? "You're here to talk about your uncle," Rabbi Ben said. "Poxl West."

"I guess I am," I said. "I guess you heard."

"Hard to miss on the 'Arts' page of the *Times*," Rabbi Ben said. "How you feeling?"

It was a simple question, but one I was unprepared to answer. I didn't have any answers then, and I'm not sure I have any answers now, decades later. Just questions.

"What's the worst of it, my man?" Rabbi Ben said. "That now Rachel Rothstein will stop paying attention again?"

"What the—" I said, and hoped he'd drop it.

"Okay, sorry," he said. "I mean, I know you know I see you looking at her. And I saw the way she looked at you when we were talking about your uncle. She even told me she'd read the book."

"She did?"

"She said she did. She might even have said she liked it. Although I got the feeling from talking to her that she was not so impressed by the way he wrote about having left that woman in Holland. I know how much you care about your uncle's heroism. But seems possible a reader like Rachel might not be so impressed by all of what he did. All of which might not matter so much anymore."

"Jesus," I said.

For a minute, neither of us said anything more.

"Okay, let me try it this way," Rabbi Ben said. There was a kind of seriousness on his face I'd not observed in him before. The skin was bunched above his hirsute brow. I could see that the smirk I often had seen in his eyes was somehow absent. "How did you feel before you learned about it?"

"Good," I said. "Proud. I mean, the guy was my uncle. He was, you know, he might as well have been my grandfather, for what he meant to my family. He'd read me all those stories before they ever even appeared in the book, and now . . ."

"Now what?"

"Now he's a fraud."

"Well, is he? I don't know any of this anywhere near as much as you do, but I read all about it. I read the book. But in terms of what he's been accused of, what did he really do wrong?"

"He didn't fly that sortie over Hamburg he said he did." I could see a flinch of smile reappear in Rabbi Ben's eyes when I said "sortie." "Flight," I said. "He didn't fly that bombing run."

"But he was telling a story, right? Honestly, I don't see what's so wrong with it. He confessed to his error. Book's still mostly true, I'd say. He's led an amazing life and told it well."

"I was basically bragging about him for months," I said before I had time not to. "I said I was gonna bring him to talk to our Hebrew class."

"And if you had, I'm sure he would've been great. Will be. Why don't you invite him?"

"Still?" I said.

"Anytime. Listen, I know you don't care so much about Kabbalah. I know you might not have time in the next little while to read much up on it. But it's my main jam. Thing. It's my main thing. You know the main book of Kabbalah."

It was called the Zohar, I said. I'd listened to him enough to know.

"It was written by this thirteenth-century Spanish Jew named

Moses de Léon. Moses de Léon went into his study every day and came out every week with new material about the *Ein Sof,* about the Sefirot—the main tenets of Jewish mysticism. He would bring them out, read them to his friends. When people asked him where it came from, he said he was translating an ancient Aramaic text. Claimed he went back to his study every day and translated a little more. But you know where he got it?"

I said I didn't know.

"Up here," Rabbi Ben said.

He was tapping at his temple with his forefinger.

"There was no ancient Aramaic text called the Zohar. There was a book that Moses de Léon wanted to write. A book based on how he saw Adonai, HaShem, the unspeakable represented by the Tetragrammaton, the God he wanted us to reach. And people wouldn't listen to it from him, so he said he was translating some ancient text— and then he just went ahead and made up his story. That's what people do when they write. They make up stories, details to fit the stories they need to tell. And people are still reading—worshiping— that book, almost seven hundred years later. I've basically given my whole spiritual life over to it."

In the picture behind Rabbi Ben, that old, big-eared Kabbalah scholar looked down at us. For the first time I looked back. I needed a minute before I could respond. A minute when I wasn't looking at Rabbi Ben. A minute when I wasn't even thinking about what Poxl West would think. A minute when it was just what I thought, directly.

"So listen," Rabbi Ben said. "I think it's time for class."

He'd never had anything but time for me. Today he'd said his piece. Maybe he thought it would be better for me not to respond. Maybe he understood what I know now: that I couldn't possibly have processed all of what had been happening in those months enough to really say anything yet. Or maybe he just hadn't ever had a rap session with anyone before and didn't know how to end it. "We should get to the classroom. But if you want to bring Poxl West to my class some time in the future—anytime in the future, my man— you just bring him."

I told him I'd give it some thought.

"Give it all the thought you want," Rabbi Ben said. "When you know, I'll know."

For a year and then another year, we didn't hear from Poxl. I went to Hebrew class and then I didn't—I was confirmed in the temple, and there was no higher step. I never did try to reach my uncle, and never extended an invitation for him to attend Rabbi Ben's class. Uncle Poxl's memory faded and that senescence was another absence, another void. No one mourns the death of a book. No fly buzzes at the death of a reputation. The prep school where he'd taught found a new teacher to take over his classroom. The Patriots were good, but not good enough to make it back to the Super Bowl. My father took me to Fenway a dozen times each summer—his firm got great seats. It would be almost two decades before the Red Sox returned to the World Series. By then, I had a kid of my own.

I found new things to write about for my senior history class. I got more interested in an art class my senior year than I thought I might, not having cared for art beyond those trips Poxl had taken me on to the MFA, where what I cared about was him and not the paintings on the walls. We studied modernism. When Mrs. Hornicker turned her brown plastic slide tray and an image of *Les Demoiselles d'Avignon* flashed up on the screen, I sat back. Here were women with a dozen faces each, all blocked in washed-out colors, as if through the scrim of a Boston winter. I read a biography of Picasso and wrote about him. I got an A+ for the first time in a year, and a "See me."

"Your interest in Picasso is obvious," Mrs. Hornicker said. "I'm going to take a small group of students up to MoMA in New York to see the permanent collection." I asked my parents. They said yes.

* * *

A month later we were walking up Fifty-third Street. It was the first week in October, and the sky was so blue it seemed to push down toward the gray city pavement. I walked through air so crisp I felt as if a hand was at my back, pushing me forward with the ineluctable rhythm that seemed to carry the millions of humans rushing through Manhattan every midday.

Inside the museum we browsed through the permanent collection. Picassos were hung opposite Pollocks and de Koonings, Duchamps and Rauschenbergs. Here we were, standing before the very works we'd just been looking at in books, set against pale gray-painted walls. I walked with determination. Where the colors of *Les Demoiselles* had looked washed-out in our textbook, now I saw the painting was covered in bright vermilions, oranges like the jack-o'-lanterns we bought at Volente's Farm every autumn. Something about that brilliance pushed me away. The ceilings of the place felt too low, painted too white. In the doorways of every room I moved to after seeing the Picasso were scowl-faced security guards. None of the faces on the myriad old women in furs who passed me was a Hepburn face. I walked around, looking for a painting with muted colors like the peach pinks I'd seen in the Picasso reproduction in my book at home.

In the last room I entered I came upon it: a watercolor of a girl with a large tuft of black hair. The canvas was beige, her face the same hue as the background. Her body was defined only by a dowdy black outline. Brushstrokes led down to blithely drawn legs. In between them, two curvilinear lines of gibbous, then concave labia. Just as my neck began to burn with my realization of their sex, as I recognized I was looking at a woman's spread legs, a voice broke in.

"It's a Schiele," the voice said.

I turned. On the bench behind me, looking at this painting, was a wizened old man. I smelled the naphthalene on his suit before I

saw him. He wore a blue Brooks Brothers suit and around his neck
a scarf with two stripes in different shades of dark green. His face
was blanched, hidden by a wiry red beard. "*Mädchen mit schwarzem
Haar, Girl with Black Hair.* Not a major work, but characteristic of
the essentially pornographic watercolors he did when he was young
and painting in Czesky Krumlov."

The speech sounded like it had been written on the placard on the
wall in the museum. This wiry man had been talking for longer than
I'd like to remember before I realized it was my uncle Poxl. His face
had undergone a transformation so violent it took me a moment to
recognize him. His nose bore bright red bulbs. The red of veins spread
back to his temples like a woman before she has properly rubbed in
blush. The whites of his eyes were yellow. They, too, bore spreading
red veins. Small patches all around his face were pocked with the
white skin of scar tissue, remnants of hastily removed melanomas.
He was still well dressed, my uncle, and he acknowledged me before
I acknowledged him.

"I'd always wanted to take you to see Schieles," Poxl said. He made
no move to get up, but he patted the space beside him. "Not this,
though," he said. "No, no, you would have to see even more than this."

I sat down next to him. For a moment we looked at the painting.
Poxl didn't turn to look at me. I started to say fifty-eight things but
they all bottlenecked. Instead I said: "You come here often?"

"What kind of pickup line is this?" Poxl said. "You want an old
man, he's yours." Space invisible as static electricity seemed to grow
between us. My uncle realized how odd this bit of humor was and
he quickly said, "For a time I worked as a docent at the Jewish Museum. That's all I ever really wanted to do from the beginning—*see*
masterpieces. I didn't have to make them. Now I just come to look
at the art."

Once Poxl started talking, it was as if he couldn't stop. He explained
that in the time after he was discovered—that's how he put it, "after

I was discovered," though it took me a while to realize he meant found to be a fraud, not discovered as a talent—he settled into an apartment he'd rented in Hell's Kitchen. It was a short walk over to MoMA.

"I felt anonymous here amid all the great paintings," he said. "All the real art."

For the past couple of years, he could do little more than hide out and visit museums. His publisher couldn't take back the advance he'd received for *Skylock*, which was just enough to live quietly on Tenth Avenue while he tutored kids from prep schools in Westchester, kids referred by friends of his old colleagues in Boston.

But he was shunned. He had no one. It was as if his attempt at a foray into public life—into the public eye, into the fame that he'd long desired, let's be honest—had negated his M.Phil, his having almost completed his Ph.D., his expertise on Shakespeare and Elizabethan drama. His ability to teach anyone anything. "Even my closest friends eventually cut me off," he said.

He stopped talking. He just stared ahead. I did, too. Had he considered my parents his closest friends? They wouldn't have thought so. Poxl hadn't called and he hadn't left a number where to reach him. And though I wasn't yet emboldened enough to say it, wasn't this one more lie? It was Poxl who had cut them off, his friends and family, us. Not the other way around. But I had to say something.

"I missed all those trips downtown," I said. "I missed the opera. I even missed the Museum of Fine Arts. I know it wasn't MoMA, but it was my introduction to the world."

A woman passed between us and the Schiele painting. Poxl had begun to turn his shoulders so he was half-facing me. I'd done the same. I had one knee up on the bench.

"Why don't you let me buy you lunch," Poxl said. "Why don't you let me take you to the Galerie St. Etienne, where we can see more Schieles, so many, and we can lunch on the way."

I looked around. I didn't see my teacher anywhere, or any of my classmates. We weren't to leave the permanent collection, on threat of a suspension from school. But here was Poxl West, sitting before me.

I told him I couldn't leave the museum but that we could eat there at MoMA if he wanted.

We went off to the museum's small café. He didn't ask what I wanted, just bought me a cup of coffee. I didn't drink coffee, so I let it sit in front of me.

"I was always going to bring you to New York City," he said. He'd just sat down and started talking like he had when he saw me back in the gallery, like we hadn't lost a beat. "I was going to finish out the tour, and then I was going to bring you down to the Galerie St. Etienne to really show you something."

"I guess," I said.

"You don't believe me?" Poxl said.

"You never even sent the signed copies you'd promised you were going to send before the book came out."

A tiny bead of sweat had formed at the tip of Poxl's red, red nose. I sat looking at him. For how long had I wanted to ask him what he was thinking, not sending us those books? Me. For not sending *me* that book. It makes me as angry to think of it today as it did then. For how long had he been in my mind and then fled? And now here he was, the great man reduced to something smaller. My uncle, for all intents and purposes my grandfather, but diminished.

"I don't know what to believe anymore, Poxl."

"Oh, right," he said. "That." I put the stirrer he'd picked up at the front of the café into his coffee and turned it around in the cup. I didn't even need to look under the table to see that his feet must again be crossed atop one another.

"When the magazine story first came out," he said, "I was despondent. I hadn't meant to hurt anyone. I hadn't meant to lie or to steal anyone's story. I sat down and I wrote a book, and people loved that book and read it and they wanted to hear me read from it. So I did what they wanted."

"But you didn't pilot S-Sugar."

He said nothing.

"You didn't drop bombs on Hamburg," I said. "You didn't fly sorties piloting that Lancaster."

"I flew for the Royal Air Force!" Poxl said. Something had changed in his face again. I could see now that the tips of both of his shoes were on either side of him, planted solidly on the floor. "I flew Tiger Moths, and I piloted RAF planes, training to be a Czech Jewish teenager attacking the Nazi nightmare!"

"But you didn't," I said.

"I did!" Poxl said. He said it too loudly; even in the din of MoMA's café, families on either side of us looked up. A smartly dressed couple said something to each other in Italian, picked up their sandwiches, and moved away.

"So I didn't fly that sortie I wrote about in the book," Poxl said, quieter now. "So I didn't enter that cloud over Lübeck. But I flew RAF planes, I trained on them. And if I hadn't been injured, I might have flown that one, too."

What was this now? Where just a minute before I'd been pushing him, not even able to get him to admit he'd forgotten to send me that signed copy of his book, I now saw that something in my understanding of him—of the world's understanding of him—was shifting. I asked him what he meant. He'd made it up, having flown over Hamburg.

"I trained for the RAF, just as it says in the book," Poxl said. "In my book. But then at the end of my training, I landed hard, went to the infirmary. I had been injured and I'd developed pleurisy, just like I wrote. Just like I told you. And no matter how many months I begged, they wouldn't allow me back to my commission. I'd met Smith and Gallsworthy and some others during training, and I kept up with them when I could. I was sent south to a desk job. When the war ended, I kept begging, until they sent me to a commission at a refugee camp in Wunstorf."

"Where you met Smith again?"

"Where I met Smith again, just as it said in the book."

"Well, not just as it said," I said.

"Smith had always given me a hard time in training, and he gave me a hard time when we saw each other again in Wunstorf. But over time we became friends. There we befriended as well a Czech Jew, a survivor. He was a man my age, Herman Janowitz. Like me, he'd lost his whole family, had been sent from his home before the annexation and made it to London.

"We'd known many of the same people—he grew up in Prague, his parents lived not far from my grandmother Traute in the Zizkov district. What were the chances of this! Two Jews who'd escaped the Nazi aggression to come and fly with the RAF. But then there was that Czech wing I'd heard of, and another Polish wing. I wasn't so unique after all, I came to see.

"I sat around for months and listened as Smith began to reveal a surprising sense of guilt at what he'd done in S-Sugar in the days after I was forced to resign my commission. And prompted by Smith's story, Janowitz told quite a story of his own: There had been a night when he piloted a Lancaster over Hamburg himself. He'd flown into a thundercloud and somehow come out the other end, flown his sortie over Hamburg just the same. He told how many of his fellow kites went down, struck by lightning, or were forced to turn around, head back to base.

"Both of these compatriots of mine had been in the air over Hamburg. Flying sorties! Flying those very bombers I might have been trained to fly myself had it not been for that damn injury. They'd gone on to kill the very Nazis I'd hoped to kill—and then been plagued with a remorse that I came to empathize with myself. I started to realize as I listened to them what I'd done to Françoise, what I'd done in leaving so many of the people I loved then. I started to realize what we'd all done, simply by listening to their stories."

Now Poxl quieted. It was toward the end of lunchtime, and the crowds moving through the café began to thin. It was the two of us sitting there, Uncle Poxl telling stories as if we were back in Cabot's, back in Boston. Only now he wasn't reading from pages in front of him. None of this was prepared. It was just Poxl West talking.

"So you didn't make it all up," I said. He continued to look down into his coffee. "But you didn't fly those planes like it said in your memoir."

"Over the course of many, many years, I wrote three drafts of a book—novel or memoir, what did I care? Each was rejected. Each was the story of the first love of my life, a woman I'd come to love in Rotterdam and whom I'd turned around at the end of the war and sought out only after I realized how badly I'd wronged her. But it wasn't enough. I'd been injured; I hadn't flown sorties myself. If I'm honest, perhaps I tried too hard to espouse those emotions when they weren't my own—it was a book of love and vengeance I'd sat down to write, not yet of love and remorse.

"And then Percy Smith died. He had no family, had lived out the last of his days in London, where I went to visit him when I could. He died a short, lonely, painful death from lung cancer, and when he died, I flew back for his funeral."

I told him I remembered—he'd mentioned the flight back during those early days of our Cabot's trips. He hadn't provided much detail then.

"That's right. I went to his funeral and thought, My own funeral can't be long off. And only he knew about Herman Janowitz. He was the only one from that S-Sugar crew left, and now he was dead. So I picked the book back up, this novel that was now going to be a memoir. I thought of Janowitz, of my dearly departed friend Percy Smith, who had once been my enemy, of the shift I'd seen in them and the shift it had evinced in me. Here was a story I understood—not just a catalog of the things I'd seen—not just a profession of love—not just a paean to Françoise—but a story of vengeance, guilt, remorse and love. And then I began to do what Shakespeare would have done. I told a story—not factually what had happened, but bearing every drop of the truth of what had happened. As Iago himself said, 'What you know, you know.'

"Do you know why Shakespeare left Stratford for London, where he gained his fame?"

I said I didn't.

"It is a tale among scholars of the Bard that he was caught repeatedly poaching deer from a landowner near his father's home. He would go onto this man's land not because he needed to, but for the thrill of it—kill his deer, slip past his guards undetected. Samuel Johnson always claimed this was where Shakespeare learned his trade later: poaching. Almost every one of the thirty-nine plays was a story from history, a story someone else had told and the Bard retold. Some were even just versions of other stories other playwrights of the time were telling and he retold.

"Only Shakespeare, he learned to tell it better. This is the very crux of telling a story: to tell it better."

"But," I said, "you were writing in the first person. You were writing a memoir. You were—"

"And they attacked Shakespeare just as they did me! The leading playwright of his day. The greatest writer in the history of the English language. They called him an upstart crow, said he was beautified by their words. William Shakespeare himself! Torn down for what he did. But what matters, my boy, is the words on the page! Did I tell the story the best I could?

"I told the story the way it needed to be told! All of this book was true, Eli. I was a Czech Jewish teenager who left his home at the moment of the Anschluss, whose parents were killed by the Nazi aggression, who went to London by way of Rotterdam and who followed love and guilt's demands back to try to find Françoise. This was my book, and I refused to go on television and be berated for it. If I wrote the book I needed to write, I'll not apologize for it. Not now! Not then!"

I was about to speak again. I was about to tell Poxl West that I thought I believed him but I needed to know more. He wasn't right; of course I get that now. The very conviction with which he made his argument raised in me both a rage and an understanding I can't explain. It strikes me now that this was what came to allow me to see Poxl in front of me for the first time right then, a man in all his sharp-elbowed contradictions. Sometimes it's only undistilled anger that accompanies comprehension. The two cannot be extricated from each other.

But he believed what he was saying. He truly did. His red face was so full of life even now in its wasted state, I still would have listened to him tell any story he wanted, consequences be damned. And the world should have, too, I guess. Or maybe not. I still don't know. But I do know that I wanted to let him know everything I'd felt and thought from the moment he came to our house during the Super Bowl until now.

But just then, I saw Mrs. Hornicker coming across the way. Her face was as red and sweaty as my uncle Poxl's face had been minutes earlier. I didn't even hear the next sentences Uncle Poxl spoke.

"Eli Goldstein, where on earth have you been?" she said.

I can tell you now what trouble I got in for having walked away, what a berating I got for having made her think she'd lost me in New York City on a field trip. Who can even imagine the fear I must have put into Mrs. Hornicker, her thinking she'd failed so miserably at her job. Just imagine if I'd accepted my uncle Poxl's invitation and left the museum with him. By the time we got back to Needham, I was in about as much trouble as I ever got in. I received a suspension. My parents were livid, concerned it might hurt my chances at getting into the right college, and when I returned, they didn't give me a chance to tell them I'd seen Poxl—and so I resolved not to. I might not have known I'd teach at a college someday, but I knew I'd get into one. Knowing what I knew about Poxl West now, and denied a chance to tell it as soon as I returned, with each day it got harder to imagine even trying to tell my parents about it. The further you get from a story whose moral you don't know, the harder it grows to tell it. Who knew if they would even believe me, or if it would simply sound like a fantastical story told to deflect the trouble I was in. And isn't that the very problem with even the simplest lie, let alone a lie the size of Poxl's? It breeds suspicion, incredulity without bounds.

But that's not what I remember of that moment.

What I remember is that Mrs. Hornicker wasn't looking at me. She was staring straight at Poxl, who was sitting there across from me in the café at MoMA in midtown Manhattan. As scared as I was of her at that moment, as much as I wanted to continue talking with Poxl West, for just one moment all we could do was look at him— Mrs. Hornicker trying to figure out what I was doing talking to this man before she pulled me from him, and I seeing him as if for the first time:

He was an old man who'd run from his parents' house without saying good-bye, who'd run from Rotterdam without saying good-bye to his first love. Only he knew what pushed him. Did Isaac sit around his father's home for years, wondering what he might ask Abraham of their trip to the top of Mount Moriah, wondering what incomprehensible flash he'd seen in his father's eyes? Once their descent was made and they were home, was it simply too complicated ever to raise the question? Or maybe he was just what he'd always been: Isaac's father. Here I am now, a father myself, remembering again for the thousandth time the moment when I could have said the right thing. Anything. I'll never know what went through his head when Poxl flew from Leitmeritz, when he flew from Rotterdam. This was the closest I would ever come. Couldn't I have said one final true thing to a man who'd been a grandfather to me, if only I'd known then what it was I should say? But I didn't. And I don't. Mrs. Hornicker whisked me away, after I'd seen him one last time. And I guess if nothing else, I know what he looked like to her.

He was just a pile of bones in a blue wool suit.

ACT FOUR

I.

The morning after my talk with Percy I went to the office of my superior officer and once and for all tendered my resignation from the Royal Air Force. I wrote Niny, asking her to send the money I'd saved, and which I'd left in our flat for safekeeping. I would arrange for a flight to Rotterdam as soon as the money arrived.

My wait lasted more than a month. Finally I found myself on an RAF air transport to Rotterdam. Even having lived in Holland for a year, I'd never seen the Nieuwe Maas from the wide view provided by thousands of feet of altitude. As beautiful as it was to see that huge port from an aeroplane, something of the image didn't comport with the trek I'd embarked upon. I'd spent so much of the years since I left Holland aloft, in an aeroplane, or thinking of flying, or remembering time aloft. The harbor appeared somehow too placid from my perch as we made our swooping arrival from the east.

A new set of cranes had replaced the ones where I'd once spent my days at work. A row of new buildings had been erected by those towers whose operation had once required the linguistic skills of a young Czechoslovak immigrant. This is little to tell compared with the new building that had accompanied the regrowth of that city after its near decimation by the Luft-waffe.

In Delfshaven, I walked every block I'd once known, knocking on doors, ringing doorbells. I found no one home at the flat where Françoise had once lived in Veerhaven. No one at Greta's and Rosemary's. Along the stagnant canals of the city, it struck me that perhaps the best place to ask after her was the Brauns'. With an adopted daughter and a dental prac-tice to look after, they were most likely not to have been dis-placed in the years of the occupation. I arrived at the house of that old schoolteacher and her dentist husband. A hulking blond golem of a man opened the door. His shoulders were as broad as the doorway. "Is this the home of"—I realized at that moment I didn't even recall their Christian names—"the Brauns, the dentist and schoolmarm?"

"No one by that name lives here," the man said in his gruff Dutch.

Though I'd resigned my post in Wunstorf, I hadn't yet ac-quired any civilian clothing. I was still clad in my RAF blues. This fact afforded me a certain courtesy of the emancipator—and burdened me with the formality paid one in a position of authority. In this situation, it kept the Brauns' door from be-ing closed in my face. This golem suggested I go to the end of his street, where an elderly woman called Van Leben knew much of the changes to the businesses and residences in the neighborhood.

I made my way to the doorway that might bring me one step closer to discovering Françoise's fate. I knocked.

The door opened.

Fräulein Van Leben was hunched and crooked, and on her

chest sat an apron below the stoic blankness of her wrinkled white face. When she opened her door, she asked, aloof but polite, that I step in over the threshold.

I asked whether she knew the couple who before the war lived in the house I'd just come from down her block, a couple called Braun?

"Ah, yes," she said. "The dentist."

She appeared reluctant to say anything more while standing at the doorway. An old woman like this had clearly experienced a fatigue of men in uniform during the war years. I explained that I knew the family acquaintances in the days before the war broke out. In those days we had shared friends—a woman named Françoise, her friends Greta and Rosemary. Did she know what had become of them?

Now she stared at me with mild contempt.

"All those types are gone now," she said. "Germans took them away very early on."

She paused. The grimace on her face relaxed. She continued, aware of the cold comfort she had offered. The day was frigid and damp. I removed my boots. She wandered back toward a sitting room at the rear of her house. I followed her and waited while she repaired to her kitchen to brew a pot of tea. This home was so similar in every way to the flats I'd entered in the period I lived there in Rotterdam. Up the center of the place was a narrow staircase identical to the one I'd ascended at that first party with Greta and Rosemary; to the back was a large picture window. It looked out upon an overgrown garden. Old Van Leben returned from the kitchen with a pot of black tea. We observed the peculiarities of the day's weather. She inquired after my uniform. My accent wasn't British. I said I'd moved

from north of Prague to a place here in Rotterdam before the
war at my father's behest. So what had become of me in those
days after I left the city where we now sat?

As would occur for many years after that day, I found a
bottlenecking of the story I might have told her. I thought to
say something about Françoise, about the details of my time in
Rotterdam. But here we were in Rotterdam! Instead I thought
to inform her of my escape from that city where we now sat,
about my time with Niny—as a squaddie—discovering news of
my parents—my injuries in training for the RAF—the great
thundercloud that struck the Lancaster S-Sugar.

Each time I opened my mouth, I didn't know what story I
would be telling. The story of a Jew who had left his home to
do—what? To fall in love? To save Londoners? To scour Western Europe in search of a woman who might be dead? To take
to the skies and exact revenge? I asked Fräulein Van Leben if
she had been in Rotterdam when the Luftwaffe bombed.

"I have been in this house since 1893," she said. "That year
I was orphaned by typhus."

From the decrepit look of the place I suppose I should have
made some such conjecture. The upheaval of the past years had
caused me to expect change, where now I was faced with a mea-
sure of permanence—or at the minimum, serious longevity.

"What I am getting at," I said, "is not so much the full span
of your tenure in this house as your specific experience during
the period of the bombing itself."

Now it was Van Leben's turn to grow taciturn. She sat back
and sipped her tea. We both looked off at the tulips growing
in their beds outside her window.

"I stayed in my basement three days," she said. "Lived there. When the noise stopped, I came up. I sat by my window, but always near to the entrance to my basement."

Van Leben stood and walked to the front of her house. I followed in my stocking feet. Two picture windows looked out on her block. They stood uncovered. Across the street was a gap in the block maybe four or five town houses wide. It had been cleared of rubble. No reconstruction had yet begun.

"The Hoffstetlers lived there since before my parents bought this house." She was pointing to some space amid the emptiness at the middle of the block opposite her home. "They had four dogs. Four beautiful German shepherds. Gustav, Gerta, Gideon, and Hilda. They walked the four dogs every day—every morning, every night.

"After the bombing I watched them carry the bodies out. Huge dogs. Heavy as men. The Hoffstetlers had a piano and many paintings. I did not see them carry out any piano or paintings. Only dogs.

"Machines came and cleared the stones and the lumber. I watched them carry away stones. Wood. Long after they carried out the dogs."

Fräulein Van Leben looked out the window to that space where the dogs' bodies and rubble had once been. She walked me to her back room again. For a long time we didn't talk, for it became apparent that what we both tacitly needed for a moment was to be around another human, while not talking. We both drank our tea and looked out again at her flowers.

"That was long before they began to take anyone away," Fräulein Van Leben said. There was something in her eyes then, a way they were moving back and forth, searching my face, that made me believe in the moment perhaps she had more to tell.

I took a cigarette from my packet and smoked it at an acceptable pace, then stubbed it out in the ashtray on her table. I thanked Fräulein Van Leben for her hospitality. If she was to remember something further about the Brauns or if she were to learn more of their fate, or the fates of my friends, I told her I would appreciate it if she'd let me know. I provided her with the address of the hotel where I would be staying, and of the café on Scheepstimmermanslaan where I could be found during the days.

As I was leaving, Fräulein Van Leben stopped me. She said that while she didn't know what she could tell me now, she did have an idea of how she might unearth something, and that I should leave her information regarding my lodgings.

From Fräulein Van Leben's I returned to my hotel room. The gaping hole in the block across from her house kept arising in mind, and alongside it an image of those brown gashes Glynnis and I had observed in the countryside outside of London. Maybe I had been wrong about the image that appears in the mirror. Walking around those old streets by the harbor, all my brain could do was imagine Françoise walking those same streets amid mortal fear of Luftwaffe bombs. I'd left Rotterdam without saying a proper good-bye. I'd left London for training and never seen Glynnis again. I'd left Leitmeritz without bidding a proper good-bye to my mother. My last letter from my parents had come years earlier. I had not attended a funeral since I'd left Leitmeritz. I had only acted and acted

and acted and acted, some delusional anti-Hamlet acting instead of thinking. And now every one of my thoughts was ret-
rospective, as if I'd set out on a new life with my gaze cast ever
backward.

2.

I rose early each morning the next week and sat at the old
café. There were new owners. Now they called it Das Amsterdam. My former employers had relocated to the countryside
along the Austrian border. They'd left the place to some rela-
tions, who promised to pass along my regards, and news of
my having outlasted the Nazi aggression. I sat and smoked,
and during those moments, I thought perhaps love's loss
would be my soul's demise. For so long I'd proceeded through
that period feeling as if I'd been acted upon: The Anschluss
had led me away from my home; Luftwaffe attacks had led
me to the seat of a bomber. But I'd acted, too, hadn't I? It had
been my decision to leave Rotterdam. I'd wronged Françoise,
and now this was the closest I would come to finding her
again: sitting in the city where she and I had met. Living as
close as I could to that memory, buffeted only by the evidence
of Luftwaffe bombs.

   My third day in Rotterdam, just as I was finishing my morning coffee, a tall girl with dark hair stopped before my table.
Standing before me was a beautiful woman, maybe seventeen.
She looked at least five years older; girls at that age are truly
already women. Her black hair fell to the middle of her back,

curled into loose ringlets, and her skin was tawny, like that of one who has spent time in the sun.

"You are Poxl Weisberg," she said. "You knew my mother."

And so Heidi Braun sat down at the café with me. This apparition, who only years earlier I'd known as a preadolescent, was Françoise's daughter. She'd found me. Fräulein Van Leben clearly hadn't told me she knew of Heidi but then had contacted her. I could see myself through that old woman's eyes in a flash—and in Françoise's. Villain. Poxl West, the villain in what he felt was his own tragedy. But here Heidi was, and here was the beginning of my chance for redemption, however meager. As she sat before me, speaking, I was struck most by the way she represented how much time had passed. I'd grown older, I suppose, but I was still the same height, same build, same size. Heidi had been a girl when last I saw her. Now she carried herself like a woman.

As I marveled at the change in her, Heidi explained that by the time she was fifteen she found her own way to utilize the calling of both her mother and her grandmother. The allure of her youth and of her exoticism would never not be desirable. For her whole life she'd been granted a greater ease of living through her adoptive parents, but when Nazi pressure arrived at their doorstep, even the Brauns couldn't keep Heidi's impure blood from Nazi scrutiny. It was in her papers.

Many like her were sent to Poland.

But Heidi was able to use her feminine power to her advantage. She found a Nazi soldier to look after her—an ineffectual soldier who ensured her safety, kept her in Rotterdam, but whom she always kept at arm's length, the relationship so clandestine that even her friends could only whisper of the mechanism of her survival, leaving her safe from the stigma and repercussions

of being deemed a collaborator like little Suse back in Leitmeritz. By the time the Wehrmacht was expelled from their city,
she'd been working three years in a store that sold fine paper.
The occupying officers had come to depend upon that paper
when they needed to send word back to their women at home.
She had learned to print, and while such fripperies were hardly
useful to the civilian population now, she claimed she could
keep at this for some time ahead.

"But what of you, Poxl?" she said.

"What of me?" I said. "What of your mother?"

Heidi took a minute to answer. Her affect was not that of a
seventeen-year-old girl—there was nothing petulant, instead
only a slow air of resignation. For the second time since she'd
come up to me, I now recognized something familiar in Heidi,
only it wasn't her resemblance to her mother this time. It was a
moment of looking at her and seeing, reflected back at me,
myself. Hers was a resignation I myself had carried upon
embarking on my new life alone.

"Only the future holds the answer to that question, Mr. Weisberg," Heidi said. A strange ambiguous look came across her
face. "My mother has been living with my stepfather in London for almost as along as you."

Françoise, Heidi explained, had anticipated the fate that
might befall a woman like herself, having seen firsthand the destruction wrought by the Luftwaffe. She'd walked the streets in
terror in the days after the bombing. Not two months after Nazi
bombs destroyed half of Rotterdam, some Brit had paid her way
to London. She had stowed away on a freighter. I told Heidi this
departure mirrored precisely my departure from Rotterdam.

"Your disappearance," Heidi said. "No one knew where you'd

gone." Now I watched as the skin on her lips bunched together. I recognized this action as I'd seen it in her mother that day I failed to grasp her explanation of how muscle memory worked in her hands. That muscle memory was now working on her daughter's mouth: disappointment drawn on her very lips.

"You must understand," I said. "My father had gotten me passage to London, and I was so confused in those days about what I was to your— I had seen that— I just."

"Do you need something more to drink?" Heidi said. I started to say something more and then stopped, not knowing what I would even say. We sat in silence until Heidi spoke again.

She told me more about her time in Rotterdam after the war. For the rest of that afternoon I found some way, as I had with Fräulein Van Leben, to avoid divulging any of the details of my life since leaving Rotterdam. When I got Heidi talking again I recognized that embedded within Françoise's resurrection, like a fissure in a rock which is over time eroded to sand, was the fact that she was now married. Heidi had kept up with her mother by post, but in the chaos of the last years of the war, she had kept in touch poorly. I took down Heidi's information, and on that same paper she included the most important informa-tion I would ever receive—Françoise's London address:

> William and Françoise Rutherford
> 128 Park Sheen
> Richmond TW 9
> England

Heidi gave me a look whose meaning I couldn't discern. She said, "There's more to my mother's state than I've told you. There

is a more pressing reason I've only been in intermittent contact
with her in the past few years. In her first year in London, my
mother was trapped in a building that was hit by a Luftwaffe
bomb. She was blinded."

"So how does she care for herself?"

"This is why I have ceased writing her, Poxl. She can read
only when William Rutherford reads to her. The things I would
like to tell her—about having met you, any material private in
the least—I cannot write."

"I could take a letter back to her for you," I said. "I'll leave
for London soon enough and seek her out."

Heidi looked down into the cup in front of her. "I'd rather
not," she said. I did not ask further after her meaning. There were
some mirrors in which I wasn't yet ready to gaze upon myself.

For the following days Heidi and I walked around Rotterdam, witnessing the beginning of its attempt to regain itself after a long period of destruction. Piles of rubble, pushed back
over their original foundations, lay between buildings with
cracked façades. Along the Nieuwe Maas the heads of massive
brick windmills lay cracked. We walked blocks, seeing only
rubble. Only in Delfshaven had most of the old brick town
houses remained intact. By the end of that week, Heidi and I
gravitated there each afternoon.

The mind desires order. Perhaps it is that which defines the
limits of vengeance: The teleology of the mind is a movement
toward order. Where no order can be found there is no retribution. Even justified destruction must trail behind itself resurrection; the only question being how long the lag. Buildings
destroyed would be rebuilt or they would become empty
space—it was a binary, nothing more. A yes-or-no question. The

restoration of a city was uncomplicated in that way. In the years after the war, when cities like Dresden and Berlin would rebuild their wrecked buildings brick by brick, Rotterdam would opt for the opposite—each building erected to replace those lost would be more modern than the next, bearing less and less resemblance to the buildings that had been there before, until they barely even resembled buildings. This city did not attempt to recapitulate herself, but to build something anew, no matter how ugly or jarring.

By our third day together, Heidi and I spent our afternoon sitting on a bench, staring off at an unbroken line of town houses that had stood in Rotterdam since the thirteenth century, the very houses from which those religious pilgrims who would first settle the United States set out in their ships to cross the Atlantic. We rarely talked of the war. I didn't want to know what Heidi had seen. At a quiet moment on our third afternoon together, Heidi said, "What did you do in the Air Force? You were a medic?"

"I wasn't," I told her. "I trained as a pilot on a Lancaster, Perdita," I said. "A bomber." I explained it was the most frequently used bomber of the Royal Air Force. Along with me were six other men. The job of these planes was to bomb Germany. Heidi sat back and again stared at the marbled sky. I looked back up, too. Where when I'd looked up when I was in Rotterdam last, I saw the sky overhead, now my brain deciphered tactical meaning: cumulous, probably twelve to eighteen thousand feet. Nimbus likely to follow, and with them rain.

Not a good day for a bombing run.

I suggested to Heidi we should get inside. At some point in the near future, rain was likely. On our way back to my hotel, we stopped for a gelato. The combination of time and the sweets rescued Heidi from her mood.

The rain I'd predicted didn't come. For the rest of that afternoon and the afternoons that followed we walked those Rotterdam streets, not raising the subject of her mother or of my military service. At week's end, by those same turbid canals of Delfshaven, a week since I'd arrived, I told Heidi I would return to London. She looked out across the way from the bench where we sat.

"Perdita, I'd like you to come with me to find your mother," I said. Heidi only continued to look out across the way. This was her home. Perhaps she would visit in due time. I'd gain no truck in attempting to change so confident a person as Heidi of anything, let alone moving to a city where she knew no one but her blind mother and her blind mother's estranged former lover.

"When you find my mother, be gentle. Be patient. You don't know how she'll respond. So much has changed for her since you saw her last, and she does have William."

I said nothing. From nothing comes nothing. I was to leave Rotterdam. Heidi walked me back to my hotel and I bid her farewell.

"One last question, Poxl," Heidi said. "Why do you keep calling me Perdita?"

I explained that Perdita was the daughter of Hermione, a Shakespearean queen believed dead sixteen years before a statue sculpted in her likeness was returned to life. She later would marry the prince of Bohemia. I stopped short of telling her that I'd read of Perdita in a cave in the countryside east of London with the mother of another woman I'd almost married. That would be too much to explain.

Something had changed in me, something I might even be able to articulate now looking back on that afternoon: For the first time in my life, I had my own secrets. When I'd met Françoise years before, the text of my life read on just one level. I could tell Françoise the story of my mother's cheating on my father, for that was all there was to tell. It was left to me to interpret, but it bore no further story. Now I could not narrate all of what had befallen me since leaving Rotterdam those years before.

3.

I set myself up in a room in the Regent London. Niny, who had taken a job with British European Airways, where she and Johana both had parlayed their good standing as WAAFs into work at RAF Northolt, greeted me at her old flat as a returning Odysseus. She laid kisses all across my face. She was wearing the earrings I'd found for her in the midst of the heaviest days of the Blitz.

"I assumed you would stay in Rotterdam with Françoise, that we might never see you in London again."

I explained what Heidi had told me: Françoise was alive. She was now married, had been blinded, and was living in a flat in Richmond. As Niny took in the implications of all I had told her, she said she would get us some tea. We could talk about what I might do now. When she returned I told her there was essentially nothing for us to discuss—after finding a permanent residence, I would go seek out Françoise.

"Six years have passed," Niny said. "A woman you fell in love and left with so long ago is now married. You need to prepare yourself for any possibility."

"I know it," I said.

"And Poxl. You need to figure out how you're going to ask for forgiveness."

"I will take it one step at a time," I said. Then I told Niny it made sense for me to find a bedsit rather than burden her again. I had Johana in mind. Before I left, Niny suggested there was little trouble for a former RAF pilot to find work flying commercial airlines. She would do what she could to find someone for me to talk to there.

My first week I found a room not in central London, as I'd planned, but not far from Niny's, either, where it was cheaper, where it would please Niny herself to have me nearby. A job came open for a flight instructor at British European Airways. Before long I was hired. It would be a number of months before the position was to begin.

Two weeks after my return I rode the Underground out to Richmond. It was forty-five minutes out, almost all the way to RAF Northolt. Soon I found myself in a small neighborhood of three-story houses and wide streets. For ten blocks up Church Street, I looked on as men and women went about their daily activities. All of them might well have seen Françoise every day since she'd been there. Up a side street, maybe a quarter mile on the left, was the little neighborhood Heidi had mentioned: Park Sheen.

At the center of the square where Françoise purportedly now lived was a small courtyard with a garden surrounded by benches, one of which I sat on while I looked up at the windows of her building, guessing which was her bedroom. Quiet secrecy was best for now, to wait here until there was some sense of Françoise and her new husband.

For three hours nothing happened. No one came in or out of 128 Park Sheen. I sat on the bench reading a play that has no ghosts but does have a woman long thought dead who turns up years later alive, *The Winter's Tale*—I'd already begun toying with the idea of returning to school. My mother might have longed for me to follow those painters she so loved; my father might have liked it if I had ventured about to restore myself to the leather-selling business. But in the depths, what I cared for most were the plays I'd read in a cave in the Kent countryside. I lugged Mrs. Goldring's old Shakespeare with me everywhere I went.

I returned home that first day without so much as walking to Françoise's door. I repeated this trip on four successive days, sitting in the courtyard of Park Sheen until it seemed impossible to stay without raising suspicion.

On the fifth day, the door to the address Heidi provided opened.

Rather than Françoise, the figure of a dwarfish, aging British man appeared. He was far older than Françoise, nearly into his dotage. In a long mac that easily covered the length of his stunted body, which opened, revealing heavy rubber galoshes that rose above his knees, he bumbled through his entranceway. No sooner had Rutherford exited his house than he was walking toward the garden, his short, childlike steps coming rapidly, and just as he was upon the bench where I sat, I thought to open my mouth before realizing he was simply attempting to pass on his way out of the courtyard.

Then he was gone. Françoise must have been alone in her flat. With William off and my heart still pounding, I set myself up opposite his door. Is it okay to knock? I wondered. Might Françoise depart this very same home and I could speak to her then? She hadn't done so once all week. I knocked on the door as if my hand were something I'd stolen, some other man's hand. On the second floor of that building, a curtain drew back. A minute passed.

The door opened.

"Yes?" Françoise said. Another moment passed. "Well, who is it, then?" Françoise had maintained her Dutch accent, the guttural Dutch rasp in her tone. "What is it you're selling?"

"Nothing for sale," I said. "It's Poxl."

Françoise closed the door.

My toe might have done some good had I thought to lodge it in the opening. I might have put up my hand to block her.

But I didn't.

After a moment the door reopened, revealing Françoise's tan face again. It was much the same, and yet in some way it was wholly changed. Thick brown-pink tissue around her eyes drew back into an indecipherable flatness. Her eyes were now blanched cataracts. Their gaze remained directed off to the left and never came near my own.

"If Poxl Weisberg does still exist, I suppose it would be rude not to admit him," Françoise said. "Take off your boots on the way in. I'll not have even Lazarus tracking all of Richmond's mud across our new rugs."

She made her way into the dark hallway of the flat she shared with her dwarfish Briton. Persian rugs in a variety of browns and rich burgundies lined the linoleum floors of the place. I found their texture coarse against the soles of my feet. I put my book down under my boots so as not to forget it there. Much as I had done with Fräulein Van Leben, who had told me of the dogs she'd seen hauled out of her neighbors' house in Delfshaven, I kept quiet.

"If in fact this is truly Poxl Weisberg, I suppose he expects me to come over and feel his face with my hands to confirm his being the same Poxl Weisberg I once knew," Françoise said.

Her back was toward the stove opposite. She made no move to approach me. Instead she used her hands to navigate around her small kitchen. Françoise used the flat of her palm to push her way along the cabinets she opened to find two porcelain teacups. She held her hands, palms out, against her counter as she made her way to her stovetop. Just as she had the first time I ever entered her flat back in Veerhaven, she brought the teacups down to the towel by the sink and wiped them once, then twice. This time she was making sure to do away with any dust that might have settled in them since they were last used.

She reached behind the stove for a box of kitchen matches, turned the gas on the stove, and went to strike one.

"Why don't you let me," I said.

Françoise had already lit the match with an expert deftness and put it to the gas. A tiny woof filled the air and then was gone—the smallest perceivable explosion.

"You'll take sugar, I suppose," she said, though she did nothing to accommodate an answer. I gave none. She passed her hand over the burner to locate the center of the flame without a flinch as the borderless yellow bulb licked her palm. The minute explosion touched Françoise's flesh. An image arose in my mind and then fled.

Now Françoise reached for the teakettle and placed it on the burner. She took a measured step to her right, then another, and passed her hand beneath the water from her faucet. Then she came and with a coarseness wholly new even to her, having not even dried her hands, she used her damp fingertips and the flat of her palm to feel my face. She pushed and prodded at my nose like an infant studying its mother. She let her hands linger for a moment on the patch of scalp where now instead of hair there was only shiny tissue. Then she promptly moved back to the stove, got us each a cup of tea, and settled back into her seat. She lifted her teacup very slowly to her mouth.

"I suppose you watched Rutherford on his way out, before having the gall to come see me."

"Heidi gave me your address," I said. "We met in Rotterdam after my discharge from the RAF. She told me about your accident."

"Yes, well," Françoise said.

For the following minutes, we drank our tea. Of course she couldn't see the tea leaves at the bottom of her cup. As she neared done she picked the dregs from her tongue and placed them on a cloth to her left, her finger coming to her mouth and then down with a certain expertise. And though I'd told Niny I'd take it one step at a time, I spoke quickly.

"Françoise, there is so much for us to tell each other, but I am, first and before other words, sorry," I said. She did not respond. I watched her lips pull tight just as Heidi's had. "I'm sure you can't forgive me now, I'm sure you will need time, but I am sorry."

"Stop," she said.

"Stop?"

Now she said nothing. A few more times she refused to hear of my life since I'd left Rotterdam. I'd hoped at least to explain my departure, to tell her of those moments of watching her on that boat in the Nieuwe Maas and seeing her at her business with that young man, stories that would lay fallow in me for decades. But each time she heard me start, she turned her blank gaze past me to the window over the sink in her kitchen, where some light source must have found its way to the remnants of what she had once been able to see. And I had no choice but to stop talking, as well. We sat that way for what felt so long I can't say how much time passed before she spoke.

"If you'd like to stay here and have this tea with me," she said, and would say repeatedly in the days to come, "I have no qualms with it. But that is all it will be. Us, having a cup." She drank her tea and I drank mine, and it was not clear if this was an end or a beginning.

Acknowledgment: Final Interlude

My junior year at college my parents called with news of Poxl's fate. He was seventy-one. He'd gone into Mount Sinai for a gallbladder operation and died from complications related to the anesthesia when he was put under. After years of skirting danger, Poxl West had been killed by something that had gone wrong inside himself. My father received the call one Sunday night when he was at home. Poxl had had the foresight to leave a will for what little he'd left behind, and he'd named my father executor. I wondered if there wasn't someone who had better be called. He must have had some family, though I realized only then I'd never heard tell of them. Everyone must have passed, or been estranged.

Apparently there was no one else.

Poxl had listed our number in Needham as his emergency contact when he went in for his surgery. Only we were my uncle Poxl's kin now, and there was an apartment to be emptied.

So while I didn't have time to leave school just then, I decided to go home.

My uncle Poxl was to be buried at the Beth Israel Memorial Park in Waltham. Though he'd given up on Massachusetts, as I'd discovered that afternoon at MoMA, Poxl's body would rest farther north. No one attended his funeral but a couple of older men I assumed to be professor friends. What old friends he had left must still have been across the sea, and none of them had come to see him laid to rest as he had gone to pay his last respects to Percy Smith years before. My father took care of all the arrangements, and maybe he simply didn't know whom to tell, or how.

A rabbi davened the Kaddish. We dropped dirt on his thin wooden box. We shook hands with the two men who'd come. One was short, with his head shaved to the skin; the other had a shock of gray hair.

"He was my uncle," I said. "Like a grandfather to me."

"He was very good to us after our father died," the gray-haired man said. "He helped Jules with our father's estate." The bald man just nodded. These were the neighbors whose father had stashed the hundred-dollar bills in his books, the failed novelist Poxl had come to tell us about that Super Bowl Sunday, which felt, now, a lifetime ago or more. But still: Jules and Willie.

Nothing would have stolen those names from my head.

I turned to tell my father that these were the sons of the novelist Poxl had told us about years earlier, but he was busy taking care of the rabbi—my uncle had hardly left a thing, but he'd left enough to pay for his obsequies—and by the time I got his attention, Willie and Jules were gone.

The next afternoon we drove down to New York to see to Poxl's estate. My father was to drive me back to campus in Connecticut and then head to Boston in the U-Haul. We arrived at his apartment on Fifty-sixth Street near Eleventh Avenue with the sun bright and painful above the tops of the buildings. By the time we'd reached his fifth-floor walk-up, shade had fallen for the day, and Poxl's apartment was steeped in a grainy half-light. I helped my father lug a couch and a dresser down five flights. We soaked through our shirts that gelid late-fall afternoon. We carried furniture and appliances downstairs and loaded the U-Haul. Some of it my parents would keep. I somehow didn't feel right taking any of his stuff.

"You don't at least want a memento of the man?" my father said. "He was your uncle, after all."

"Not my real uncle."

"We were there when he needed us," my father said. "And no matter what happened later on, he was there when we needed him. We'd grown to be family, Eli, and you know it. He was like a grandfather to you. He had put us down as his only emergency contact, for Christ's sake."

"I saw him once, you know," I said.

"You saw him lots of times."

"No, like, I saw him after the whole thing with his book."

The corners of my father's mouth turned down. This twitching thing happened under his left eye that I recognize in myself when my kids have angered me. That dim smell of naphthalene I'd caught on Poxl back at MoMA years earlier lifted into the air from some indeterminate corner of his half-vacant apartment.

"When I was in New York, my senior year," I said. "Remember I got suspended? You guys thought I might not have gotten into college because of it."

"You might not have."

"You were so pissed those early moments after it all went down, I couldn't tell you. And the longer it went on, the harder it would've been to tell you. But I ran into him, at MoMA. In front of a Schiele painting. He explained to me what had happened with the book—why he'd made that stuff up."

My father didn't say anything. It was a lot to take in all at once and especially right after a funeral.

I lifted a chair and moved it to another side of the room. It needed to go downstairs. My father didn't follow. I walked it back over toward him. I sat.

"So he admitted it," my father said. "Even to you."

"It was a lot more complicated than that," I said. And I proceeded to recount to him just what Poxl had told me. Telling it then, saying it aloud after years of rehearsing it in my head, trying to think how I'd tell it to someone, in which exact words in which exact order and with what inflection when I finally did, I felt as if a kind of constriction in my chest had let itself go. It was as if the words were coming out of me on their own, in their own syntax, as if the language had coalesced around the story in the only way they possibly could. There were no choices to be made anymore. None of the questions of inflection or order I'd considered so carefully remained. Now there was just the old ineradicable rhythm of the story—a story I haven't told or known so well since. I wondered if this was what Poxl had felt in those days when he tried to write his memoir one last time, when he took Herman Janowitz's story as his own.

"It's a lot for him to have held inside, alone, for all that time," my father said.

"Alone," I said. "Why was he alone after all?"

"He never told you."

I asked him what—I was sure Poxl had told me everything there was to tell, some of it even true.

"One day in the early seventies, when he was still living in London, his wife was hit by a car. Died instantly. They'd never had kids, and she was all he had. He really never got over it. Before we learned about his war stories, it had kind of come to define him, that sadness. Now we understand it was just the last in a long line of losses, but it was the most immediate. They'd been married twenty years."

We both sat there in the faded light, amid the smell of mothballs. From the apartment one floor down some loud heavy-metal guitar buzzed on the floor, one final insult to the myth of Poxl West's private life.

"That's why we always let him spend so much time with you, Eli. Poxl was a good friend of your grandfather—your grandfather was the dean who hired him, and they became fast friends soon after Poxl arrived in the States. After the accident, Poxl could never bring himself to return to London. He'd suffered one too many losses, I guess. Couldn't even bear to be in London at all anymore, except to go back for a wedding or a funeral when duty dictated he had to. He'd told us he had cousins who'd survived, unlike so many of their kin, and that they had returned to Czechoslovakia after the war. But he'd grown estranged from them because of their returning. They'd gone back to a city that was now called Litomerice, but that wasn't the city he'd grown up in. His was called Leitmeritz, the German for it. He found a place here, and a job, with an ocean between him and those awful memories.

"So after Grandpa died, when Poxl asked if he could take you into town to see plays, to go to the museum, to go out and listen to him at Cabot's even, of course we always said yes. Like I said, he and his wife had never had kids. I think it fulfilled something for him, spending that time with you. I'm sure there was something in those outings that let him talk about one long, momentous period of his life that had previously been too hard to remember. Lots of those from his generation didn't want to talk about it, but now Poxl did. We felt it had to be a good thing. I'm sure writing it down in that memoir, having it acknowledged—his love, his experiences, no matter what he fabricated—must have freed something in him."

"Well, why the shit didn't he ever tell me that?" I said. When I started talking I was sure I would feel the anger of it having been kept from me. But there wasn't enough air in my lungs. I felt light as a cirrus cloud, jittery. The question came out thin—so lacking in conviction, my father could hear it.

"We did, Eli," my father said. "I think you just didn't hear it."

"He could have talked to me about it."

"Could he have? Talked to a fifteen-year-old about the pain of losing his wife after years of marriage, a memory that stayed so present it was as if it wasn't past? That's different from telling war stories. Maybe war stories are easier to tell than simple tragedies. Or harder. I don't know. I guess in the end it was easier for your uncle to tell the stories from back then—Nazis killed his kin and so he tried to kill them back. That might not even have been quite how it was, but he could remember it that way. Why would he have told you about a car up and hitting his wife, years later? That's a different kind of story altogether. It would take a whole other novel to tell it."

I started to say that he was wrong. Or that he was right. Or that as I thought about it now, I wished that my uncle Poxl would have loved me enough or trusted me enough to have confided that pain. I could quote three dozen historiographers and theorists to him now, but not one of them would have helped me to have something to say that evening. It would take years of trying to process what Poxl West meant to me in those days and even after all those years; the best I could hope for was a glimpse of the truth of a feeling I'd had when I was a teenager. Is that a truth best gazed at up close, pretending the tectonic weight of years hadn't passed deep below the surface? Or from the other end of a telescope, one big world made round as a shooting marble by distance, and a trick of light? Neither of those have made it knowable to me.

Not one thing I could have said then would have been right.

I know that now.

I was a teenager back then, and Poxl West had been a red old Ashkenazi Jew in his dotage. What he needed from me he needed from me. I was lucky he needed anything from me at all. Luckier than I could have expressed. Luckier than I can conceive even now, no matter what percentage of it was fact. Maybe that's the one thing I do know of that time: Whatever pain or confusion it brought then and brings still, I wouldn't give back a minute of the time I'd spent with the hero, the writer, my uncle Poxl West.

Finally I picked up the chair and took it down to the U-Haul. We lifted and lugged. We didn't say anything more about Poxl.

All through the evening I kept eyeing his library. I had forbearance of some kind, by then twenty and not a kid watching a Super Bowl, and not yet the man I am now. As I say, my uncle Poxl's stories stuck with me over the years, and though I flirted with a degree in art history, I don't have that kind of visual memory—not like Poxl—and the images didn't take hold. History did. I took my Ph.D.

in nineteenth-century European history. I've always had a hard time answering why that period was the one I settled on. Maybe I've known all along: There's a comfort in living with the period before all the tumult Poxl lived through. Eighteen forty-eight wasn't 1944. It was a period of wars and revolutions and upheaval, but distant enough to be history and stay history. It had no living survivors.

When we finally did come to dealing with Uncle Poxl's library later that evening, even after all I'd just learned, my palms prickled—desirous, intemperate. Only the day before I had seen Jules and Willie, whose father had failed as a novelist before scraping by as a book reviewer, but who had filled his books with bills. What might Poxl West's books hold? What lessons had his neighbor taught my uncle all those years before, my uncle Poxl, whose brief fame had fled and left him in penury, an old man on a bench staring at Schieles and confessing his most public trespasses to a teenage kid while still hiding his sharpest pains?

I pulled his old Shakespeare, the very copy Mrs. Goldring must have left for him in that cave east of London, off the shelf. It was travel-worn and smelled of mildew. Its leaves fell against one another with a whish. They flapped, heavy with possibility.

Nothing.

I turned the book to inspect it further, *All's Well That Ends Well* to *The Winter's Tale*, only to find so many notes covering those pages, it was rendered nearly illegible. I remembered the notes Poxl had written about, notes Mrs. Goldring had made in that book decades ago, and a knot drew up in my throat as I turned to *King Lear*. Here I was about to find evidence of a lie or a truth on the pages in his book, a verifiable, incontrovertible truth. Or lie. I turned to Act 1, and on the second page, when Cordelia has just so unwisely shunned her father's love, when she has publicly shamed him for refusing to say she loved him most, there it was. Next to the Lear lines, in a wavering pen but clear and distinct:

"Pocksall."

The airy cold breath of a ghost seemed to huff against my neck. My head felt light, and then my father said, "Eli, come give me a hand here," and I had no choice but to put the book down. Before I left that night, I put it in my backpack. That book would be mine.

We packed twenty-three boxes with Poxl's books that evening. I put eighteen copies of his book into a single box and with a fat Magic Marker labeled it:

"Nonfiction."

Before taping the box up, I turned to the back of the last copy I encountered. My name was still there, typed in black ink. Just above it was a paragraph I'd never paid much attention to before—I'm sure I must have read it, put the words through my head—how could I not have?—but I'd never really taken in. Every time I'd turned to that page, and I must have done so a thousand times, maybe more, my eyes went reflexively for that place where my name was in print, simply skimming everything before and after it. I'd been acknowledged, and when you've been acknowledged, it's hard to pay much attention to anything else.

"For my love, Victoria, the last I lost," it read. "All these stories came after you."

My father passed in the hall outside. I flipped the book shut so hastily it fell from my hands with a clamor before I could keep it from hitting Poxl's hardwood floor.

ACT FIVE

I.

Françoise hosted me weekly for chamomile tea. She never accepted any help with the preparation of the tea, or of the traditional British foods she'd learned to serve William Rutherford's guests—cucumber finger sandwiches, scones and heavy cream with strawberries and currants—foods she'd rarely encountered when I first knew her, but which now were central to her existence. Once a week, on Wednesday afternoons, she gathered our teacups, lit the gas and passed her hand over that open flame on her stovetop, and then ran cold water on her singed palm.

With time Françoise allowed the range of our conversation to broaden. She sat before me and fingered her teacup. Now her face was somehow less dynamic and a far greater mystery than it had been those years earlier. One depends so much on the subtle movements of another's eyes to perceive her thoughts— the face is so much more than simply the façade of a building.

Françoise's thoughts were now entirely her own. What her mouth didn't say, her eyes couldn't reveal.

What Françoise would say was only that she was interested in current events. She allowed me to tell her what had transpired in the Pacific Theater, what was in the papers, in the political decisions which followed from the treaties at Yalta and a conference at Potsdam, in the austere postwar days of rationing and bedsit living in London. Within a year I was working three days a week as a flight instructor for British European Airways, as it was then known. Wednesdays were not a possibility, and as an RAF veteran, I was given no trouble with this request. I first set out as well on attaining an A.B., for which I was able to apply some of the courses at Leather-sellers College early in the war. Much later, in the evenings after work, I was able to attain an M. Phil. I went on to a program for a Ph.D. in English literature, with a specialty in Elizabethan drama, and completed the course work and began a dissertation on Shakespeare. With the focus I've given to writing this memoir—and then to teaching, and to life—to this day I've not completed it. I still hope one day I will.

During this same period Richmond began to call me with ever greater frequency and, its being in the direction of RAF Northolt, was a natural way station on my daily commute. For a period a lull in training at British European Airways allowed for Fridays off as well.

On those days the bench outside Françoise's window beck-oned. I sat and waited for her to open her curtains. There were blackout curtains installed during the Blitz. William left their flat at nine in the morning, and at ten Françoise stood at her second-story window—not looking out, of course, for she couldn't see, but standing with the sun on her face. She had changed so acutely since those days in Rotterdam. The deep scars around her eyes seemed to shift the whole manner of her person. She had now a slick burn mark across her brown left cheek. Her front teeth no longer had their gap—they'd been replaced.

I wondered how extensive the damage to her body was. Her hair was still so long and dark, her frame so full. Her nose was still flat, the most prominent feature on her face, and it still bore those brown islets her eyes had lost.

For five minutes, maybe ten, Françoise would stand by that window. At some point she would recede back into her room. I don't know what my purpose was during those days, only that being granted a view again of Françoise, what I'd wanted for so long, I had no interest in leaving. It wasn't clear to me what my love for her was now. I knew only that Park Sheen was the sole venue where I might discover what it had become. I would sit on the bench and read plays and sonnets, and often when my eyes grew tired, I'd move to the center of the courtyard to deadhead the gardenias, pull off hollyhock blooms that were beginning to suffer from rust, so the whole plant would not be infected.

Sometimes the tremolo and woof of a mandolin would arise from Françoise's window. Her muscles had not forgotten how to make chords, how to pick that instrument. I would sit very still, and in not moving, I could hear her voice. It was much quieter now, but it still carried that warble I remembered from her days performing with the Tennessee Sisters. I listened as she sang Bill Monroe's "What Would You Give in Exchange for Your Soul?" If it occurred to me then that I might be cuckolding this William Rutherford as my mother's painter had once done my father, it had not stopped me.

One day while I was in the midst of my deadheading in Françoise's garden, an old man approached and inquired after my interest in those flowers.

"I have a certain fascination with making things grow," I told him. He suggested that he could provide a small fee for my looking after those plants.

Soon, on the Fridays when British European Airways wasn't in need, I would go to Park Sheen and, in khaki pants and knee pads, with a spade and a shovel, some fish emulsion procured from the receptacles out back of the local seafood market, and some gloves, I would look after those flowers. At lunch it was the bench and Mrs. Goldring's old copy of Shakespeare, and awaiting Françoise's drawing back her curtains so I might listen to her singing; after she'd let them fall again, I would read a single act of one of the plays, or half a dozen sonnets, and then return to gardening. Some days, William Rutherford even waddled past in his Falstaffian way, but he never acknowledged me.

The gardener is an unseen force. The better he is at his job— the better he is at making things grow and making it appear as if they've grown on their own—the less he is seen. He is wholly unlike the bomber, whose nacelles cried out for miles across the German countryside, and in whose wake lay only irrevocable destruction.

2.

I'd like to pause for a moment before this life history draws to its natural conclusion, to say a thing or two about my life after returning to find Françoise in London, which needn't be mysterious any longer. She and I did not reconcile. We did not marry. She stayed with William Rutherford, and I had no choice but to leave.

I believe to this day that Françoise and I were very much in love, that I never stopped loving her even after I was forced to abandon any dream of a life with her again, maybe even after I married, even after I left London for good for a life in the United States. But there are some events in our lives that *do* change irrevocably who we can be, what we can be. The damage I'd done in leaving Françoise, the years we'd had apart sitting on those indiscretions, had caused too great a chasm. It took some time for me to comprehend that, but in time I did. I don't know to this day if Françoise loved William Rutherford. I do know now that it was her life and she would live it. It was not mine.

Once or twice in the years since that initial postwar period, I've gotten my horns locked with older survivors of that war and its attendant atrocities, survivors with whom I've joined groups in the interest of solidarity, those middle-aged men like myself who in the forties experienced things they can't really bring themselves to speak of. They, like me, might have a manuscript locked away in a closet somewhere, reams running through a typewriter, pages they're likely to show only to their family—or pages they have no interest in showing anyone, which they'll then share only with the utmost reticence. Those memories are far from mind most days, and yet the scratch of their talon leaves its unalterable mark on the skin of daily life.

We are sometimes willing to talk about those times. Generally we simply play bridge or discuss some history we're reading, but at times someone will begin to tell a story and find himself unable to stop until he's finished. Once or twice, on a bad year, I'll provide a truncated version of my loss in exchange. They'll hear some expurgated version of my story, hear that I flew a Lancaster bomber. Usually they'll say, "What I've heard described—firebombing over Germany—you say it was a total destruction by fire. How do you handle it? Thinking of it? Speaking of it?"

I understand their implication. We all live with what we live with. What you know, you know.

There were decades ahead for me after I returned to London. Freed from trying to find Françoise, I traveled to Leitmeritz to see the remains of Brüder Weisberg. It had fallen badly into disrepair. Seeing it so made me somehow happy. I traveled to Vienna. In the Österreichische Galerie Belvedere, I saw a portrait of my mother as a young girl hanging alongside the most famous Schieles and Klimts. Some people fought to get paintings like this one back. I liked that it hung where anyone could see it.

Like every one of the things I'd lost in that period, I couldn't have it back.

At times, always unexpected, the flames of the past will come and burn a hole in my day. I read a lot of poetry in my summers when I've got some free space in my head and I return to the poetry written during that time when I first met Françoise. I knew then that T. S. Eliot had been a fire watcher in one of those central London stations near where Clive Pillsbury and I worked as squaddies. Perhaps I saw him once. Perhaps I passed him on the street that night in December when I first met Glynnis Goldring. Perhaps I saw Françoise in those last months before she lost her sight, simply passing her on the street somewhere, seeking out fires and not seeing her because I wasn't looking. Running around all of London in those last days before I decided to fly sorties to kill tens of thousands. Perhaps if I'd found her then, before her life settled in Richmond, I could have won her back, could have had her as my wife.

I came through those years of war wanting only one thing. But I understand now that it wasn't Françoise. It was the Françoise I knew before I left her, before I'd made the worst decision I'd ever made in my life, one that I regret today more than anything I've ever done. The Françoise I'd met in Rotterdam before I left for London, as she was then. I could not return to Leitmeritz and take over Brüder Weisberg; I could not go back and choose to attempt to help my mother and father reconcile. I could not go back and sit out the bombing of Rotterdam by Françoise's side, allowing her whatever she needed to be allowed. But I had found her, and now she was in fact William Rutherford's wife and she was going to stay, bodily, William Rutherford's wife.

3.

I have written a book through the scrim of memory, seeking a freedom that can be attained only through acknowledgment. I do not know if I've succeeded. But allow me to back up just once more and recount to you one last memory, to return to one moment before things were settled with Françoise, in want of liberation.

One Wednesday in 1947, in the winter months, during which British European Airways and the weather kept me from Françoise's garden and before it was settled that she'd continue on in her life with William Rutherford, I arrived at 128 Park Sheen, only to find no answer at the door.

A week later I returned. Again I found the flat vacant. Mail lay piled at the door, letters Françoise couldn't have read if she'd wanted to. I wondered if one even arrived from Heidi. But I would never know. I was alone for so much of those years after I left my home in Leitmeritz, but never in all that time was I as alone as I was during those weeks. They began to accrete: I'd lost forever the sedentary love of my parents. I was certain at that time I'd been all but disabused of the hope for romantic love.

Still I returned each week to Park Sheen with the hope Françoise might admit me again for tea. On the fifth Wednesday after Françoise had ceased to answer, I knocked, and she answered. She saw me in. She took me to her kitchen as if no time had passed. In the span of our relationship, I suppose it hadn't.

She took out the teacups, lit the flame, cooled her palm in the sink, and served our tea. Sweat began to collect on my brow. I was about to say something when I looked at Françoise and recognized she was about to speak. This fact was signaled by a tightening around her eyes.

"My ophthalmologist is in Vienna," she said. "I was being checked out. William set it up. He knows a man there. There's scar tissue behind my left eye. My right eye is gone. Just glass. But the scar tissue behind the left must be cleared from time to time. While we were there we stayed to see *Don Giovanni* and to see a psychotherapist I've come to trust.

"Well, not see, after all. But.

"I had reason to talk with him this past month. There appeared to be some chance of restoring sight to my left eye. There was response from the optic nerve after the scar tissue was cleared this time."

"You might have mentioned you'd be going," I said.

I didn't say it particularly kindly.

"I might have said a lot of things. I might have told you how confused I was in the days after you left Rotterdam, when Veerhaven was bombed to dust. When many died. When I was left alone to deal with it, wondering where on earth you'd gone. Do you know what it feels like to be abandoned again? I can no longer see, but I haven't forgotten what color looks like. How often do I think of that afternoon when we biked to the tulips fields, when I told you of the American who bought me my mandolin, who left me without explanation. And then there I was, again, left alone. Without a word. Even after you knew it was my greatest fear to be abandoned. Some actions you can't take back, Poxl. Most of them, in fact. Mostly we do things in our lives and they affect the people around us. You. What you did. To me. You ask for forgiveness? You offer apology? As if that could undo what's been done.

"Greta and I were lucky to live. You weren't there. It was only through William's generosity that I was able to come to London. One man, one person who finally did what he said he would do. There was always a promise of a different life. Only William took action. Was it what I most wanted? Was this the version of my life I'd have chosen? I'd even fallen in love, really in love, with a Jewish boy from Czechoslovakia at one point, but he flew from me without a word. After the bombing that spring, I would have done anything to leave. Do you know what it is to wait out nights in a basement, waiting to be burned as if you were in a kiln? There's nothing I wouldn't have done to get away. Nothing.

"William had a flat in Knightsbridge. We made it all the way through the heaviest nights of the Blitz without being hit. I was finally away from Rotterdam. I was finally safe. We were lucky. Neighbors were left homeless. Plenty of scares. Our town house remained intact. Months passed. Soon there were no longer scares even—there was no more real fear. We let ourselves believe it. What we can let ourselves believe if only we want to believe it badly enough. The rumbling of buildings being hit, the hiss of incendiaries, those became the natural sounds of life.

"One night in February we were to go into London to see some friends. William hired a car to pick us up. At the last minute he decided he would shower. Would I mind looking after the car? I said I wouldn't.

"Now, you might wonder—didn't I know better than to stand by a window? My life had grown so circumscribed. Sometimes I allowed myself indiscretions. I didn't even want to acknowledge the war was going on outside. For just one evening I would stay in our flat without the blackout curtains pulled, the lights out in the room but the curtain open that I might look on the park across from our building, which reminded me so of those parks I'd loved in Delfshaven. A late-night walk in that park, even, if William was at hospital.

"That night, I allowed myself to stand by a window without the blackout curtain drawn.

"The first thing I thought was that the wall had somehow

fallen and hit me in the face. A rush like a conch shell up to each ear. My eyes were closed. I couldn't press my face off the wall. Then I realized it wasn't a wall; it was the floor. I couldn't get up. I could hear William calling me. All I could think was to henpeck at him for his tardiness, to say, 'Finish your damn shower; the cab's coming.' Even when I came around in hospital the following morning, even when my body knew I wouldn't be able to see any longer, in my mind I felt anger at William, wishing he'd finish that bloody shower."

She made a little sound, not a sigh really, but a kind of harrumph I'd not ever heard her make before. Then she stopped. She fingered her teacup, and it appeared she wouldn't say anything further.

"I was a squaddie in those days," I said. "I drove around looking to save people like you." Françoise didn't say anything. "Later I flew a bomber. I trained on planes that bombed Germany. Bombers that flew deadly runs on Hamburg. That destroyed entire German cities."

It was meant as a complement to the story Françoise had just told. An exchange of information. A chance at retribution. One of us was in her flat in Knightsbridge when a Luftwaffe bomb stole the visible world from her. The other trained on a bomber a couple of years later that either exacted revenge, or perpetrated the same evil upon Germany. Whichever it was—vengeance or villainy, quid pro quo or quid quid quid—I know only that in that moment I honestly thought she wanted me to tell her my story in exchange for hers.

Behind the skein of scar tissue that surrounded Françoise's eyes the muscles in her face twitched. They'd gained their own new memory. Her eyes stayed fixed in their sockets, both the eye she'd been born with and the glass eye, identical in every way. Her eyes were open, but their senses were shut. Their rheumy stare was still directed over to the window above her sink.

"I might ask how that was for you, but to be honest, I don't want to know," Françoise said. "We all did what we needed these past years. I'm not here to conduct a postmortem."

Françoise's words suggested liberation, but in hearing her talk, I understood that what she needed to be liberated from was her past. Françoise was not a ghost; she did not do any haunting. She was haunted by a ghost of her own. Her ghost was a capricious young Czech kid who came into her life and flew just as he came, without explanation. What Françoise needed was the very liberation I thought I'd come to gain from her. From the pain of events long past.

From me.

In those moments, I began to understand something that wouldn't grow in my conscious mind for months: I would have to stop. I had found Françoise and one day I would have to leave her. But that did not keep us from talking now. I could attempt to apologize once more, but now I understood something new about the nature of apology: It is the request for a gift. Forgiveness. It was not a gift I deserved.

"In the time before I found Heidi in Rotterdam," I found myself saying, "I worked at an internment camp in Wunstorf. There I encountered a German youth who told me of his life in Hamburg while RAF bombers were dropping those very bombs on his city. It was awful."

Françoise seemed to be looking at me. I know she could not see, but some atavistic instinct had placed her gaze upon me. Her whole face, for the first time since I had found her here in Park Sheen, was directed at me.

"And how was he?" Françoise said. Her meaning wasn't clear. "Was his skin sloughed off from the flames? Had he lost his sight, a limb?"

I told her I hadn't thought of it.

"No, no," I said. "He didn't bear any physical mark from the bombing."

"Well, tell me, then, Poxl. Which of these things has made you understand? What do you make of seeing me here?"

"What really *have* I seen of you?" I said. "Not what I've wanted."

"What do you want?" she asked.

"More," I said.

And so I did what I'd yearned to do for so long then it might express the underlying momentum behind every emotion that had coursed through me since that day I found Heidi in Rotterdam: I stood. I walked across the room. I took Françoise by the shoulders and made her stand. Then I took each button of her blouse between my thumb and forefinger.

I removed it.

I removed her bra and then her skirt. I stepped back. All across her chest, above her breasts and on them, too, was that tan-pink watery flesh of the burn victim, that flesh that grows anew to replace what's been stolen by fire. What the war had stolen was not replaced as it had been, but was replaced by slick, tight, shiny flesh. The nipple of her left breast was obscured by just such scar tissue. That is where I began. I began to kiss, just as I had previously kissed, what shrapnel had stolen. I kissed her and kissed her and kissed her: new Françoise. Some other man's Françoise. A Françoise I'd wronged so badly, she would never be able to forgive me.

More Françoise.

She did not stop me, knowing as well as I did that this would be the last time. She did not express fear that William Ruther-ford might return and find us there, as I'd found my mother in her anteroom a decade earlier. She took her arms so that the crook of each elbow was against the very center of my neck. She flexed so I couldn't breathe and it did not matter that I felt pain, that I was getting what I deserved, that the brittle cartilage of my throat made audible sounds against the sharp bone of her elbows. Neither of us even acknowledged it was happening. She placed kisses atop my head, where new tissue had come to re-place the eruption where lightning had passed from my head into the electric cloud above Lübeck.

I moved to the nipple that was untouched by new tissue, but Françoise moved me back again. I pushed her down against the cold tile of that Park Sheen floor. Her arms released my neck. I opened my eyes and saw she was wearing no earrings. I thought for the first time since I'd again found Françoise that now maybe I had supplanted my mother's suitors, all of them. I'd not been up this close to Françoise since I'd returned to London and I never would again, but I could see that, where when I saw her last her lobe was taut, now the hole had drawn long, and there were four little creases like I'd first seen those years before in Prague but I had only a moment before I had to close my eyes again, as both of her hands were rubbing me, then clutching me, one moving up and down and one moving in circles and for far too short a time—it had, after all, been so long since I'd made love erotic and romantic, love as brief as

lightning and sedentary as family—we moved against each
other, I moved inside her and she within me, and we moved
and moved and moved until we were, until the end but never
again, lovers.

Acknowledgments

My immeasurable gratitude to:

My editor at St. Martin's, Hilary Rubin Teeman, who apparently was born with better judgment and a keener sense of how a story should be told than anyone on the planet. I can't thank her enough for taking a chance on this book, and for putting in so much time while her sweet new little one was on his way into the world. And her assistant, Alicia Clancy, who clearly knows how to steer the ship.

My agent, Brettne Bloom, whose faith in early drafts can't have been anything but that: faith. This novel wouldn't have found its ideal reader (or a worthy title!) without her tireless efforts.

Willing readers and dear friends, for their counsel and care with a mercurial manuscript: Eric Rosenblum, who has been an ideal confidant and friend. For reads early and late, and for all their support: Rebecca Curtis, Deena Drewis, Laura Farmer, Miciah Bay Gault, Cordelia Jensen, Adam Levin, Adrienne Miller, Hilary Plum, Lauren Goodwin Slaughter, Daniel Smith, and Thomas Yagoda. Tyler Cabot and Genevieve Roth have provided friendship and advice over the years.

My mentors, the first among them George Saunders, whose generosity, time, and wisdom is more than a person should receive in a lifetime—I owe every good decision I've made to his advice, his example, and the hospitality he and Paula have offered. And all the writers at the Syracuse MFA program: Arthur Flowers, Mary Gaitskill, Amy Hempel, Mary Caponegro, Brooks Haxton, Bruce Smith, Mary Karr, Michael Burkhard, Sarah Harwell, David Yaffe, and Terri Zollo.

The English Department at Syracuse University, which made possible travel to the Czech Republic, Holland, Germany, and England. The team at the Jewish Book Council have provided support, as have the people at the Foundation for Jewish Culture. Lunches in Midtown with JBC director Carolyn Hessel have been a joy and an education. The people at the Samuel Johnson House in central London offered access and information.

My colleagues and students in Bryn Mawr College's Creative Writing Program. Karl Kirchwey has given me opportunity, mentorship, friendship—and a read of this novel. Karen Russell has blessed me with support, friendship, and the generosity of her prodigious talent and mind. Robin Black has offered now years of her time and wisdom. Bryn Mawr's English Department, Arts Program, and the college's president, Kim Cassidy, have provided collegiality, encouragement, and creative support. Lisa Saltzman, in the college's History of Art Department, lent advice on Schiele and his milieu. Kate Thomas grew up in Kent, and she provided invaluable details about the UK in the forties—with an assist from her parents, Michael and Elizabeth Thomas.

The relatives in my diaspora family, who made trips to Europe feel like trips home: Bibi and Charles Hope opened their homes in both England and France to me. John and Reni Carson gave a room in their home in Dominica, and shared stories of London in the forties. Thanks also to their daughter, Ann Tempier. My aunt, Kathy Bristow, made all the introductions. My Hungarian grandparents, Steven and Maria Torday, and my father's Aunt Traute Reiss, all of whom passed before they could read this book.

My cousin Honza North, who lent me the hospitality of a room in London, and whose generosity with stories of his experiences during the war in Czechoslovakia, Holland, the UK, and Rhodesia offered me a glimpse into an experience I didn't know existed. Without his inspiration this novel would never have materialized. I'd give any number of my days to fulfill the wish that he hadn't passed before I could show him this book.

My parents, John and Barbara Torday, who have never shown a second of doubt that it was reasonable to want to give the better part of a decade over to writing a novel. And Nicole Torday, who has always been a loving sister and aunt.

Finally, where it starts and ends: my wife, Erin, and our beautiful daughters, Abigail and Delia. It's always for you, and always and only because of your love and support.